BATTLESTAR GALACTICA

Flagship of the 12 Worlds' Warfleet, she was as large as a planet, yet as swift as the Starhound fighters she launched from her bays. For generations the vast ship had led the thousand-year war against the Cylon for control of the known Galaxy. Now that war was in its last phase, and *Galactica* had one final mission, win or lose: blast through the deadly grid of the Cylon Starfleet and dash for deep space in a desperate attempt to find the legendary "Stonehenge" of the universe—the lost planet the ancient microfilms call "Earth."

BATTLESTAR GALACTICA

BY GLEN A. LARSON
AND ROBERT THURSTON

TROLL

'BATTLESTAR GALACTICA' A GLEN LARSON Production

Starring

RICHARD HATCH · **DIRK BENEDICT** and **LORNE GREENE** as Adama

Written by GLEN A. LARSON

Directed by RICHARD A. COLLA

Produced by JOHN DYKSTRA and LESLIE STEVENS · Executive Producer GLEN A. LARSON

A UNIVERSAL PICTURE

FROM THE ADAMA JOURNALS:

More than a thousand years ago, the war with the Cylons began abruptly—without warning, without even a formal declaration that war was to be. Like pirates, showing no threats and cowering beneath false colors, the Cylons opened fire on our merchant ships without even an invocation to heave to, or a cautionary blast from a laser cannon. They came to destroy, and they destroyed our ships by the thousands. A fleet of their warships, base stars as they are sometimes called, headed for the twelve worlds. Arrogant beings that they were, the Cylons did not anticipate that we would be ready for them. We *were* ready for them and for the next thousand years we continued in battle readiness.

But a thousand years is a long time, even when the duration of some years is compressed by the time twistings of space travel. We forgot the extent of Cylon treachery. Instead, we became slaves to our own myths. We could not be subjugated, we were resourceful people who loved freedom, we welcomed adventure. When the Cylons offered peace just as abruptly as they had initiated hostilities, we had forgotten that they were not to be trusted. We embarked on the peace mission with hope, with the expectation that ten centuries of

1

unceasing warfare would finally be ended. Peaceably we had explored myriad diverse worlds of the universe, peaceably we had established the system of twelve worlds that became our main colonies, peaceably we would live again. Joy grew in our hearts. Those of us whose lives had been totally committed to the war should have known better, should have perceived that the joy in our hearts had a strategic significance. The more we moved away from the facts that formed the structure of our design, the more we became like the politicians who governed us, men and women who had so clouded their minds with the *words* of power that they misunderstood the words of the powerful when they smilingly offered peace.

I keep saying that *we* should have known better. That is the fallacy of the democratic instinct. *I* should have known better. Coping with an alien mind that was not understandable had always been my special ability. For once it failed me. Afterwards, I vowed it should never fail me again.

CHAPTER ONE

The contact sensor implanted in Zac's jumpsuit at mid-back sent waves of tingling impulses up and down his spine. The sensor system detected an anomaly in this sector of space; its mild, pulsing stings notified Zac to check it out. Excited anticipation joined the induced impulses as he keyed in the automatic search and watched data, both in numbered and diagram form, accumulate on his scanner screen. When he had first returned to the battlestar *Galactica* as a green ensign grown overconfident with the informational input of space-academy training, Zac had been counseled by his father, Commander Adama, not to become too excited about the war or anything connected with it. The war had been going on for a thousand years, Adama had said, no need to welcome it as if it were your best friend. However, Zac had never been able to lose the thrill of zooming through space in his very own sleek-lined fighter plane and blasting Cylon craft into pieces of infinity. Now that he was a lieutenant, at 23 years old way past his majority, he still felt the same eagerness for battle he had known on his first launch from the *Galactica*'s spacedeck.

His scanner now displayed the flaw that the warning

system had located. Two unidentified aerial devices hanging near an old moon, called Cimtar on the star map, that orbited around the decaying orbit of the single planet of this out-of-the-way, never inhabited solar system. A perfect spot from which to ambush the Colonial Fleet. As part of a vanguard patrol for the Fleet, it was Zac's duty to investigate this bizarre, lurking threat.

"Something..." said the voice of Apollo. Apollo's whisper was so sibilant, his words were so precisely enunciated, that Zac could have sworn his brother was right there in the cockpit with him instead of scouting in another fighter some distance away.

"Yeah," Zac said, "I see them. What do you think?"

"We'll think about it after checking it out. Might be a Cylon patrol."

"Maybe. Awful long way from home, though. Where's their base ship?"

"No base ship maybe. Long-range reconnaissance craft, refueling vessels carrying extra Tylium. Strange...."

"What, Apollo?"

One thing Zac had learned as a cockpit jockey was to listen to any of his brother's suspicions.

"I'm not picking up anything but static on the far side of those guys, Zac."

Apollo was right. Zac glanced at his scanner, saw only the two mysterious blips and an odd, steady field of static interference beyond them. The static appeared to indicate a storm, but no storms had been charted earlier for this sector.

"See what you mean," Zac said. "I thought there was something off with my scanner."

"Could be a storm, though that doesn't make...."

Apollo's voice drifted off, leaving behind a note of puzzled concern in the staticky silence. After a moment, Apollo said, "If it *is* a storm, the Fleet'll be coming right through it, and soon. We'd better go have a look. Kick in the turbos."

"But Apollo, the standing orders on conserving fuel specifically forbid use of turbos, except under battle conditions or making the jump back to base."

Zac could have predicted his brother's irritated response.

"Kid, don't let that peace conference back of us interfere with your judgment. Until we get official notice of a signing, anything goes. These are still the front lines."

On his ear-receptors, Zac could hear the thunderous acceleration of Apollo's ship as final punctuation to his rebuke. Okay, he thought, let's get to it. Pre-battle tension enveloped his whole body. It felt good. Zac ferociously pushed the trio of turbo engagement buttons and shoved his foot down on a pedal. The resulting thrust drove him back against his seat.

As they hurtled toward the old moon, Apollo felt uneasy that there should be any kind of disturbance within the unpopulated Lianus Sector. It just didn't check out. The orders his father had sent out specifically commanded that all ships, whether war or merchant, should transmit their exact locations at all times. There was no reason that any of them should have forgotten, no strategic or trade reason for them to take the dangerous chance of hiding out. When you eliminated all the known twelve-colony ships, including outlaw craft, there was only one solution. Cylons. It wasn't a solution Apollo particularly wanted to come to.

Zac's voice came through the com.

"Hey, brother?"

"What is it, kid?"

"I know why I drew this duty. Tigh's shafting me—no, mark that out—Tigh's teaching me a lesson for that little rest-and-recuperation escapade with Paye's chief nurse in sick bay. But how did you get stuck with this patrol?"

Zac always had to know everything. Sometimes his youthful curiosity annoyed the hell out of Apollo.

"Oh," Apollo said, "I was figuring that, once the armistice is signed, they'll be turning out all of us warriors, sending us to one of those planets where they force you into so much organized leisure you go out of your mind with boredom. So—I just wanted one last bite of a mission."

"Uh huh," Zac said. "Say, it wouldn't be because you wanted to ride herd on your overeager young brother, would it? I mean, watchdogging me for the duration of this—"

"Stop that, Zac. I'm not watchdogging you. Not at all. Like I said, I—"

"You sure, *big* brother?"

Apollo hated the sarcastic emphasis on the word big. Sometimes his kid brother could be a royal pain in the blast-off tubes.

"Don't be silly, Zac. You've got a fine battle record—not

to mention the tiresome old datum that you came through with the highest marks in the history of the academy. I don't need to ride herd on—"

"Forget it, Apollo."

The com crackled in silence for a moment, then Zac spoke again:

"Say, what're you going to do when the armistice *is* signed? *Really* go to one of those boring leisure planets?"

Apollo smiled. He was not sure that Zac, who always needed somebody around to talk to, would understand what he was about to say.

"When the war's officially over, I don't think I want to settle down on *any* planet. Just long enough to refuel and relaunch."

More crackle from the com before Zac's voice came through again.

"Well, what *are* you planning for the postwar time, Apollo?"

"Not sure. But there's a lot of space still to explore. That's the real challenge, Zac—deep star exploration. Who knows what we'll find beyond the twelve colonies?"

"Long as it's not more Cylons. They give me the creeps. You looking forward to peace with them? I mean, *really*?"

"If you mean, do I believe in peace with the Cylons, especially one that'll last until the ink dries on the treaty, my only answer is, I don't know. But I don't think we'd better be discussing it over the com. If we're being monitored, it might be a little embarrassing back aboard the *Galactica*."

"Yeah, how about that, *Galactica*? Your face red, Colonel Tigh, sir?"

"Stop that, Zac. Keep your mind on the patrol. Cimtar's just ahead. Let's roll over and have a good look, huh?"

"Roger dodger, old codger."

In an instant they were hovering over their objective, a space vehicle that was large and ponderous, wasted looking. It seemed to float aimlessly, bobbing like a baitless fishing lure in its own portion of the sea of space. Above it was the old moon, below it a purplish layer of clouds that Apollo did not recall as being a normal feature of the barren, uninhabited planet.

"What is it?" Apollo whispered.

"Tell ya in a flash," Zac replied.

● ● ●

Zac punched out the combination that would identify the vehicle pictured on his scanner. The intensity of the scanner picture changed as various profiles of existing airships were compared with the antiquated conveyance under study. A match was quickly made and the identification appeared in printed form below the picture.

"Warbook says a Cylon tanker," Zac reported. "Scanner reads it empty."

Apollo's voice became agitated.

"An empty tanker? What in the twelve worlds is an empty tanker doing out here?"

"And where's the other ship, the one that—"

"Screened off by this one apparently. Under cover, far as I can make out. Funny—wonder what they're hiding."

"I don't know, but it's awfully close to those clouds."

Zac felt impatient, not ready to wait for his brother's orders. When he made captain like Apollo, he could give the commands. Of course, by then Apollo would be an admiral or something, and probably still be telling Zac what to do. Even though he had looked up to his gallant brother since childhood, even though his own prestige at the space academy had been enhanced by the tales of Apollo's heroism that he had recounted to his classmates, Zac was eager to get out more on his own, perform the kind of seat-of-the-pants flying exploits that had made Apollo so famous on all the battlestars.

Why was he thinking like this now? Here his father and the other great leaders of the twelve worlds were on the *Atlantia* working out a peace agreement, and Zac was still hoping to become a great war hero. Something askew in his thinking there. He would have to talk it all out with Apollo later, when they got back to the battlestar and had their regular post-mission talk.

"Well, kid," Apollo's voice whispered softly in his ear. "We came to look. Let's get up closer."

"Be careful, Apollo," Zac said, and was immediately astonished by his own uncharacteristic caution. "I have a funny feeling about this."

"Funny feeling, eh?" Apollo's voice was now warmer, touched by a note of brotherly affection. "I always told Dad you behaved more like a native of Scorpia, that you didn't seem to belong on Caprica."

"Still, I have this funny feeling...."

"You're not old enough to have funny feelings, pilot!" Zac nodded even though Apollo couldn't see him. It wasn't unusual for him to have such an immediate physical reaction to a rebuke from his brother. "Anyway," Apollo continued, "while we're stuck out here on patrol, Starbuck's pulled a couple of those Gemons into a card game, and I want to get back before he cleans out those suckers."

Looking out his sideview, Zac watched Apollo's viper peel off in order to sweep around the ancient freighter. Feeling very much the younger brother, Zac set his flight pattern to follow, hitting at the course buttons angrily.

Commander Adama's angular cheekbones seemed the work of a skilled diamond cutter. But his cold, penetrating eyes could not have been designed by even the finest of artisans. The members of his crew feared Adama as much as they loved him. There was a popular superstition aboard the *Galactica* that, when the commander became angry, those powerful eyes retreated into his skull and gave off rays that made him look so inhuman he might have just materialized as a god from some new alien mythology. Although tall and strong, he had none of the muscular man's typical clumsiness in normal movement. His gestures were smoothly graceful, and there was an ease in his bearing that made even his enemies comfortable with him—at least when he was comfortable with them.

He stood away from the others, his fellow leaders from the Quorum of the Twelve. Their toasts to their new-found peace rang falsely in his ears. In front of him, as if arranged for his own private viewing, the millions of stars visible through the *Atlantia*'s starfield reminded him, as it reminded all contemplative men, of his own insignificance in this universe. And, even more, of the smallness of the historic event being enacted behind him. Men fought wars, cheered the coming of peace, then always seemed to locate another war to keep the peace from becoming too comforting.

This peace, especially, disturbed him. There was too much strain to the enthusiasm, too much simplicity in the negotiations. He didn't like the fact that the absent Cylons were controlling the event like distant puppet masters—sending a human go-between and arranging the ultimate rendezvous for treaty signing at their own chosen coordinates in space.

President Adar, looking every inch the wise man of tradition with his long gray beard and flowing toga, had called the settlement the most significant event in human history. The array of candlelight on the banquet table, catching the blood-red jewels on his silver chalice, had lent a religious aura to the official toast. And the subsequent unctuousness of Baltar's response to the toast left a bad taste in Adama's mouth. Why had the Cylons used Baltar as their human messenger for this conference? Although a self-proclaimed count, Baltar was little better than a trader, a dealer in rare items. He was rich, yes, overwhelmingly so, but not a fit liaison between the humans and Cylons, not the proper carrier of sacred trusts. Why send a corpulent merchant whose unhealthy skin suggested the tarnishing of coin when power-hungry diplomats were available?

Who could ever know what went on in the alien mind? There might have been some reasoning among Cylons that led to the choice of the overweight, soft-looking trader. And, besides, who was Adama to judge the facets of the peace? He had never known peace; he had geared his entire life to the fighting of the war. He knew nothing, factually or philosophically, about peace.

Adama returned his attention to the celebration, which was in its final stage of formality. Adar embraced Baltar. The trader's ornate, colorful garments, especially the long, flowing velvet cape, made the president's simple robes appear rustic. The two men seemed alike only in the high boots each wore—a bizarre link, since Adar's boots clashed so strongly with the austere lines of his white silken toga. Even in this respect, Baltar's footwear, with its scroll-like decorations, appeared more sumptuous. It was ridiculous, the President of the Quorum of the Twelve having to warm up officially to the merchant-messenger. Adar's voice boomed across the *Atlantia*'s dining room:

"You've done well, Baltar. Your tireless work has made this armistice conference possible. You have secured yourself a place in the history books."

A place in the history books, indeed! Adama thought. The man didn't even deserve a decent burial within a footnote.

It always annoyed Adama to hear his old friend Adar speak so officiously and with such an overtly political manner. They had gone to the space academy together, Adama and Adar. The alphabetical proximity of their names

had continually thrown them together in classes, a solid
example—they always claimed—of fate cementing a valuable friendship. Their comradeship had been secured later
when they had both been assigned to the same battlestar fleet
as fighter pilots. After being elected President of the Quorum
of the Twelve, Adar had continued to rely strongly on
Adama's advice. Until now.

The obsequious look of humility upon Baltar's face forced
Adama to concentrate again on the starfield. His shoulder
muscles tightened as he heard the trader's reply to Adar.

"The Cylon's choice of me as their liaison to the Quorum
of the Twelve was an act of providence, not skill."

Party noises intervened and Adama could not hear Adar's
subsequent remarks to the trader. Good, he did not want to
hear any more politicking. He had had enough of that
already today.

"You look troubled, old friend," Adar said. Adama had
sensed the president's approach, but he chose a bit of petty
insubordination by not taking note of it. Suspecting Adama's
antagonism, Adar spoke with the patronizing nasality that
was his trademark when he was opposed. Fussily stroking his
full gray beard as if he were considering shaving it
immediately, he said, "Well, I see the party isn't a huge success with *all* my children."

Although he rankled at Adar's patriarchal phrasing,
Adama decided not to reply in kind.

"It's what awaits us out there that troubles me," Adama
said, pointing toward the bright starfield. Adar smiled his
best condescending smile.

"Surely," he said, "you don't cling to your suspicions
about the Cylons. They asked for this armistice. They want
peace. For myself I look forward to our coming rendezvous
with the Cylon representatives."

Adama studied the president's bland, confident face, and
considered addressing him in the blunt vocabulary of their
space-pilot days. No, Adar had been too far removed from
the field for too long to understand plain language any more.
Adama resorted to diplomatic phrasings.

"Forgive me, Mr. President, but—but the Cylons hate
humans deeply, with every fiber of their existence. In our love
of freedom, of independence, our need to feel, to question, to
affirm, to rebel against oppression—in all these ways we are

different from them. To them *we* are the aliens and they'll never accept our ways, our ideas, our—"

"But they have *accepted.* Through Baltar, they have sued for peace."

There was a finality in Adar's voice, a this-is-the-end-of-the-discussion command. Adama stared at the bearded man who, even though they were contemporaries, looked so much older. He knew there was no point in opposing him at this supposedly joyous moment. As in any battle, there was also a logical point of retreat in political disputes.

"Yes," Adama said, "of course you're right."

And of course Adar had come to him requiring this capitulation. Pleased, the president stopped stroking his long beard so nervously, and grabbed his old comrade by the shoulders. The man radiated confidence. Adama wished he could be that assured, but Baltar's vigilant stare only added to his present uneasiness.

Leaving Adama alone, Adar strutted back to a group of the more jubilant Quorum members. Adama, sullen, walked along the rim of the giant starfield which composed nearly one-half of the dining chamber. He stopped at a position from which he could observe his own ship, the battlestar *Galactica.*

He took great pride in the unanimous acknowledgment of the *Galactica* as the greatest fighting ship in the Colonial Fleet, and the most efficiently run of the Fleet's five battlestars. Commissioned at least two centuries before its present commander's birth, and commanded by Adama's father before him, the *Galactica* had survived thousands of rough encounters with the enemy, no mean achievement when one considered the notorious Cylon deviousness. With the destruction of the *Atlantia*'s sister ship, the *Pacifica*, Adama's craft had become the largest fighting battlestar in the Fleet. And since he had taken over command its record had become as impressive as its size. The most heroic exploits, the most suicidal missions, the highest number of Cylon kills were all now part of the *Galactica*'s gallant history. If this peace lasted any time at all, the battlestar would surely be declared a monument to human achievement.

While it appeared to drift placidly, the *Galactica* was actually "idling" at near light-speed. Its slowness was due to the fact that it had, as guardian to the *Atlantia* during the peace conference, to keep its pace down to the Command Battlestar's speed. No wonder. Where the *Atlantia* was a hive of bulkily designed sections, the *Galactica* was a slim-lined, multi-level vehicle whose functional components allowed for the rarely achieved combination of size with speed. In regular space it could traverse distances nearly as fast as the fighting craft launched from it. Its fuel system provided the most power possible from the mixture of Tylium with lesser fuel sources. Its launching decks could be activated within minutes, emerging as long extensions from the cylindrical core of the vehicle, and its guidance systems had been refined—at Adama's orders—so that his pilots could land on an InterFleet Memo without smudging a single letter.

Adama was equally proud of the efficient social system within the ship. A commander could not wish for a more cohesive crew—amazing when one considered the thousands of people required to keep a battlestar going. His daughter Athena was always saying the crew worked well because they knew they had a fair and understanding commander. While he chided her for the sentimentality of the observation, he was pleased that the skillful performance of everyone on the *Galactica* testified to the abilities of Adama as commander. (His father had predicted that Adama would surpass his own achievements after he regretfully retired from active command, and the prophecy had proven out—so far.) Yes, it was a fine ship and a fine crew. Even his impulsive children— Apollo, Zac, Athena—shaped up when it came to the needs of the *Galactica* and its commander.

Now, though, more impressive than his battlestar's efficiency within or without was the image of beauty it created set against the background of flashing stars. So delicate were its lines, so multifaceted the jewel of its blue-gray surface that a casual observer looking out from the viewing wall of the *Atlantia*'s starfield would not in the least suspect that its dimensions were so monumental, its overall size so huge. Adama recalled his father saying that the *Galactica* was the size of a small planet, that a traveler could use up most of a lifetime walking its corridors without having to retrace a single step. He had learned later that the old man's description was somewhat exaggerated, one of the outrageous tall tales he had so savored in the telling. Still, the

Galactica would be a mighty challenge for the dedicated hiker. Viewing it now, he was struck for a brief moment by the feeling of disbelief that it was his domain, his world. He had felt that way when command had originally been transferred to him two and a half decades ago, and he now felt it quite deeply again. He grew impatient to return to the *Galactica* as soon as possible, to escape from the emptiness in the joyous sounds of the Quorum's victory celebration.

Starbuck didn't have to look over his shoulder to know that a gallery of onlookers had formed behind him. When he had a pair of rubes like these two on the line, word always spread through the ranks of the *Galactica*, and people came running to the ready room. It was considered a privilege to be in on the kill. Starbuck's gambling acumen had become so famous that his name was now a part of fighter-pilot slang. To be starbucked meant that you had allowed yourself to be maneuvered into a situation in which your defeat was inevitable. It was in the vocabulary of battle as well as in that of the gambling tables.

Like an actor, the handsome young lieutenant knew how to play to an audience. He let his face, so clean-cut for a man so diabolically shrewd, assume a mask of naiveté, as if he had just boarded the battlestar fresh out of space academy. Awkwardness substituted for the normal grace of his movements, and he leaned into the table like a man who wondered how he had gotten himself into this mess in the first place. All part of the setup. The gallery knew it, just as they knew he was ready to sweep down on his foolish opponents like a Cylon patrol from behind a cloud cover.

This time his marks were a pair of Gemons from the planet Gemini. Apparently Starbuck's notoriety had eluded them, for they held their round cards with a cavalier sureness characteristic of men positive their hands are the winning ones. Like all Gemons they resembled each other, even though their features were quite dissimilar, one thin-faced, the other with a hint of chubbiness. Something in the expression of the Gemons, a placidity bordering on inanity, seemed to make all of them look alike. Gemons were among the most intelligent members of any battlestar crew, but when it came to gambling they were often the easiest victims of all.

Starbuck was ready now. He could feel victory on the smooth surfaces of his cards, as if it had been encoded there as a private communication for his hands only. Keeping his voice steady, he announced:

"Just to keep the game instructive and because you're new to it, I'll only wager...oh, say, this much."

Coolly he pushed out half his stash, an evenly stacked high pile of square gold cubits. His dark blue eyes hid the mockery of his opponents which he felt inside. The two men looked quite astonished. Simultaneously, and with a duplicate raising of eyebrows. As they had done all game, they passed their single hand of cards back and forth, while whispering together about their next move. Some smiles and a pair of chuckles activated the previously stoical gallery. They all had a stake in each of Starbuck's strategic moves. As each of them had arrived, Starbuck's buddy, Boomer, had collected cash from him to add to Starbuck's cubit-pile. Now they were sensing their own profits.

"Despite the humbleness of this hand," said the Gemon who now held the cards, "for the *honor* of our home colony, we must challenge you."

"Honor. Challenge. Gemini," said the other Gemon. Whichever one spoke, the other usually echoed the main points of his statement.

The Gemon with the cards pushed forth a pile of cubits equal to Starbuck's wager. Starbuck could feel the gallery tense. He was about to speak, say it was time to call, when the Gemon quietly spoke again:

"And for the *glory* of Gemini, another equal measure."

"Glory. Equal. Measure," said his partner, who now took the hand back and himself pushed the pile of cubits that would double the stakes. Feeling the nervousness of his gallery, Starbuck knew it was important to continue feigning his relaxed manner.

"Well," he said, fingering some long strands of his cornstalk-yellow hair, "in the name of *our* planet Caprica and for *her* everlasting glory, I'll measure your increase and double it."

If they hadn't been packed so closely together, some members of the gallery might have passed out and fallen to the floor. Starbuck shoved in all his remaining cubits and sat back confidently. He felt a tap on his shoulder, and he looked up into the tense black face of his buddy, Lieutenant Boomer. Who else but supercautious, never gamble unless it's surer than a sure thing, intellectual Boomer?

"Where is the remaining portion of your bet?" said the cardholding Gemon.

"Remaining. Bet."

"Just a moment," Starbuck said. "Come on, guys, up with the rest of it."

The gallery seemed to take a collective step backward. Boomer acted as its spokesman:

"Could we speak to you for a moment? In private." Turning to the Gemini, he said: "Only be a flash, fellas."

With an exaggerated courtesy, Boomer led Starbuck away from the table. Out of sight of the Gemons behind a nervous wall formed by the onlookers' gallery, they were joined by Lieutenant Jolly and Ensign Greenbean, the Mutt and Jeff of the fighter crew, whose physical appearances made it clear why the *Galactica*'s crew had awarded them such descriptive names. Jolly was hefty, a strong but overweight young man—while, of course, Greenbean was tall and thin. The conference among the four men was conducted in heated whispers.

"Are you crazy?" Boomer said. Boomer, who rarely sweated, now wiped away lines of glistening perspiration from his brow.

"Were you listening?" Starbuck said. "This is for the *glory* of Caprica."

"Glory, Caprica," Jolly said.

"Are you a Gemon, too?" Starbuck said, smiling. "Look, have I ever steered you guys wrong?"

The faces of the three men, especially Boomer's, displayed the message that of course he had.

"All right," Starbuck said. "Once or twice. But this is the real goods, I can take these guys. Look at it this way, we'll double our money. They're trying to buy the pot."

"You told us they didn't understand the game," Jolly said.

"Evidently they caught on fast," Boomer growled, but he sighed. He was always a pragmatist, whether in gambling or in a furious encounter with the enemy. All that reading on his bunk viewer had made him a thoughtful analyst of any situation, and for this one he could see that cutting losses was simply just not practical—the investment was much too high.

"We've got to do what Starbuck says or we lose everything we've already got in the game."

Boomer moved among the gallery, forced its members to cough up enough to cover Starbuck's impulsive wager. Handing a neatly stacked pile of cubits to Starbuck, he told him to go to it. Starbuck nudged the cubits to the center of the table and turned his cards over.

"Beat that," Starbuck snarled, his voice sending up an unsettling echo through the stillness of the room.

The Gemon smiled and revealed his cards. The gallery stared at the tragedy revealed by the pasteboard circles, then collectively they sagged as they had to watch the Gemon rake in the golden cubits.

For a brief moment Apollo got a good look at a second tanker, the one that had been revealed as the companion of the first on his and Zac's scanners, before it disappeared into the cloud layer. He couldn't tell whether the move was a strategic one, or whether the apparently empty ship had simply drifted into the portentous clouds.

"There's the other ship tucked in nice and neat," he said to Zac. "Now what is she and what's she doing?"

He restrained his urge to chase after it. He wasn't ready yet to follow a possible ghost-tanker into possible jeopardy. Not until he had made every other kind of check first. However, as soon as he tried to punch out a scanner program, the scanner's screen began presenting a meaningless jumble of symbols. It was as if something inside those clouds were trying to lure him inside, one of the space Loreleis so dear to saloon storytellers. After trying every check he could think of, he told Zac of the failure of all his sophisticated equipment to get a fix on the mysterious clouds.

"I get the same mess from a scan of that tanker back of us," Zac said. "Whatever I try, just a jumble."

"Somebody's jamming us."

"I don't know. Warbook says they're both freighters."

"My foot. If they're jamming us, they're hiding something. There's no choice. I'm going in there."

"But the cloud—"

"I'll take the chance."

"All right, but I'm not sure I like the idea of us flying in blind."

"Not *us*, kid. *You* stay put."

"I can't—"

"If I need you, I'll call you to come in after me, *Lieutenant.*"

Apollo headed his viper ship directly into the cloud mass. He heard Zac's agitated voice over his communicator:

"This jamming's knocking out my scanner now."

Inside the clouds Apollo tried to work his own scanner again, and received the same jumble.

"Nothing but a harmless cloud cover," he said. "Not heavy at all, not as dense as it looked. I don't see why they'd send up all that electronic—"

Breaking through the other side of the clouds and looking down, he suddenly saw why. Below him was an immense Cylon staging area and he had flown right smack into the middle of it.

"Apollo, what's going on?" said Zac.

As far as Apollo could see there were Cylon warships, with their odd curves and arclike limbs. In one of the ships he could see the usual triad that composed a Cylon fighting crew. Two helmeted pilots sat side by side. Their tubular shaped helmets covered what Apollo knew from a closeup examination of Cylon corpses to be many-eyed creatures with heads that apparently could alter shape at will. In the center of the helmet was a long but narrow aperture from which emerged fine concentrated beams of light. No human had ever discovered whether the light was generated by the Cylons themselves or was some facet of the helmet's technology. Now, as Apollo stared at this particular trio of Cylons, he was startled to see one of their helmet lights swing upward toward his viper. At the same time the Cylon observer motioned to his fellows to follow his gaze. Apollo punched a reverse loop on the directional touch plate. His ship rolled upward and over, and screamed off in a tight turn. At the same time, he radioed to Zac:

"Let's get out of here!"

"Why?"

He caught sight of Zac's ship as he came out of the clouds.

"I'll explain later."

Zac's viper promptly rolled over to follow his brother's accelerating craft.

"Apollo," Zac said, "for a couple of harmless tankers, it seems to me you're burning up an awful lot of unnecessary—"

Zac's voice was interrupted by the sound of explosions.

"What is it, Zac?"

"Ships. Cylon ships. Coming at me. They're firing. Hold on, I'm coming...."

Checking the scanner, Apollo could make out four Cylon ships pursuing his brother's plane. He punched in the direct-com line to the *Galactica*, got only static in reply.

"They're jamming our transmission, kid. We've got to get back to the Fleet, warn them. It's a trap, an ambush. They've got enough fire power to destroy the entire Fleet."

"But Apollo, there's the peace mission, the whole Quorum of the Twelve, they couldn't—"

Apollo heard an explosion through his earpiece.

"What is it, Zac? Are you all right? What's wrong?"

Zac's frightened voice responded.

"Apollo, they hit my port engine."

"Take it easy. Look, we're not going to make it showing those louses our backs. I can see four ships on the scanner. How many you make out?"

"Same. Four."

"Darn the Cylons. They only sent four after us. It's insulting."

"Maybe, Apollo, but they're doing awfully well."

"Only because they're behind us. Okay. When I count three, hit your reverse thrusters and maximum breaking flaps. We'll give them a little surprise. All right?"

"All right."

"One...two...*three!*"

While the sound of his own craft's reverse thrusting was deafening in his ears, the subsequent silence of the Cylon fighters flying past him was disconcertingly eerie. Although he could not see his helmeted enemies, Apollo was sure they were confused by the abrupt maneuver. He could picture them scanning the sky, their beams of helmet light going every whichway, trying to locate him and Zac.

Narrowing his eyes, he put his finger on the firing control button of his steering column. One of the Cylon ships came into range.

"Right here," he whispered, "you wretched, slimy creature."

He squeezed the trigger. The Cylon ship disintegrated, transformed immediately into space debris.

Zac's fighter came into view, pursuing another of the Cylon ships. Knowing his brother's moves, Apollo could sense him lining up his target and firing. The second Cylon vehicle disintegrated. The remaining two fighters divided and veered off. The element of surprise had gained Apollo and Zac two direct hits.

"Not bad, little brother," Apollo said. "Okay, you go after the guys on the right...."

Apollo directed his viper ship at the Cylon fighter on the left. Before it could swing around to attack position, he lined it up on target, squeezed the trigger, and blasted it to the far reaches of space. As he swung his craft around he could see Zac again, just in the act of firing at, and missing, the last of the Cylon attackers. Heck, Apollo thought, the kid was so often a shade too eager, too quick on the trigger. Zac's prey veered off, did a tricky loop that Apollo recognized as a skilled maneuver only the best Cylon pilots could execute. Before Zac realized what had happened, his enemy had taken up position behind his plane.

"Apollo...." Zac said.

"I can see. Keep them interested just a little longer. I'll be right with you."

"Interested? Believe me, they're interested!"

As Zac tried to pull away from his pursuer, his ship was hit again.

"There goes one engine," he said.

Apollo's viper swooped in on the Cylon fighter from the side, heading toward it on a perpendicular course.

"Steady," he whispered, "steady. Just don't look this way, guys."

He thought he saw one of the Cylon pilots become aware of him a moment too late, just before the ship exploded.

Sighing, turning his ship toward Zac's, Apollo said, "The day those guys can outfight us without a ten-to-one margin—"

"Apollo," Zac said, "better look at your scanner."

He looked, saw that a larger attack force had emerged

from the clouds. What looked like a solid wave of Cylon dreadnoughts was heading their way.

"Ten to one, yeah," he said, "but a thousand to one, that's not fair."

"What does it mean, Apollo?"

Apollo laughed mordantly.

"It means, little brother, there isn't going to be any peace. The peace mission was a trap right from the start. We've got to get back, warn the Fleet."

"Do it, Apollo. I'm short an engine, you know. I won't be able to keep up with you."

Apollo was impressed by the note of courage in Zac's voice. He was a member of the family, all right. But *family* meant more than forced bravado.

"I can't leave you, Zac. Together we'll—"

"No, not together. You have to go. I'll be all right. I'll keep ahead of them, don't worry. I'll put my foot in that turbo and make it back ahead of them. Go on. You've got to warn the Fleet. There's no other choice."

"Okay, partner. Meet me in the ready room, I'll have the coffee warm."

"I don't need heat right now, thanks. Got enough coming my way."

"Good luck, kid."

Before the turbo thrusters engaged, Apollo took one last look at his brother's viper ship. Then the turbo kicked in, and the viper seemed to vanish immediately from the dark, suddenly somber sky.

The farther away his shuttlecraft took him from the *Atlantia* and its unpleasantly cheerful set of politicians, the more relaxed Adama felt. It was always good to return to his own ship. He longed to take one of his famous tours, go down among the crew for some casual chatting and perhaps a few slugs of the sort of brew that did not often find its way into command cabins.

"You're thinking the kind of thought you always refuse to tell me about," Athena said, swiveling her pilot seat around toward him.

"Keep your mind on your work, young lady, and let the old man maintain his privacy."

She assumed a fake pout, then laughed as she swiveled

back. For a moment Adama examined his daughter's profile. He knew she was considered beautiful, especially by Starbuck and the other young officers who competed for her attentions. However, even as a loving father, he had difficulty perceiving Athena as beautiful. For one thing, she looked too much like him and too little like her mother, who was the real beauty of the family. Athena's face was angular like her father's, but the overall effect was softer, less granitic. Her nose displayed the same hint of aquilinity and her mouth the same thin-lipped straightness. Although he imagined these features as showing the world a firm look of determination in himself, he didn't think they blended well with Athena's lustrous blond hair and the one good feature she did inherit from her mother, her eyes. Every time he caught the look of his wife, Ila, in those glowing blue eyes, he found himself glancing away to avoid the longing that always accompanied his memories of Ila.

In their married life, he and Ila had been apart for more time than they had been together—this time it had been almost two years since his last return to Caprica—and that enforced separation was the one requirement of the military career that he had always despised. If it had not been for the war, they could have had the kind of balanced, happy life that now came only at well spaced intervals, although, as Ila often argued, perhaps their love was intensified by the long disruptions. Without them, she said, she and Adama might have become dull old married folks, never really acknowledging each other's existence. Instead, they remained bedazzled, youthful lovers who still appreciated each other's virtues. Adama had replied that she was just saying that absence makes the heart grown fonder, albeit in a more roundabout and loquacious way. Of course, she said, that— and a little more.

As he looked at his daughter now, intent on her duties, he saw a feminine version of himself. Even her body, with its attractive and clearly sensuous features, seemed to suggest useful strength rather than useless coquetry—or perhaps that was merely a father's clouded view. He loved her, would always love her, but would never in the twelve worlds be able to see her as an object of intense interest to gentleman suitors.

The communicator light flashed on and Athena quickly

donned her headset. Her brow furled as she listened.

"Something's wrong," she said.

"What is it?"

"Don't know, but they just put the *Galactica* bridge on alert."

"On alert, why—"

"Ease up, Dad, we'll find out what's up on the old bucket soon enough. Just let me get this crate onto the landing deck safely."

She engaged the landing hookup and checked out her equipment. Everything okay. The landing deck came out of its pod, expanded, and seemed to ease itself under the descending shuttlecraft. Large strobe lights were an arrow to point the way in. Athena guided the small craft to the final stopping point indicated by a flashing red deck light. When the shuttlecraft settled to a stop, both father and daughter were out of it and running.

On the bridge Adama found his aide, Colonel Tigh, squinting at his scanners intently. Tigh, a short, wiry man who had been through many battles with his commander, was not one to panic easily, yet he seemed very apprehensive and jumpy at the moment.

"What is it?" Adama said.

"Patrol ran into trouble," Tigh responded. "We're picking up signals but can't make anything out of them. Jamming of some sort."

"The trouble, what is it?"

"Can't tell yet. Pirates could be. Smugglers. Or. . . ."

Adama could read Tigh's real conclusion in the man's eyes. Cylons. Definitely Cylons! Looking out the starfield at the placidly drifting command ship, he ordered the radio man to connect him with President Adar at once. When Adar answered, there still was the sound of partying in his voice. Adama cut that short.

"One of our patrols is under attack, Mr. President. We're not sure by whom."

Adar's face on the monitor altered so quickly, Adama thought for a moment there was interference affecting the picture's resolution. The skulking figure of Baltar, his chubby face showing a concern that seemed feigned to Adama, moved into the picture.

"As a precautionary measure," Adama continued, "I'd

like to launch intercept fighters."

Like to? he thought. That was the kind of mealy-mouthed
phrasing Adar expected from the more servile members of
the Quorum of the Twelve! In the old days Adama would
have said he was determined to send out the intercepts. His
stomach churned as he watched Baltar lean in toward the
president and whisper in his ear. Adar nodded.

"Quite right, Baltar," he said. "Commander—" Where did
Adar get off addressing his oldest friend so formally? Why
did he put on such official airs in front of the despicable
Baltar? "Commander, as a precautionary measure, I *insist*
upon restraint."

"*Restraint*? But—"

"Commander, if this turns out to be an encounter with
some outlaw traffic, we could jeopardize the *entire* cause of
peace by displaying fighters when we are so close to our
rendezvous."

To Adama the Cylon choice of rendezvous point seemed
more suspicious than ever.

"Mr. President, two of my aircraft are under armed
attack."

"By *unknown* forces. We must receive proper information. You're not to launch until the situation is clearer."

"Sir, may I at least urge you to bring the Fleet to a state of
alert?"

Adama's throat tightened. He hated to plead like this.

"I'll consider it. Thank you, Commander."

The screen went blank abruptly. Adar's afterimage
seemed to take on sinister overtones in Adama's mind.

"He'll *consider* it," Tigh said angrily. He had never been
able to keep his feelings in. It had lost him a starship command post at least once. "Has he lost his mind?"

"Colonel—"

Tigh looked around. Clearly he was a bit embarrassed at
the way the bridge officers had become ominously silent,
listening to them.

"I'm sorry, Commander," Tigh said. "It's just that . . .
well. . . ."

"Yes. What?"

"The patrol under fire. It's, well, it's under Captain
Apollo's command."

"And if I can't depend on my own son, who can I—"

"Zac's with him. One of the men took sick and, well, Zac was on the bridge at the time and, well, there was this little matter of a disciplinary nature, a nurse, and, well, I—"

"Enough, Colonel. I understand your concern. But Zac can take care of himself as well as his older brother can."

He turned away from his aide, afraid that the man might read in his eyes that he didn't believe a word of what he was saying. In action Zac had good instincts, good moves, but was too impulsive—always had been, ever since he was a wild kid stealing rides from every shuttle or freighter that he could stow away in. The fact that Zac had raced off on patrol was still another of the wrong things that had gnawed at Adama's nerves from the beginning of this strange peace junket.

For the next few minutes the crew of the bridge worked silently, aware of the explosive tension that surrounded their commander like a minefield. Adama and Tigh spoke only to issue orders. When there were no more commands, Adama spoke to his aide.

"Anything?"

"Still nothing from the fighters, Sir. One thing I'm sure of—their transmission is being jammed *deliberately*. If we don't launch soon—"

"We cannot launch when it has been expressly forbidden," Adama said, measuring out his words carefully. He could feel the eyes of the entire bridge crew staring at him. "This might, however, be an appropriate time to order a test of our battle stations drill."

Tigh smiled and the rest of the bridge crew followed suit.

"Sound the battle stations alert, Colonel!" Adama shouted.

The identical smugness on the faces of the two Gemons infuriated Starbuck. The main goal of his life had just that moment become to wipe that self-satisfaction off both their faces. Sitting down at the table, with the remains of the gallery's cash reserves overflowing in his big hands, he grinned his best country-boy grin at his opponents and pushed the large pile of cubits to the center of the table.

"Okay, guys," he said. "The showdown play, right? One hand. Sudden death."

The Gemons frowned simultaneously and whispered

together. Even though he was not up on their dialect, he could tell by the quarrelsome sound of their voices that they were debating the odds. They came to their agreement, nodded at the same time, and pushed the equivalent amount of cubits into the pot.

"Sudden death it is, pilot," one of them said.

"Death. Pilot," said the other.

Smiling genially, Starbuck began shuffling the cards. When the hands were dealt, one of the Gemons picked up theirs immediately while the other leaned over his shoulder to inspect it. Starbuck waited a beat before picking up his hand. He knew the nonchalance of such a pause could unnerve the already anxious Gemons and affect their play.

As he regarded the hand, he realized with a surge of exultation that he hadn't needed to employ such elaborate play-acting. His cards were all one color, and all the same symbol, the highest ranking—the pyramid! He could sense the electrified crowd reaction behind him, and started to lay out the cards for the Gemons to read and weep.

"You may never see another one, fellas," he chortled. "A perfect pyramid."

Both Gemon mouths dropped open in perfect unison. The cardholding Gemon was about to throw in his hand.

The alert-claxon blared loudly through the ready room, jarring everybody's concentration and sending several crewmembers into immediate action. A woman reading a book on a corner bunk dropped the volume and started running. A sleeper flung himself out of a chair near the card table and, awakening a moment after his instinctual rise, he plunged sideways as he tried to avoid the running woman. In plunging, his body bumped against the table. The cards, including Starbuck's perfect pyramid, slid and fluttered in all directions, some falling to the floor. When they were already dispersed, Starbuck made a futile grab at their ghosts. The Gemon watched the cards scatter, exchanged a look, then smiled together.

"Unfortunate," one of them said. "We'll have to replay hand at later date."

"Wait a minute, you—" Starbuck cried.

"Duty calls," said one Gemon.

"Duty," said the other, while picking up his battle helmet from the floor (brushing off a couple of round cards that had stuck in ridges along its surface), and scooping their half of the pot into it. Their bodies tense in battle readiness, the two rushed out of the room.

"Come back here, you little—" Starbuck shouted. "Hey, somebody stop them!"

But it was too late to stop anybody. After their collective moment of shock, even members of the gallery started charging for the exits, gathering up their helmets and flight kits on the way.

Starbuck shrugged his shoulders, pocketed his half of the pot, made a mental note to distribute the cash back among his contributors (but only if they asked), and hurried to the flight-prep corridor.

Running along the luminous ceiling of the elongated chamber that was the catapult deck, a transparent vacuum tube revealed the even rows of the *Galactica*'s fighter ships, side by side in their powerful launching cribs. As the vehicles were thrust out of the tube onto the deck itself, their pilots emerged from chutes that had carried them from the flight-prep corridor. Each pilot raced on foot to his individual ship, while ground crews activated the sleek, delta-winged craft for launch.

Starbuck emerged from his drop and sprinted to his ship. After jumping onto a wing, he executed his famous into-the-saddle leap into the cockpit. Jenny, his ground-crew CWO, belted him in. Her darkly attractive face showed extreme concern as she closed the form-fitting cockpit over him.

"What's going on?" she screamed.

"Nothing to worry about," Starbuck replied. "Probably just some kind of, I don't know, aerial salute for the president as they sign the armistice or kiss the Cylons or something."

Jenny frowned.

"That's revolting!" she hollered.

"Revolting? What's revolting?"

"The idea of kissing the Cylons, that's what, it turns my stomach."

"Don't knock what you haven't tried."

"Get outta here, bucko!"

Jenny hit the main power switch and Starbuck felt the familiar thrust backward that always accompanied the engagement of the flight systems. He took the controls and taxied to his launch point where, his craft joining the titanic array of the *Galactica*'s iridescent vehicles, he waited tensely for orders to launch or return.

Although Adama had to keep aware of the information on all of the wall screens in front of him, his eyes inadvertently kept returning to the one that showed Apollo's ship coming into physical range of the battlestar.

"Starboard landing deck ready for approaching single fighter, Commander," Tigh said.

"Sir," one of the bridge crewmen said, "long-range scanner picks up large number of craft moving this way at high speed."

Adama and Tigh glanced apprehensively at each other, then rushed to the scanner screen toward which the crewman pointed.

"Get that pilot up here as soon as he lands," Adama ordered, checking the progress of Apollo's approach to the landing deck, "and get the president back on the codebox."

He tried to discern some meaning in the screen revealing the wall of ships coming their way, some proof of the awesome threat he felt emanating from it. The president's face, looking a bit less smug than before, came onto the communications screen.

"Yes, Commander," Adar said blandly.

"Mr. President, a wall of unidentified craft is closing toward the Fleet."

Baltar's puffy face appeared at the edge of the screen, smiling oddly.

"Possibly a Cylon welcoming committee," the trader said.

"May I suggest that at the very least," Adama said, "we launch a *welcoming* committee of our own?"

"Mr. President," Baltar said, "there remain many hostile feelings among our warriors. The likelihood of an unfortunate incident with all those pilots in the sky at once...."

"A good point, Baltar," Adar said. "Did you hear that, Commander?"

Adama could barely hold in his anger, but his voice remained steady as he replied.

"No, Mr. President. I can't possibly have heard correctly. Did Count Baltar suggest we allow our forces to sit here totally defenseless, that we—"

"Commander!" Adar's voice was unusually sharp. "We

are on a peace mission. The first peace man has known in a thousand years."

"Mr. President—"

Tigh touched Adama's shoulder, a printout report clutched in his hand.

"A lone ship is coming under attack from the main approaching force," Tigh said.

As his plane seemed to limp through space, Zac could see on his scanner the rate at which the Cylon fighters were narrowing the gap. His information, displayed at the bottom of the screen, indicated that he had no real chance to get back to the *Galactica* ahead of the Cylons, and there was no way he could pump extra speed into his damaged craft.

"I may have to turn and fight," he said aloud. He was a little disturbed that Apollo was out of communication range and could not respond to his younger brother's bravado. Even though he often resented the tight leash Apollo kept him on, Zac wished he would return now to tell him what to do.

The Cylon ships opened fire and Zac's ship lurched— another direct hit. His scanner flashed, then went blank. A strange oscillating whine filled the cockpit, and the fighter slowed even more. Zac pushed on the throttle, tried to force speed out of the ship.

"Come on, baby, not much farther," he said. "Give me all you got!"

The ship vibrated as it took another hit. Zac felt the blood drain out of his face and his heart began beating rapidly.

Enraged, Adama ripped the printout sheet from Tigh's hands and waved it toward the screen, which showed Adar's now troubled face.

"Did you hear that, Mr. President?" he shouted, feeling in control of the situation now, as his anger at the officious politicians erupted. "Your *welcoming* committee is firing at our patrol."

Adar backed away from the camera, his body looking as if it had collapsed inside the tent of his toga.

"Firing," he said. "But ... *firing* ... on our patrol ... that can't ... how do you explain this, Baltar?" He looked around frantically for Baltar, who no longer stood smugly at his side. "Baltar...Baltar!" He looked back at the screen. "He's...he's left the bridge. Adama—"

"I'm ordering out our squadrons," Adama said. The defeated man on the screen nodded sheepishly.

"Of course," he said. "Yes. Immediately. Now."

Before Adar had spoken, the bridge crew of the *Galactica*, responding to Adama's rapid gestures, had swung into action. Adama scowled at the screen showing Zac's fighter under heavy attack from the Cylon ambush party. He could sense what was about to happen, and his throat tightened. Zac's ship was within range of the Fleet now. The static caused by the Cylon jamming diminished, and Zac's voice suddenly reverberated loud and clear across the *Galactica*'s bridge.

"—they're up to...I don't think I can—wait a minute, I see you now, *Galactica*. My scanner's working again. Everything's A-OK. We made it, we made it!"

Even as Adama felt the wave of happiness at his son's joy, he saw the three Cylon fighters moving in for the kill.

"NO! Watch out, Zac!" he hollered at the screen. Tigh shouted, too, in echo.

Obviously not receiving from the *Galactica*, Zac's voice became coolly businesslike.

"Blue flight two. In trouble. Request emergency approa—"

The Cylon ships fired simultaneously.

Zac's ship exploded, became a flash of light, disappeared.

All around Adama there was silence. Only the sounds of equipment could be heard. On the screen next to the one that had pictured the destruction of Zac's plane, the array of Colonial Fleet fighters ready for launch spread as far back as the camera eye could detect.

"What was that?" Adar's voice broke the silence. For a moment Adama could not figure out what the president was talking about. What was what? He had a flash memory of Zac smiling, in battle-gear, so engagingly eager to make a heroic name for himself. Then he turned toward Adar's image. His voice was low, bitter, crackling with suppressed rage.

"That was my son, Mr. President."

Tigh gestured crew personnel into action as the attacking fleet of Cylons came into view and opened fire. Adama turned away from the small screens and examined the massive starfield. Hundreds of Cylon fighters streaked by, firing salvo after salvo of their laser-particle torpedoes. The starfield—ablaze with the marks of flame, explosion, destruction—had suddenly been transformed into a deadly fireworks display. Two Fleet battle cruisers exploded together. Tigh looked anxiously toward Adama, waiting for his command.

"Launch fighters!" Adama shouted, "All batteries commence fire. I say again—commence fire!"

As the claxon aroused the ship and the noises of counterattack began, Adama's tightly clenched fist slammed against empty air.

FROM THE ADAMA JOURNALS:

We often debate the differences between individual death and mass death. People say there is more sorrow involved in mourning the end of a loved one's life, than in mourning the tragic annihilation of hundreds or thousands or millions of victims whose identities are unknown to us. I'm not sure that's true. I have viewed the death in action of a son and also been forced to consider individual deaths and mass deaths that were all part of the same insidious event in history. It seems to me all the deaths were intricately connected to my sorrow in ways that I could never explain. The tangled, subdued sorrow over the multiple deaths of some mass disaster is, I believe, no less intense, no less meaningful, no less important, than the more dramatic outward show of grief for a person who has had the considerable misfortune to die alone.

CHAPTER TWO

As Adama directed the launching of the *Galactica*'s counterattacking forces with growled commands and fierce, violent gestures, his counterpart on the enemy side was in a calm state of meditative relaxation as he maintained complete surveillance of his meticulously planned battle strategy. He was sitting in the exact center of the Cylon equivalent of a battlestar, a circular vehicle which tapered down almost to a point through several dark and metal-webbed deck levels. Power for the ship emanated upward from the nether point, where highly volatile liquid Tylium was mixed with neutralizing fuels and forced into the generational systems by the action of what appeared to be revolving pinwheels. Humans who had glimpsed the formidable Cylon base ships up close had unanimously described them as spinning tops.

The Cylon commander, whose name would translate into Adama's language as "Imperious Leader," sat above his officers on a huge pedestal whose sides were marked with hundreds of sharp-edged and barbed points that sent off sporadic threatening gleams in the shifting light of the immense chamber. On his many-eyed, knobby head, whose surface colors were various shades of gray, like shadows without sources, he was now wearing a helmet that was the Cylon version of the massive communications panel aboard the *Galactica*. All the same informational units that spread across one side of the *Galactica*'s bridge were contained in miniature in the helmet. With it Imperious Leader could keep track of all phases of the battle simultaneously. At the same time the helmet was feeding him the necessary abstract information from which he could formulate the proper improvisations on the basic strategy. All of this information was being transmitted to him from a contingent of executive officers who circled the pedestal and dispatched their data in invisible beams upward to the leader's helmet. The Cylon officers were also in helmet contact with each other, so that trifling and unnecessary bits of information could be filtered out before transmission to the leader. If the transmission beams had been visible, the headquarters chamber of Imperious Leader would appear to the casual observer as an impossibly intricate spider's web. In spite of all the communication activity, the dimly lit room, populated by unmoving figures cemented in sitting and standing positions, suggested a rigid serenity, an alien gentleman's club with members engaged in apparently harmless contemplations.

In his third-brain, the one that monitored the functioning of his other two brains, Imperious Leader enjoyed a deep flow of satisfaction. His entire life had been pointed toward this moment, the final and overwhelming defeat of the alien pest that had infected the perfect unity of the universe. He had been born at a time when the war had been going on, in human measurement, for about seven hundred years. His first-brain, replacing the rudimentary one that trained and educated him in his early years, had been awarded him at the proper ceremony marking his passing from childhood to maturity. First-brains were the basic guidance system of both the Cylon citizen and warrior. Since the first-brain's activities concentrated on perceptions related to information gathering and efficient performance in whatever job had been assigned the individual Cylon at the maturity ceremony, only the simple interpretive powers were implanted in it. In Imperious Leader's case, his childhood achievements, especially the physical ones, had qualified him for the coveted job level of warrior. Even better, he had quickly ascended to fighter pilot status and won the name that would have been (loosely) translated into human language as "Ace of Aces." As a result of his mastery of warfare techniques, he had been awarded his second-brain much earlier than his peers. The second-brain gave him the abilities necessary for Cylon officers, particularly the gift of analyzing and interpreting information. When the second-brain operated in conjunction with the first-brain integrally, as it always did for Imperious Leader, one rose to the level of executive officer. He had become one of the youngest executive officers in the history of his race. He knew now that, if he removed his helmet and let his many eyes survey the officers surrounding the pedestal, he would be besieged by keen memories of himself doing their jobs, interpreting and filtering data for previous Imperious Leaders.

When the most recent Imperious Leader had reached the end of his reign (each Leader held power for a specific term; about three-quarters of a century in human time, although the Cylons used no such constricting measurements of linear time), he dictated his selection as successor. Whatever his choice, no grumbling would have been heard from the Cylon executive officers because there was no aspiration to power. Cylons believed that the decrees of their superiors at any level or in any position originated in a master plan known completely only to the Imperious Leader. For them it was only logical, since Imperious Leaders were the only Cylons with a third-brain and therefore the only Cylons in possession of all information.

Even though he displayed his reaction to none of his fellow officers, the present Imperious Leader had been mildly surprised when his predecessor had selected him. The awarding of leadership generally went to one of the officers senior in command experience. He had served long and well, but did not consider himself eligible for the supreme echelon until the next time of selection. However, with the same stoicism with which he would have reconciled himself to death in battle, he accepted the awarding of the third-brain. As soon as it had been implanted, he understood why his predecessor, who now communicated with him telepathically, had selected him. Besides being part of that telepathic network connecting the few third-brain holders who had not as yet selected their time of death, he now possessed, according to Cylon belief, the capability of limitless wisdom. While the second-brain had allowed him a substantial amount of understanding about what happened, why it happened, and how it happened, the third-brain allowed him to transcend the tyranny of mere facts, to rise above the limitations of trivial speculation, insight, and idea. With the third-brain he could connect his first-brain information and second-brain interpretations of the information to a vast accumulation of knowledge going back in time very nearly to the beginning of the Cylon culture. He discovered that not every Cylon could admit the third-brain into his body and, in fact, most of his compatriots would have involuntarily rejected it. For that reason primarily, the selection of successor to Imperious Leader was always carried out with extreme care. Tests at the implanting of the first-brain indicated the few Cylons who had third-brain potential. Those who qualified were kept under intense scrutiny during the ensuing years. Some were weeded out when certain character instabilities emerged in difficult test situations, while others were merely killed in the war—a high number, since third-brain qualifiers tended to take high risks in warfare. By the time the present Imperious Leader rose to the executive staff, he was one of only six survivors eligible for third-brain implantation. The final selection was made by the Cylon in command, advised by all the former living Imperious Leaders, supplemented by analyses based upon memories of dead Leaders whose brains were preserved in the historical tanks. When he had awakened from the third-brain implantation, knowing immediately why he was the choice, he agreed thoroughly with that decision.

All of this, plus the entire history and accumulated knowledge of the Cylon race, was his in an instant.

Now he reviewed the progress of his scrupulously designed diversionary battle against the human Fleet, and he looked ahead to the main plan that was about to commence. The enemy was sure to be routed. His victory over the humans would assure his place in Cylon history. He could expect to hand over command to a successor in the far future with satisfaction, knowing he would continue to be an influential Leader, even in voluntary stasis.

His base ship now approached the main target, the most important of the twelve targets to which he had deployed the massive forces under his command. He wished to supervise personally the destruction of the planet Caprica. His spy network had informed him that it was the home planet of his chief human enemy, Adama, and he wanted the pleasure of causing its destruction for himself.

It was odd, he thought, how dealing strategically with humans as enemies for so long had forced him often to think like a human being. His predecessor had warned him that it would be necessary to utilize a portion of the massive third-brain for the contemplation of human ideas, in order to counter the enemy's moves in battle. He could not deny that the ability to copy human thought processes had been invaluable in fighting this stubborn, irrational race that was the enemy, but he had never liked the times when he had to engage that part of his brain which contained the essence of human knowledge, the clumsy stronghold of unreason that housed human philosophies. Even now, as an image of the present state of Caprica was transmitted to him from several sources, he could not help seeing the coming annihilation of the humans in their own terms. Good and evil, that was the kind of concern that perplexed single-brained, inefficient human minds. If one of them had his abilities and could penetrate the limitless dimensions of the Cylon three brains, the human perceiver would have been appalled that such simple dichotomies as good and evil just did not exist for the Cylons. What was essential to all Cylons was preserving the natural order of the universe, and they were relentless guardians of that order. For that reason the humans had to be wiped out. Their adventuresome ways and overriding need to explore areas where their mere presence threatened universal order had irretrievably destined them for elimination at Cylon hands. Imperious Leader believed peace must be returned to the universe. The humans' unfortunate tendency toward independent thought and action could no longer be allowed to disturb the inhabitants of worlds whom they visited without invitations.

Good and evil! He detested the human portion of his mind for forcing him to consider that subject. He envisioned the deaths he would cause, the cities he would demolish, the worlds he would reduce to rubble—and saw that from the human viewpoint all of this *necessary* warfare was evil! The Cylons were evil. He was evil. He detested the very concept of evil, as much as he despised the concept of good. They were not opposites, and they were not mutually exclusive. Even most humans knew that. First-brain Cylons sensibly accepted the consequences of warfare as essential, and neither mourned their own deaths nor felt triumph in killing humans. Nevertheless, before initiating the destruction of Caprica, Imperious Leader found it necessary to disengage all his human philosophies, so that he could concentrate on strategy.

Two executive officers strode toward him, stopped before the pedestal, and formally communicated the request to attack, a ritual that went back to early Cylon history.

"By your command," the first officer said.

"Speak," said Imperious Leader.

"All base ships are now in range to attack the colonies," the second officer said.

As the ritual demanded, the leader removed the communications helmet and stared at his minions, his many eyes glowing with a rare moment of elation.

"Yes," he said, "the final annihilation of the alien pest, the life form known as man. Let the attack begin."

The two subordinates made perfunctory bows and rejoined the spider web of fellow executive officers. Even before they regained position and Imperious Leader had redonned his helmet, large apertures had opened all around the main circle of each Cylon base ship. Cylon warships emerged in precise sequence from each aperture and flew to their pre-battle positions, where they formed a twelve-tiered, coruscating wall that, when fully constructed, divided into waves, each of which had a human world as its eventual target.

No other Colonial Fleet battlestar had been able to launch full contingents of fighting craft in time. The Cylon attackers now picked off easily the ships, sitting ducks, that were catapulted out. Adama realized with mixed sadness and anger that only the *Galactica*'s fighters were left to lead the fight against the immense attacking force. Outnumbered, they alternately dodged and flew at Cylon fighters. Laser cannons fired and cross-fired, their radiant, thin lines changing to spectacular eruptions of yellow and red flame when they found their targets. As usual, Fleet warships fought with more skill and better accuracy, but the overwhelming odds of this battle—this treacherous ambush—seemed to be working against them, and Adama experienced a sharp pain in his gut each time Cylon fire destroyed one of his ships. The Fleet would lose many pilots today, perhaps all of them. They had already lost Zac. Adama told himself to stop thinking of his son's death. He *must* stop thinking of it. It had been painful enough to watch it happen while he stood helplessly by, watching it on a screen like one of the entertainment cassettes he often watched in his quarters. There would be more pain later, but now, like all commanders who had tragically lost sons in battle, going back in time through the many devastating wars the race had endured, Adama had to keep his mind on his duties.

Apollo rushed onto the bridge, and Adama hastened to his side. The young man was out of breath and he spoke in a staccato fashion:

"Cylons . . . ambush . . . they ambushed us . . . had to leave Zac . . . no other option . . . had to leave . . . didn't want to, but had to . . . he's disabled . . . I'm going to go back and lead him in. . . ."

"I'm afraid that won't be possible," Adama said. His mind raced, searching for a way to tell Apollo of Zac's death. The two brothers had been devoted to each other and there seemed no gentle way to break the news.

"Father," Apollo said, desperation in his voice, "I left him . . . just hanging there . . . his ship was damaged . . . I didn't know what else to do. I've made my report . . . if I don't go back. . . ."

Suddenly, staring into his father's eyes, Apollo perceived their sad message.

"Zac?" he said in a weak voice. Tigh came to his side and spoke.

"Captain Apollo. Zac's ship was destroyed just short of the Fleet."

"But . . . but . . . I left him."

"You had no choice," Adama said gently.

Apollo turned away, his face pale. Adama recalled the few times when Apollo, as a child, had shown such excruciating pain. He wished he could take the man into his arms as he had once embraced a crying boy. But Apollo would, he knew, only brush off any sympathetic touch at this moment, and

Adama knew enough to let his son come to terms with his own pain. Telling Apollo again that he had had no choice, the commander quickly scanned the screens of the communications panel and ordered Tigh to report.

"Captain," Tigh said, "we must know how many base ships we're dealing with."

"No base ships," Apollo replied, some strength coming back into his voice as he attended to duty. "Only attack craft. Thousands of them. I saw them hovering over—"

"You must be mistaken, Captain," Tigh said. "I mean, fighters couldn't function this far from Cylon Warbase without base ships. They don't carry sufficient fuel and—"

"No base ships!" Apollo shouted angrily. "Just fighters. Fighters lined up from here to hell. I saw them. Maybe a thousand, maybe more, maybe—"

"How do you explain it, Apollo?" Adama said, forcing his voice to remain normal in order to quell his son's natural anger.

"I don't know," Apollo said, his voice calming. "We picked up an empty tanker on our scanners. My guess is the Cylons used it to refuel for the attack. They flew to the tanker from wherever their base ships are right now."

Adama's brow furled as he processed the information Apollo was providing. It was just the data he needed, it shed light on the elusive riddle of this sudden ambush and the fake peace conference. The thought that had been nagging him ever since the alert had been sounded came into the forefront of his mind. Tigh was speaking.

"Why operate so far from base ships when—"

"It makes sense," Adama said. "It's more important that the base ships be someplace else. Get me the president. Now!"

The president's blood-drained face flashed onto the proper screen before the echo from Adama's shouted command had faded from the bridge. Behind Adar, fire raged on the *Atlantia* bridge. Adar was frightened—Adama hadn't seen a look like that on his face since that day at the academy when they sweated out the senior finals.

"Mr. President," Adama said, striving to control his voice. "I request permission to leave the Fleet."

"Leave the Fleet!" Adar screamed hysterically. "That's a cowardly—"

"Adar! I've reason to suspect our home planets may face imminent attack."

The president, his eyes clouding with desperation, moved out of view for a moment. The *Atlantia*'s camera readjusted, caught the broken man leaning against a wall.

"No," Adar muttered. "You're mistaken. Got to be. It's not—not possible—I couldn't have been that wrong. Not that wrong."

"Adar, this is not time to debate the—"

"Shut up, Adama. Don't you . . . can't you . . . I've led the human race, the *entire* human race to ruin, to—"

"Stop considering your place in history. We've got to act, man! We've—"

"I can't . . . can't act . . . can't even think straight . . . can't—"

"Look, Adar, it's not your fault. You didn't lead us to this disaster. But we *were* led."

"Led? But wh—Baltar?"

"Of course Baltar!"

"No, Commander, that couldn't be. I don't believe it. I won't—"

A deafening explosion drowned out the rest of Adar's sentence. The camera, blown off its moorings, momentarily caught a picture of a section of the command bridge being ripped open, then engulfing flame rushing across, then nothing. Adama shifted his attention to the starfield, where he could see the flagship cruising in the distance. Fires could be seen blazing inside it. Suddenly, with a burst of blinding light, it blew apart, disintegrated into thousands of pieces. After a moment, there was emptiness where the *Atlantia* had once been.

Activity on the *Galactica*'s bridge came to a halt, as the crew looked on in stunned silence. However, Cylon warships closed in on their own ship now, and there was little time for reverent silence. Tigh now stood beside Adama, the inevitable printouts in his hands.

"Look, sir, our long-range scanners have picked up Cylon base ships here, here, and here. That puts them well within range—striking range—of the planets Virgon, Sagitara, and—"

He could not say it, so Adama finished the sentence for him.

"I know. Caprica."

Athena, who had been helping plot the course of the *Galactica* and the enemy base ships on a large, translucent starfield map, turned suddenly at her father's words.

"Caprica," she whispered.

"Helm," Adama said, not looking at her, "bring us around. We're withdrawing. Colonel, we're heading for home. Plot the proper—"

"Father," Athena interrupted, coming to Adama's side, "what are you doing?"

"Sir," said Apollo, from his other side, "our ships—"

"This is necessary," Adama said. "We'll leave our ships behind to defend the Fleet."

"But they can't return to us," Athena said.

"Yes, it is possible for them to return. They can use refueling stations to—"

"If the refueling stations haven't been destroyed, too," Apollo said bitterly.

"Well," Adama said, "those with enough fuel, those that can obtain enough fuel, they can, well, they can catch up as best they can."

"Sir, I must protest—" Apollo said.

"Later, please," Adama replied.

"We should tell them, transmit our intentions—"

"No. If we have any advantage left, any advantage at all, it's surprise."

Adama briefly felt anger toward his two children as they sulked back to their positions on the bridge, then he suppressed all emotion as he crisply gave the orders that transported the *Galactica* away from the embattled colonial forces. He tried not to notice that most of the power ships in the Fleet were in flames.

When they had moved out of range of the battle, a bridge officer announced that all electronic jamming had ceased.

"They're clearing the air for their electronic guidance systems," Apollo said.

"That means the attack is under way," Tigh said.

"No, sir," said a bridge officer, "we're picking up long-range video satellite signals. Everything looks perfectly normal at home."

Everybody's attention centered on the monitors that displayed scenes of Caprica. Adama concentrated particularly on an aerial view that showed Caprica's beautiful, pyramidal architecture to a particularly good advantage. He had a similar view in his work room at home, not far from the scene he was watching. Ila had given the holoview to him. He must not think of Ila now.

Clearly, it was a beautiful day in Caprica's capital city. A downtown area bustled with shoppers, a row of residence pyramids appeared serene. The communications board was picking up broadcast transmissions. It all looked so peaceful, so much like the scenes they had all anticipated returning to at the conclusion of the peace mission, so ordinary that Adama for a moment considered that the battle behind them had been proven a lie, a dream, and instead they now flew toward a glorious reality.

"Commander," Tigh said quietly, "perhaps—perhaps we're in time. Or maybe, maybe the Cylon attack on our Fleet was just some action of a dissident faction, a small anti-peace movement trying to cause trouble...."

"Not likely, Tigh," Adama said. "Not likely."

The wave of Cylon warships appeared suddenly, as if from nowhere, on a screen adjacent to the home-planet views.

Serina's eyes teared from the steady glaring light bouncing off the fronts of the all-glass shopping-mall buildings. In the middle of giving orders to her technicians about where to set up the TV equipment, she whispered into the microphone of her makeup kit, told it to come up with something to alter the tear level in her eyes. It produced a sturdy, treated tissue with which she dabbed away the offending moisture. Besides acting as a sponge, it also medically soothed her eyes' irritation.

As she attended to her work, many startled passers-by stopped to stare at her—the price of being a media personality known all over Caprica. For herself, she had grown tired of the face known to millions. It was beautiful, sure—with all that auburn hair, plus the green eyes, and the full sensuous mouth, not to mention the slim, curvaceous figure that had become the Caprican ideal of beauty—but when you had to check it out daily, almost hourly, on monitors, verifying that it was suitable for general viewing, you could easily get sick of such comeliness.

Her ear-receiver announced thirty seconds to air time, and she got into position in front of the camera. As the count worked down to zero, she spot-checked the scene immediately behind her. She was pleased with the beauty of the flower arrangements, especially the raised quarter-circle of brightly colored flowers spelling out the word PEACE. Above the word were spread the flags of the twelve colonies. *How impressive*, she thought, *and what a marvelous backdrop for the celebration that's going to break loose when the peace is officially announced.* The count reached zero, the red light came on, and Serina began her speech.

"Serina here, at the Caprica Presidium, where preparations continue as they have continued through the night for the ceremonies that will commence when the long-awaited announcement is beamed here for the peace conference. Even though it's early dawn here, large crowds of people have gathered all around the Presidium complex. Anticipation is growing as Capricans ready themselves to usher in a new era of peace. So far, details of the armistice meetings are not coming in as hoped for because of an unusual electrical interference blocking out interstellar communication. We've not yet even received official announcements regarding the rendezvous with the Cylon emissaries. However, as soon as information is available you will see first pictures of what has been described as the most significant event since—"

The sound of a distant rumbling explosion was followed by a closer earsplitting noise of shattering glass as windows and door panels all around the Presidium broke simultaneously, sending shards of glass flying everywhere. The cameraman pointed in a direction behind Serina and to her left. She turned and looked that way. People near her had stopped working. Most of them looked back toward the area where the explosion had occurred. A few hurried past her, toward the mall exit. Farther away some raucous shouting began. Serina beckoned toward her cameraman and soundwoman, while still addressing the camera.

"Excuse me. Something's happened. C'mon, Morel, Prina, let's see what it is. Excuse me sir, madam, could you let us by please? I don't know what it was, but it sounded to me like some kind of explosion. Perhaps some sabotage from dissidents, if there are such a thing as dissidents on Caprica. Listen to that crackle of glass underfoot. You picking that up, Prina? Yes? Fine. I really don't know what—wait, here comes someone. Ma'am, could you tell me what—I guess she's not telling anybody anything. She looked scared, I thought. Maybe you noticed. Wait a minute, let's see if we can—excuse me, pardon me."

Elbowing her way through the milling crowd while maintaining continual check to see that her crew followed her, Serina forced her way to an open spot. Morel, her cameraman, quickly set up the camera and nodded to her to begin.

"I still haven't figured out what—Oh no! Morel, get that on camera, quick!"

Morel pointed the camera where she directed, at the horizon beyond the city where a huge brilliant fireball was rising like a drifting but erratic sun. It was followed by another, just as huge and just as bright.

"A tremendous explosion," Serina said, looking toward her soundwoman to make sure it had been recorded. When the aftershock rumble faded, she resumed her commentary. "Two explosions. You saw them on camera. People are beginning to run in all directions. This is terrible, horrible."

She hoped her voice was not giving away her feeling that it was exciting, also.

"Nobody seems to know—"

She was interrupted by a Cylon warship streaking across the sky, shooting bursts from laser weapons into the crowd. Around her people started to fall. Oh my gosh, Serina thought, this is real! It's war! It's not just a disaster, it's—

A pyramid to her left exploded with a thunderous roar, a monolithic building farther away started to fall forward, splitting away from its foundation, pieces of it falling onto a running mob. The whole street began to rock and Serina fell unglamourously into a clump of greenery. She looked up; Morel was steadily aiming the camera her way.

"Not at me, Morel. The explosions, the fire. This is terrible. Ladies and gentlemen, it's terrible, someone's bombing Caprica City. It looks like Cylon—"

A fighter swinging low over the city made her duck her head into the bushes. It fired in her direction. A young woman running by her plunged to the ground. Standing up, Serina started to go to her aid, realized suddenly she was dead.

"She's dead. She's—Morel, Prina, we better get under cover, we better—"

Throngs of people ran by her, jostled her, almost made

her fall again. More explosions, screams, planes firing. Morel continued to point the camera at her.

"It's hopeless," she said. "People are dying all around me. I don't even know if we're still on the air. I see a small child over there, running for his—Look out! Look—"

Another low flying plane released another volley of laser fire. Morel was hit along with his camera. Sparks flew from the splitting camera as Morel fell to the ground. Prina started to run, abandoning her soundboard. Serina threw down the microphone, ran toward the young boy she had seen chasing after an animal. Another swooping attack fighter came directly at them, its laser cannon at full blast. Diving, Serina pushed the child away from the burning laser path before it reached them. Holding the trembling child close to her, she watched an entire wave of fighters scream by, their weapons indiscriminately adding to the awesome destruction. A pillar of concrete crashed a few feet away. Serina tried to ignore the yells of pain amid the rubble. Something fell upon her, and suddenly there was no air.

One of her arms was still free and she could move it. She began frantically digging toward the surface, resisting the driving impulse to take a breath. Her arm broke through. She frenetically shaped an escape hatch in the dirt and pulled herself and the child into the air. After taking a quick inhalation, she pulled the child all the way out of the hole and checked him over to ensure he was all right. He was a small boy, about six years old.

"Don't try to move for a minute," she said to him.

The boy began to cry and Serina pulled him to her, comforting him.

"Everything's going to be all right," she said.

"Muffit," the boy said, "where's Muffit?"

"Who?"

"My daggit. My daggit. Where is he—"

"Your daggit. Oh, I'm sure he's fine."

Daggits, animals native to Caprica, had been easily domesticated by the first colonists and had become the favorite choice of pet among younger children. Parents liked the four-legged, short-furred rascals because, in spite of their playfulness, they always protected children. Serina smiled. She was continually amazed by the unique ways children focused their concentration. This boy, unaware of the meaning of the Cylon invasion, was more concerned about his lost pet than the devastation around him. He probably thought finding the daggit would set everything right again.

Although the Cylon fighters no longer flew across the sky, the dust from their attack was still settling all around Serina and the boy.

"Muffit! Muffit!" the boy hollered.

"I'm sure he's fine, honey," Serina said, trying to make her voice sound as if she believed every word.

A tall man ran toward them, his bloody left arm hanging limp and useless at his side.

"Move everyone," he shouted. "Move! Evacuate the center!"

"My daggit," the boy said, "where is—"

"This isn't any time to think about—" the man said, but Serina waved to him to shut up.

"Come on," she said softly. "We have to go. I'm sure your daggit is all right."

"Please, miss," the man screamed desperately. "The building there'll topple at any moment."

Serina looked in the direction toward which the man's functioning arm waved. Before she located the about-to-collapse building, her eyes fixed on a pillar from which what looked like a daggit's limbs stuck out. Shielding the boy's head, she maneuvered a few steps toward the pillar. It was the daggit, all right, crushed underneath the pillar, its pointed snout buried in dirt and rubble. Turning her body so that it screened any possible view the boy could have of the dead animal, she pointed in the opposite direction and said:

"There he is, must've been him, running that way. Let's go have a look."

"I want Muffit. Is he all right?"

She picked up the boy, held him close.

"Sure, he's all right. Everything is all right. Everything is going to be just fine. Just fine. What's your name?"

"Boxey."

She wiped some of the dust from the boy's face. He was a cherub-faced child, with large brown eyes and a shock of curly brown hair hanging down on his forehead. She imagined that shock of hair was continually getting in his eyes.

"Hello, Boxey," she said.

She looked past him, at what remained of the city. Not much remained. The buildings that still stood were rocked with explosions, bursting with fire. The wounded man pulled at her with his good arm and, still carrying Boxey, she began to run. She did not look back at the sound of the crashing building behind her. As they hurried past the place where her camera had been originally set up, in front of the floral arrangement spelling PEACE, she noticed that the flowers had been completely buried and that the flags of the twelve colonies were in flames.

Athena kept glancing covertly at her father to check on his reactions to the dreadful slaughter they were all helplessly viewing on the *Galactica*'s multi-screened communications console. Most people would have expressed the opinion that Adama was emotionless, that he didn't react at all to the holocaust, but Athena knew better. She detected the somber pain in his eyes. He stood stiffly, nodding at the reports of his officers, but Athena could tell he was thinking of her mother, who lived in a suburb of the smoldering Caprica City. She wished they could leave their duties, be father and daughter again for just a minute, go to a quiet room and hold each other. But that was not possible. Mother's got to be all right, she thought, she's got to be!

Tigh had moved to his commander's side with the latest report.

"Sir," he said, "long-range scanners are picking up Cylon base ships. Launching to all outer planets."

Athena, hearing this, wanted to slam her fists down on the panel of gauges in front of her. A conversation she had had just a few days ago with Zac and Apollo came back to her vividly. She had been arguing with them about the coming peace mission, contending that the Cylons could be trusted. They were at the very least an intelligent race. Apollo said Cylons might have technological prowess but he wasn't so sure they could be described as intelligent, at least in human terms. It was an old argument, one that she had had countless times since joining the service. Cylons might be intelligent, but they were certainly not compassionate; they were hardly, in fact, emotional at all. Apollo, like many others, believed that the ability to feel was necessary for intelligence. Athena held to her belief that the Cylons *must* have feeling, *must* have emotion, it just wasn't describable in human language. Since their cultural systems were so entirely different, she argued, we must search for and discover the other differences, too.

Their argument had become quite heated, even though she and Apollo knew the debate itself was ancient, almost ritualistic. Zac broke it up by laughing suddenly and saying they should all get falling down drunk in order to make their argument more logical. They all laughed. Their father, walking in on the hysterical trio, chided them for silliness below the call of duty. It had been a nice moment, a fine moment, the last time they'd joined in warmth as a family. Now Zac was dead—and Athena didn't want to think deeply about that just now.

She tried to shake the sorrowful thoughts out of her head by taking a reading of her equipment. However, she couldn't help but watch the monitors often. Planetside, things were worse. Fires everywhere. Buildings still falling. Corpses tucked into doorways and corners of rubble as if arranged for viewing. The scattered survivors moved slowly, sluggishly, in a collective state of shock. Adama turned away from the terrible pictures, his shoulders slumped in defeat. She knew that she looked just as miserable. She felt comatose; the nightmare had to end soon, she must wake up. A hand gripped her shoulder. She looked up, into the grim face of Apollo. She pulled away from him, feeling illogically angry at his pain, furious at the downcast look of her father. She could no longer hold her feelings in and she raged at Apollo.

"First Zac, now this! They trusted us to protect them!" She sensed her father looking distressfully her way. "How could we let it happen? Why were we guarding a bunch of corrupt politicians instead of our homes? We let it happen, we just let it happen."

She looked toward Adama, saw the pain in his face again, wished she hadn't spoken. He was commander. When she said how could *we* let it happen, she knew that inside he heard why did *you* let it happen. She wouldn't be able to take that back. It was true, but she wouldn't be able to take it back.

For the next few minutes she performed her duties still in the dream state. But all the concentration she could work up would not push the gruesome memories of destruction out of her mind. If only Starbuck were here to cheer her up, she thought—but she didn't even know where *he* was. They had left him behind with the others they had—they had *abandoned*. He had to come back. At least Starbuck had to come back. She needed him now.

Tigh called everybody's attention to the largest monitor screen. The Cylon base ships had now been located. One of them could be seen in closeup, the other two in the distance. All of them were launching more fighters. Another officer locked in scenes from all of the twelve worlds. Each picture showed Cylon fighters on bombing runs.

"What are the reports from the twelve worlds, Colonel?" Adama asked.

"No hope, Commander."

"There's always—what about Sagitara? They have the most sophisticated defense system in all the worlds. Perhaps there's still time—"

"Sorry, Commander. The planet is in flames."

Athena had never seen her father so pale, so close to collapse. She took a tentative step toward him. He saw her and waved her away. He turned to Tigh.

"Prepare my shuttlecraft," he said. Tigh appeared as startled as everyone else who heard the commander's request.

"Shuttlecraft—?" Tigh said.

"I'm going down to the surface of Caprica, Tigh."

"That's out of the question, Commander. You can't."

"Prepare the—"

"Sir, if the Cylon scanners should pick you up when you get out of our camouflage force field—"

"I'm going with you," Apollo said.

"Yes," said Athena. "I, also."

Adama touched her arm, spoke softly:

"You stay here. We'll be all right."

"But I want to—"

"You're needed here."

She capitulated to the firm tone of command in Adama's voice. As elder brother, it was Apollo's right to take this particular trip, even though it was usually her job to pilot the shuttlecraft for her father.

"We'll go in my fighter, father," Apollo said. "You're the last surviving member of the Quorum. If we run into a Cylon attack ship, at least you'll have a chance—"

"The captain's right," Tigh said. "And, since I'm the one who has to fill your shoes if anything happens, well, I insist you go down in the fighter, Commander."

Adama nodded at Tigh.

"You proceed to rendezvous with the survivors of the Fleet. Make all necessary preparation. You must proceed as if I might not return."

"Not return?" Tigh said. "You'll return, Commander."

Tigh extended his hand and the two men, old friends as well as fellow officers who had served together for more than three decades, clasped each other's wrists as they shook hands.

FROM THE ADAMA JOURNALS:

Nobody likes being called a coward. I didn't even understand the misconceptions placed on my withdrawal of the *Galactica* after the Cylon ambush.

There is a legend that goes back so far in space lore no one knows its origin. A moon miner in the original solar system that contained the fabled Earth works the natural satellites of the various planets. A miner is like no other, braving the desolate areas where normal humans would cower in fear, just to dig out materials vital to human progress. Moon miners, according to legend, live more fiercely and celebrate more ferociously than any other heroes in the space fraternity. At a party on some outworld of the system, honoring one of the usual holidays devoted to harvesting or history, a group of moon miners party happily. Suddenly their celebration is interrupted by the roar of a loud, ugly voice. A strange, ugly man, dressed in a bizarrely colorful variation of the basic green mining outfit, strides into the center of the party. No one has ever seen him before or knows where he comes from. Immediately he chides the miners for their cowardice and offers a challenge. They should, he says, choose the bravest of their number and he will allow that designee a shot at him with any weapon he chooses. Our hero, named Gavin in most of the versions of the story, springs forward and makes his choice. In many versions it's a vehicle, usually a bulldozer equipped with the surface-mining scoop. Aiming the bulldozer at the rude intruder, Gavin runs it at him full force. With the scoop he knocks the villain so high in the sky that the man goes into temporary orbit. But he comes down, lands on his feet, and tells the miner-hero that they'll meet again, on the next occasion of the holiday, and it will be Gavin's turn to receive a blow. But where will I find you? Gavin asks. It'll be your business to discover that for yourself, the villain responds. Among moon-miners the implication of cowardice is the worst insult, and so our hero spends the next year, experiencing many adventures, including the usual romantic dalliances, in search of the domain of the rude intruder. But no one he meets seems to know where the villain lives.

Finally, the legend has it, the moon miner comes to the original moon, the one that circles Earth. He's never been there before, never known its magical properties, never even glimpsed the planet of humankind's origin from the vantage point of its own moon. If he finds the villain and lives through the experience, he vows to descend to Earth, perhaps spend his remaining days there.

On the moon his adventures continue, but he begins to despair of ever finding the goal of his quest and taking the return blow. However, on the day fated for their meeting, he encounters an old hag nestled in an abandoned scoop within a manmade crater, and she instructs him. The villain dwells in an orbiting castle in the sky above the moon, and Gavin must launch himself there. Why launch? he asks. Why can't I just hop the daily shuttle or a passing freighter? She says that the boastful villain claims that the miner will *prove* himself a coward if he comes up by shuttle or any safe conveyance.

Gavin secures himself upon the track of a mass-driver, a long, beltlike device used to launch products of the mines to a precisely located receiver-scoop vehicle, called a catcher, where it's transferred to an orbiting space station. He sets the mechanism going, and he begins to be pushed along the mass-driver track. At first slowly, then faster and faster. As his speed increases he gradually rises a few feet above the track of the mass-driver, and then a few feet more, kept from flight only by plates designed to prevent a payload from being flung into space ahead of an exactly computed time. With acceleration he speeds up the final launch slope. Restraining plates drop away and he is thrown into space, into the dark sky above the moon. A living corporeal payload, Gavin speeds through the vacuum of space. His rate of speed increases to six hundred miles an hour. In front of him, the villain's floating green space castle appears, as if out of nowhere. At the last minute it puts out its own catcher and rudely interrupts the moon-miner's flight.

Well, of course, our hero would have been broken into a million pieces, just like a mining payload—but this is legend, and he awakens in the bedchamber of his host. The villain now extends his hand in friendship and says that the debt is paid. Gavin has verified his bravery, he is no coward. And—who knows?—in stories where villains are instantly transformed into comradely hosts, perhaps Gavin the moon miner does realize his dream of visiting Earth.

There were times when my own apparent cowardice made me feel like the moon miner, as I faced the destination where I might be broken into a million pieces. However, I could not count on awakening comfortably in my opponent's bedchamber.

CHAPTER THREE

When the *Galactica* withdrew from battle, Starbuck almost fell out of his cockpit in anger.

"What's going on?" he radioed Boomer.

"Don't ask me. Commander's calling the shots."

There was an edge of sarcasm in Boomer's voice, the tone of the hardbitten pilot who knows full well you cannot trust anybody in power.

"But he can't leave us hanging out here like—"

"Hey you guys," Greenbean's voice broke into the transmission. "What's up? The *Galactica*'s pulling out."

"You noticed!" Starbuck said. "I don't...it must...there's gotta be a good reason."

"Sure there is," Boomer said. "It's dangerous around here. A guy could get—heads up, Greenbean, you've got a pair on your tail."

"Pull up yourself, Boomer," Jolly's voice cut in. "You're in somebody's sights yourself. I'll try to get 'em off."

As Starbuck zeroed in on the sinister fighters pouncing on Boomer, he looked back at the departing *Galactica* and muttered more to himself than to anybody who might be listening.

"There's gotta be a good reason."

He had scant time to be introspective about the mystery of his parent ship's hasty departure as scores of Cylon fighters impolitely demanded his attention. Several times he was nearly trapped in one of their insidious and dreaded pinwheel attacks, in which a dozen Cylon vehicles surrounded their target and each, in a complex, intricate sequence of arclike sweeps, bore down on the human flyers. A pinwheel was a particularly tough style of attack to evade, but Starbuck had been up against every deceptive tactic known to the vicious, iniquitous Cylons and could time his own moves to match theirs—and wipe out many of them in the bargain.

Time and the fact that the Cylons greatly outnumbered the humans took their toll. Soon Starbuck discovered that his weapons charge had diminished to a dangerously low level. With no *Galactica* around to return to for recharging, he could become a sitting duck for even the greenest of Cylon warriors. He searched the sky for another battlestar, where he could make an emergency landing for new fuel and new armament charges. He found the *Solaria*, but it was under fierce attack by a Cylon warship. Starbuck could see, through its portals, the flickering of hundreds of fires inside the battlestar. He directed his own fighter toward the besieged *Solaria*.

"I'm with you," said a voice in his ear. Boomer, streaking by just above him. The Cylon pilots hadn't seen either of them yet. They zeroed in on the target.

"I got him on the left," Boomer said.

"And me on the right," Starbuck said.

Boomer and Starbuck released their laser torpedoes synchronously. A second later the Cylon ship exploded, leaving thousands of lazily floating metallic traces in its sector of space. Another Cylon fighter emerged from the far side of the *Solaria*, took aim at the battlestar, fired a massive charge, and hit it amidships. Starbuck could see the *Solaria* begin to split in half as the Cylon fighter pulled away. Cursing venomously, he bore down on the enemy and, relishing vengeance, sent the ship to smithereens with what seemed to be the last good shot he had left.

"Nice shooting," Boomer said.

"Yeah, but a little late," Starbuck snarled, as he watched the final stages of the *Solaria*'s disintegration.

He located another Cylon fighter in the distance and started toward it. But his common sense took over from his rage. Testing the firing button on his steering column, he heard the faint whine that told him that the weapons charge was now below efficiency level. He veered his own ship to the right, to escape any attack the Cylon craft might attempt. However, to his amazement, the several enemy ships he could discern now all went into an abrupt arcing turn and headed away from the human forces.

"What's up?" Starbuck said.

"Total defeat is what's up," Boomer said. "The *Solaria* was our last battlestar. Minus the *Galactica*, of course, which seemed to find it militarily necessary to turn tail and—"

"Stow that, Boomer. We don't know what happened yet."

"Okay, okay. Whatever, they've destroyed the fleet, the slimy louses, and there's no use hanging around."

Jolly's voice cut in.

"They're turning tail. Let's go get 'em!"

"No," Starbuck cautioned. "We've got barely enough reserve fuel as it is."

"To do what?" Boomer said. "To joyride around this sector? Where do you propose we land, *Lieutenant* Starbuck? There's nothing left for—"

"The *Galactica* has left," Starbuck said. "I suggest we try to find it."

"Right," said Jolly, "and when we do—"

"We shoot it down," said Boomer.

"Tone it down, Boomer," Starbuck said. "Let's take time to hear their side. They must've had a good reason to pull out when they did."

"Yeah," said Jolly, "they're cowards."

Starbuck heard Boomer's soft malicious laughter in tacit agreement with Jolly's accusation.

"How do we propose we get to the *Galactica*, flyboy?" Boomer said. "You gonna take us all by the hand and guide us home?"

"We'll find it, don't worry. First, we've gotta make it to one of the fueling space stations or we're not gonna get off the pot."

"What makes you think the Cylons didn't take out all the fueling stations?" Boomer asked. "I mean the question with all courtesy, of course, skyrider."

"We'll just have to find out, won't we, Boomer?"

"You say so."

Boomer's plane banked and swept off from Starbuck's portside wing. Jolly followed suit. After a moment of hesitation, so did Starbuck.

Fortunately the fueling stations, which were hidden from Cylon view by camouflaging force fields, were all intact, and the squadrons were able to refuel. With the scanner transmission no longer jammed, they worked out the coordinates for the *Galactica* right away. Starbuck was puzzled by the fact that the battlestar was in the region of their home planet. That location only seemed to support Boomer and Jolly's accusation that Adama had taken the *Galactica* away from the fray for cowardly reasons. During the long trek back, as they made two more hops to fueling stations, Starbuck convinced Boomer, Jolly, and the other fuming pilots of the need for caution—not only to wait to find out what had happened, but to save themselves *and* their planes. Still, he could feel his own rage build to a boiling point.

As they neared the *Galactica*, Starbuck ordered the flight patterns set on a direct line to the battlestar's landing deck. When he pushed his own course button, however, sparks from the control panel flew suddenly all over the cockpit. At the same moment a piece of the instrument panel popped out and dangled from its moorings. The ship started to waver from the dictated flight path. Trying to keep it straight manually, Starbuck had to deal with the electrical shorting directly. His mind telling him to work slowly, he forced his fingers to keep wires apart and try to sort out the problem.

"Reading you, Red leader one," said a voice on the communicator. "From here something appears to be wrong with your craft."

"Darn right something's wrong. In trouble, in trouble."

Tigh's voice cut in.

"We read you, Red leader. How can we assist?"

Starbuck tested his portside stabilizing rocket. Normally its thrust could be controlled by a lever on the instrument panel. But this time, pressing the lever, he found it wouldn't respond to his touch. Instead, it coughed and swung about in an erratic rhythm.

"Battle damage," Starbuck reported. "Stabilizer won't keep steady thrust. Put a systems analyst on the line."

"On the line," said a voice immediately. Starbuck recognized it as Athena's. He glanced quickly at the small, round picture of her he had pasted as a souvenir at the top of the scanner panel, and could see her in his mind scowling over the gadgetry of the guidance system. "What's your condition, Starbuck?"

"This is no time for trainees, Athena. I'm in real trouble."

"I'm the best you've got right now, pilot. You'll stay in trouble if you keep talking like that. What's your fuel?"

He glanced at the gauge.

"Low."

"All right. Run the check with me. Alpha circuit, close and alternating to left servo circuit...."

Reaching deftly past the sparking circuit board dangling from beneath his instrument panel, he closed off a circuit switch.

"Alpha circuit closed and alternating," he said, "to left servo circuit."

He checked the stabilizer, which was now dead, not responding a bit to his touch on the lever.

"No response."

"Omega C circuit," Athena said. Her voice was calm, aloof, sounding much like it did in response to his sly proposals in the ready room. "Closed and alternating to servo support circuit...."

"Alternating to servo support circuit."

He felt the sweat becoming roaring cataracts down his brow. The stabilizer was still not responding.

"Does not respond."

A small choking sound—the engine beginning to misfire.

"Fuel zeroing out," he said.

Tigh's voice cut in again, addressing Athena.

"Bring him at zero thrust, with all stabilizers cut off. There's no choice."

"Wait," she said. "One last check. Is your right stabilizer steady?"

"Right stabilizer steady."

"Cross patch right servo to left."

"Cross patching right servo to left."

Working as patiently as possible, Starbuck made the cross-connections on the panel. He looked out again at the stabilizer. It teetered limply, stone cold.

"No luck," he said. "I can't reverse thrust. Get everyone out of the way, I'm coming in hot."

There was a pause before Athena's answer came.

"All right, you're cleared to come in."

Her voice sounded apprehensive.

"You'll be coming in like a missile," she said. "The deck is cleared for an emergency."

"Thanks for the comforting thoughts."

"Don't mention it. See you on deck."

"That's a date."

Boomer's voice cut in.

"Would you listen to this guy? He loses one lousy stabilizer and he's gotta have all the ladies out to watch him ventilate the flight deck. If the ladies'd only—"

Jolly's voice interrupted.

"Good luck, Starbuck."

"Thanks, Jolly. Red leader to flight deck. I'm coming in hot, ready or not. I hope you guys aren't counting off for neatness."

His sweat felt like a raging sea in a torrential storm. The deck swung out from the *Galactica* way before he was ready. He knew the deck hands inside the battlestar were in readiness for disaster, ready to mop up his blood if that turned out to be the necessary duty.

He could lose this one. Well, the famous Starbuck luck had to run out some time. He engaged all the devices on his instrument panel that still functioned. His ship careened down to the deck. He could feel himself on the verge of blacking out as he made his descent, and he shook his head to clear it. Just before landing, he was able to turn the viper to something resembling the correct entry attitude. He knocked out a series of landing strobes as the viper touched the deck. Sparks flew in all directions. As his ship shuddered into the entry port and hit the emergency force cushion, he did black out....

... When he came to, after only a few seconds of darkness, he saw the small emergency vehicles racing out of pockets in the walls toward the crashed viper.

Everything was okay. He was in terrible pain, but everything was okay. The Starbuck luck was still as good as gold. He headed through the air lock.

"Starbuck, are you all right?" Athena cried, as she ran up to him and into his arms. He hugged her perfunctorily, released her abruptly, and started walking toward the elevators.

"For a guy who just had a whole fleet shot out from under him, I'm fine," he said. "No thanks to your father."

Athena hurried after him.

"What are you saying about my father?" she said. "Do you realize what we've been through?"

"Yeah? You should've seen how we spent our day. Joyriding, just joyriding. Keeping the Cylons off your necks while you took off on a pleasant little cruise away from—"

Athena stopped him in front of the elevator.

"Starbuck," she said, "don't you *know* what's happened?"

He guided her into the elevator, a bit roughly.

"Bet your life I know what's happened, little darling. You should get a scan of what this baby looks like from out in space when she quietly catfoots away from the scene of battle. A beautiful sight, serene—unless of course she happens to be your base ship picking up and sneaking away, leaving you high and dry like a—"

"Stop it! Listen! The colonies, Starbuck, they're all gone. *All* of them. Wiped out by those Cylon—"

"Wait, what are you talking about? Destroyed? How's that—"

The elevator door opened, and the raucous noise of the bridge drowned out the remainder of Starbuck's question. Angry, he stormed into the room. Nobody noticed him. The voice of one of the bridge officers rose over the clamor.

"Fighter ships coming in on both decks, sir."

Tigh moved toward the officer and said:

"Give me a full report. What's the count?"

Tigh? Starbuck thought. What's he doing giving the orders? Where's Adama? There can't be anything wrong with Adama! He felt disoriented, thrust into some alternate world where Adama no longer existed and the terrible cowardice of removing the *Galactica* from her proper place had somehow been transformed into heroism.

"Sixty-seven fighters in all, sir, twenty-five of our own."

"How many battlestars!"

The officer paused before revealing the information.

"None."

"What?!"

"We're the only surviving battlestar."

"My God." Tigh looked shocked. When he spoke again, it was in a choked voice: "Make the pilots from the other ships as welcome as you can."

Starbuck strode up behind him and said:

"Little late for that, Colonel."

He heard Athena, keeping pace with him, whisper:

"No, Starbuck, not—"

He could sense all the bridge officers staring at him, as Tigh turned toward him.

"For some of those guys you want to welcome," Starbuck said, "it was a tossup to them whether to land here or blow the *Galactica* to pieces with a bellyful of torpedoes. Maybe they got talked out of it, or maybe nobody had any left, but—"

"What's the meaning of this insubordination, Lieutenant?" Tigh barked.

"He doesn't realize what's happened yet," Athena interjected. "I told him some of it, but it doesn't seem to be sinking in. I don't think any of them really know."

Puzzled, Starbuck looked around him. He noticed Boomer and Jolly, looking just as furious and frustrated as Starbuck felt, just arriving on one of the elevators.

"Realize what?" Starbuck said. "That the old man turned tail and ran, leaving all our ships to run out of fuel, making—"

Tigh's angry gesture compelled Starbuck to stop in the middle of his sentence. The Colonel nodded toward one of the officers.

"Put the tapes of the transmissions we monitored back on the scanners. For our young *patriots* here."

Starbuck started to complain further, but the pictures that came abruptly onto four of the screens on the console effectively silenced him. The pain of watching the disaster on a single screen was stretched to unbearability when multiplied by four. Starbuck's fists clenched in frustration as he became aware that there was no chance he could climb back into his cockpit and battle these Cylon warships that had worked their grisly havoc hours before.

"I'm sorry," he said, "sorry."

Behind him he heard Boomer and Jolly, muttering sadly, joining him in his remorse.

Adama stood on the old familiar hill, inspecting the line of the new, unfamiliar battle scar that ran in a deep rut across his land. The line seemed to go off to infinity, or at least to the base of the row of fires that raged at the edge of the crumbling, far-off city. Every building there must be ablaze by now.

He headed down the hill, unaware of Apollo following close. A faraway sound of many voices was growing rapidly louder. Glancing over his shoulder, Adama could see the flickering of a dozen torches beyond Apollo's viper. Roaming mobs already. Well, he would deal with them when they reached him. Unless they had some kind of fanatical, wild-eyed leader, he believed he could handle any mob.

He turned back and resumed his walk down the path, the one he had so carefully laid, stone by stone, in the first year of his marriage to Ila. The broad, deep battle scar cut across it, too, running all the way toward his home. He kept his eyes away from the house for as long as he could, but finally he had to look. Once an attractive series of living units—he had laid out its interlinking half-circles himself, as diligently as he had put down the stones in the path—it too was now sliced down the middle by the straight-line scar of battle. On one side of the line much of the dwelling still stood, but the other half, the half containing Ila's sitting room, was now charred rubble. All lingering hope of Ila's survival left him as he stared at the damaged structure. There was little chance Ila had wandered off by herself. She knew his first impulse when free would be to return to her here, and she would wait. If she were here now, she would have run out of the house into his arms. What was her schedule for the time of day when the attack had occurred? Late afternoon. That was the time she usually took a nap. She had probably been asleep then, or been awakened by the shrill squeals of diving Cylon fighters. He did not like to think of her in terror. It was unlikely anyway. In recent years Ila had become slightly hard of hearing, although she didn't like to admit it. Anyway, she could sleep through anything, no matter how loud. She had probably stayed asleep.

Stop this rambling! he thought. *She's dead! Admit it to*

yourself. She has to be dead! There's no other possibility.

Adama felt the tears well up in his eyes. Walking into the house, he didn't have to stop for the scanning device, which had been reduced to a knobby lump of debris and dangled by a wire from a jagged hole in the wall. The front door hung uncertainly from a single hinge. He went directly to the living room, to the row of holographic photographs that had been implanted into a wall years ago. There was a single source of light in the room, a rectangular candle with each of its twelve permanent wicks ablaze. Each flame represented one of the twelve worlds, and Adama felt a momentary odd surge of joy when he saw they all still burned, as if the candle were saying to him that the colonies must, and will, survive.

He remembered the pleasure Ila had found in that candle when she had discovered it in a nearby town bazaar. She always delighted in searching for bargains, and would often go too many uneconomical miles out of her way and come back arguing that her latest purchase was especially economical. The flickering light from this special candle cast strange auras on the series of pictures she had so carefully selected before arranging for the laser procedure that made them part of the wall. There were photographs of the entire family, he and Ila, Athena and Apollo and Zac. Zac. He could not bear now to look upon the eager hopeful smile of Zac, nor could he examine the chronological half-circle of photos that traced Zac from child to adult.

Adama recalled a recent conversation with his youngest son, one of the last talks they had had. Zac, somewhat drunk from a glass of the unusually potent Libran wine which always tasted so mild but provided such a heady kick, had revealed to his father his intention to eclipse Apollo. He said his whole life was directed toward bettering his brother's achievements. When Adama had begun to provide soothing fatherly advice, Zac had interrupted him by telling him he simply didn't understand.

"Father, all the time I was growing up, it was Apollo this and Apollo that, every second thing I heard about was some big heroic Apollo exploit. Well, okay, don't get me wrong, I'm just as proud of him as you and Mom are, as Athena is, but don't you see we all have somebody we have to beat. Sometimes it's just some idealized role model, sometimes it's somebody real. With me, it's Apollo. I love him, but I've got to beat him."

Adama had tried to convince Zac that there was more to life than a stratified sense of competitiveness, but the boy wouldn't listen. He had left his son that night feeling a vague sense of failure. Had he invested his children with a distorted ambition to succeed? Or was it the war that fired up his heroic ambitions? Perhaps Adama had devoted so much of his life to the war, hardly taking note of his own considerable achievements in it, that he had failed to give his progeny a proper perspective on life. Perhaps he had made Zac and Apollo, even Athena, pale copies of himself. All of them were geared to perform heroic acts, make important decisions, assume leadership as naturally as others went about daily tasks. Years ago Adama himself had accepted such responsibilities as natural consequences of being his own father's son. Was it possible that the cracks in a life devoted so completely to military matters would start emerging in the third generation? No—he was being too hard on himself. Zac may have been unreasonably ambitious, but he was also young. Adama suspected that at the age of twenty-three he might have been similarly oriented toward success and just as energetic in talking about his future hopes. And his other children, Apollo and Athena, showed no signs of personal or psychological problems. Apollo, combining bravery with intelligence, was a fine fighter pilot, one of the best, and Athena's sharp-witted ability to synthesize information in order to come to a quick decision seemed to destine her for a command post.

As he looked away from the pictures of his children, Adama realized that he was exaggerating Zac's slightly besotted declarations because of his own deep sorrow. Zac had just shown a natural, youthful desire to flee from the nest. But even as he told himself that Zac's aspirations were not his fault as a parent, Adama could not quite rid himself of the nagging thought that perhaps they were.

For a moment he wished that all these pictures were not embedded so firmly in the wall. He would have liked to turn them around, face them toward the wall, as angry people did in the ancient novels he often scan-read during recreation periods.

Finally, he had to look at the pictures of Ila.

The poses in the neat circle depicted her at several ages from seventeen to fifty. The most recent photo showed her smiling broadly at her fiftieth birthday party the previous year. In the background he and the three children stood, their figures dimly lit, perhaps put in shadow by the glow of her pride. He reached out to touch the figure in the foreground of the picture, was surprised at the framing glass which blocked his hand from the three-dimensional figures inside.

He and Ila had both drunk a bit too much wine the night of that birthday and had foolishly speculated on the far-off future—on the day when Adama would have come to the end of his usefulness to the Colonial Fleet and could pension himself off to his home on Caprica. Even as they had spoken, they knew how absurd their hopeful speculations were. As long as the war continued, Adama would have refused retirement and pension, and was likely to serve in at least an advisory capacity after he became too feeble to command. In Ila's last letter, which arrived just before the beginning of the peace conference, she had written that if the conference was successful then perhaps their absurd hopes for the future might be realized after all. He had enjoyed a moment of hope—but just a moment. That was all the Cylons allowed, one moment.

He looked at the youngest Ila, the oldest photograph, taken just before their marriage. Memories of that time came back to him in a flood. When he met her, Ila had been a dedicated career woman, determined to become one of the Quorum of the Twelve. At the age of seventeen she had run for, and won, a seat on the local council. Her radical ideas had already drawn attention to her, especially her plan to reduce her city's contribution to the overall Caprican military budgets. Because she was gleaning some support from the populace, themselves tired of the war which was then almost a thousand years old, certain military and political circles concluded that she should be investigated. Adama, then a young ensign on TDY to the Caprican training base, was dispatched to check out the mild agitation in the boondocks, and see what he could do to smoothe it over. Caprican law would not allow Ila's right of free speech to be interfered with, but there was nothing in the books that said a handsome young ensign couldn't positively influence a beautiful young agitator. The insight of the military higher-ups in this matter proved to be extremely prescient. Not only had Ila been positively influenced by the ensign, he had fallen head over heels in love with her, from the first moment he saw her making an impassioned speech to her council. He had always preferred women with strength of character, and Ila turned out to be one of the strongest women he had ever met. Her inner strength had saved him time and time again during the course of their marriage, especially during those moments when he had to be told no as he leaned toward some ridiculous course of action.

Each separate likeness of Ila he looked at started similar waves of memory. He saw her beauty in all its stages, could remember his love growing through all the years. Suddenly he broke down, began to cry.

"I'm sorry, Ila," he sobbed. "I was never there when it mattered. Never there when—"

Inevitably, he thought of all they might still have accomplished together, all they might have done in the past. The pain became too much to bear. He willed the tears to stop, willed himself to turn away from the wall of photographs. When he looked up, he saw Apollo standing in the doorway. Obviously he had been there watching for a long time. Adama had forgotten that Apollo was with him; he was disoriented for a minute. With his fingertips, he brushed away some of the remaining tears and struggled to control his voice as he addressed his son.

"I didn't—didn't hear you come in."

"Forgive me, Father," Apollo said. "I should have gone away, left you...."

"No, no, that's all right. I was... was just gathering a few remembrances."

There were some nonholographic photos spread on the mantel below the arranged pictures. He picked one up, offered it to Apollo.

"You want this likeness of you and Zac?"

Apollo drew back. When he spoke there was a clear edge of bitterness in his voice.

"No," he said. "Look, there are crowds coming. They probably saw our ship land."

"I'm not worried about them. I'll be a few more minutes here...."

Clearly the decision was against Apollo's best judgment, but he nodded stiffly and started to leave. In a second he was back in the doorway, saying:

"Maybe she wasn't here, maybe—"

"She was here," Adama said with finality. "She was here."

Apollo muttered, "Yes, of course," and left.

• • •

Standing by his ship, Apollo watched the angry crowd of people approach. They moved like a mob, disorganized, with a lot of arm waving and jostling. Their voices, pitched high and shrill, made their hostility clear. Apollo wondered if his father had judged correctly in staying around. A mob like this one might kill the both of them, and what good would that do? Perhaps he should have insisted more strenuously, rushed the old man back to the plane and taken off before the crowd's arrival.

Adama might, after all, be too overwrought right now to make a decision wisely. It certainly didn't seem rational to Apollo for the old man to mourn quietly before a bunch of old photographs. Apollo didn't like photographs. They were just ice sculptures that would melt away if you refused to look at them, and the last thing Apollo wanted was to look at pictures of Mom and Zac. He had refused his father's offer of the photo from the mantel—and that picture had once been his favorite—because he couldn't bear to look at it, to see Zac's smiling face and their arms around each other's shoulders. If he kept that picture, it would definitely call up the memory forever of their last battle together, definitely force him to speculate about his possible error in leaving Zac out there all alone. The kid wasn't ready to be left on his own and, in spite of the fact that all military wisdom dictated that Apollo return post-haste to the Fleet with his information, he would always wonder whether or not he should have turned and flown back to Zac, helped the kid out when he really needed it. With the present desolate condition of the war, it was a memory he could not afford.

The mob stopped about fifty yards from the ship. Some of them pointed toward it angrily. Apollo walked forward, trying to gauge the depth of their enmity. Some of the people who were doing the pointing turned to point toward him. Gradually the entire mob took notice of Apollo coming out to meet them. A man came forward, shaking his fist, shouting.

"Where are they, the rest of your fancy pilots?"

Another man, just behind the first speaker, hollered:

"Where were you, lad, when they were killing everyone? What were you doing?"

Other men and women separated from the crowd and edged toward Apollo. They were angry, as if they would like to tear him apart and spread the pieces from here to the burning city.

"Wait," called out a woman who was running to the front of the crowd. The front ranks parted and she stepped forward, leading a small boy by the hand. "Let him talk." She turned to Apollo, and walked a couple of tentative steps toward him. Apollo was struck by her beauty, which shone through the dirt marks on her face and the dishevelment of her hair and clothing. "Before they jump at your throat, I'd like to know a few things. Where you were. For that matter, where was everybody, the entire military force? Where were all of you? Even after the battle had begun, we prayed for relief, but you never came."

Her words were enunciated precisely, with a theatrical projection. This lovely woman could be the real danger to him, Apollo thought. The mob he could handle by tactics learned in training, but one intelligent person could combat such tactics easily. To give himself a moment to think, he looked down at the boy beside her. The child's face almost couldn't be discerned through all the dirt on it, but his innocent eyes were clear as they stared upward at him.

"Most of us are dead," Apollo said, trying to speak as matter of factly as possible. The crowd quieted down. "We were ambushed. There *is* no more fleet."

First there was a collective gasp in the crowd, then individual reactions of anguished crying and angry despair. The woman looked around at the mournful people, her face showing the confusion she felt.

"But," she said, "but why—I mean, you're here. Where did you come from?"

"The battlestar *Galactica*."

"Survived...."

"Yes...."

"Well, what of the president, what about the Quorum of the Twelve? And the other colonies. We can fight back surely. We're united, all twelve colonies, after hundreds of years. Our combined strength, it can't possibly be defeated, that's what we were all taught, what we learned from the cradle."

Adama, standing by the wing of Apollo's craft, moved into the flickering light and spoke.

"Our unity, our strength, came about too late."

The woman clearly recognized Adama, and her head made an automatic bow.

"Commander Adama!" she shouted.

Others in the crowd reacted to the name.

"Serina," Adama said.

His mere appearance seemed to bring home to Serina and the crowd the impact and scope of their defeat.

"Then it's true. They've beaten us. We're doomed."

Adama's look was stern, magisterial. Apollo turned away from it and looked down at the boy who was, inexplicably, smiling as he looked up at Apollo with admiration.

"Can I ride in your ship, mister?" the boy said.

Apollo bent down and picked the boy up. The child was lighter than he looked. As he replied to the boy, he thought of Zac and he had to look at his father as he spoke.

"Fighter ships are no place for boys."

Adama must have understood the meaning of his son's glance, for he looked away, some hurt in his eyes.

"They're going to have to be if our people are going to survive," Serina said.

Adama walked slowly up the hill and turned his attention toward the burning cities. Serina moved up behind him. Apollo followed, still holding the boy in his arms.

"Commander," Serina said, "we're going to have to fight back. We can't—can't simply give up."

A long silence followed. Both Serina and Apollo stared at the commander, searching for signs of decision. When Adama looked their way again he seemed to look past them.

"Yes," he whispered, "we're going to fight back."

Those in the crowd who could hear his declaration told those closest to them. Word spread quickly. As the knowledge was shared, the crowd reacted variously, with cries of satisfaction, frustration, vented anger.

Adama took a couple of steps toward Apollo before speaking again. When he talked to his son, it was as if the crowd beyond them didn't exist. The intimacy was a combination of father speaking to son and commander addressing captain.

"But we can't fight back here, and not now. And not in the colonies, not even in this star system. We must gather together every survivor from each of the twelve worlds, every man, woman, and child who's survived this infamy. We must get word to them to set sail at once, in any vehicle that'll carry them, no matter what its state."

"Father," Apollo said, "there isn't time, not enough time

to arrange provisions. I'm sure the Cylons will be sending landing parties to eradicate the survivors. What we should do—if we could just send in our remaining fighters—"

"No! Too many of them, too few of us. There's a time to fight, but not now. We must withdraw, fight another day, it's only—"

"But—but there's no way to board the entire population on the *Galactica*, and we have no troop carriers any more. Those vehicles—they'd be, well, just a ragtag fleet. Their potential for conversion to hyperspace capability is marginal at best."

"You're thinking logically, yes, but this isn't the time for logical thinking. We'll use what we do have. Every intercolony passenger liner, freighter, tanker, even intra-colony buses, air taxis, anything that'll carry our people into the stars."

"And when they've gathered in the stars?" Serina asked softly.

"We will lead them. And protect them until they are strong again."

Adama's eyes glowed with such powerful confidence that, for a moment, Apollo couldn't be sure whether he was facing a madman or a savior. From the confused face of Serina and the curious looks emanating from the mob, it was clear that they weren't sure either.

Apollo tried to picture what his father proposed. All manner of ships rising from planets in flame—as he had called it, a ragtag fleet. The survivors of all the colonies, the Aeries from Aeriana, the Gemons from Gemini, the Virgos from Virgon, the Scorpios, the Leos, the Picons, the Sagitarians. It just didn't seem possible. But judging from the determination displayed on Adama's face, Apollo wasn't going to pull forth any doubting auguries.

Apollo nodded, said they had to try it. Serina agreed. Soon the mood of the crowd had changed from puzzlement to confidence as they cheered their leader.

FROM THE ADAMA JOURNALS:

The assembling of the survivors! What a miracle that was. Word went out over all the secret channels. Somehow people on all the twelve worlds received it. I'm told that the waves carrying the message only had to burn their way through the thinnest beginnings of planetary atmosphere before messengers on the surface were dispatched in every direction. Get to a rallying point, salvage every ship with sufficient thrust to reach the chosen coordinates, sneak around, above and beneath the Cylon patrols that were scouring the ground and weaving webs in the sky.

Not every refugee made it to our secret rendezvous. We have, in fact, no way of knowing how many failed. In the aftermath of a holocaust like the Cylon massacre, there's no time to arrange for the proper memorials, no cenotaphs that can be planted in airless space. Some made it, some did not. They came to our designated assembling point, around which Apollo had neatly improvised an enveloping camouflage force field that made us invisible to the many Cylon search patrols that passed near us. How no ship led the Cylons directly to us is simply another facet of the historical miracle that took place.

Divine intervention was suggested to some by the fantastic chain of events that brought thousands of survivor ships to us. Whether it's interpreted secularly or mystically, the miracle happened.

CHAPTER FOUR

The Cylon Imperious Leader had learned long ago to overcome his distaste at the sight of a human being. In the rare times when he had needed in the uncomfortable course of duty to actually face a captured enemy, he had felt sick for a long time after the interrogation. They greatly disturbed his sense of unity. He was never sure why, but he absorbed small doses of their irrationality when forced to be physically near any of them. Now, self-discipline and the deliberate suppression of certain portions of the third-brain enabled him to encounter a human without undue reaction afterward. However, the human being standing before him at this time threatened severely to restore the old irrational responses. While trying to figure out why this particular human was so particularly unsavory, he carefully shut off those parts of his mind that could be significantly affected by the being's mere physical presence.

The answer to his growing feelings of revulsion might be the simplest, the most obvious. The man, Count Baltar, was a traitor. Traitors deliberately disturb order for their own selfish gain. They were the vilest of a vile race. And Baltar was surely the greatest traitor of all, since his betrayal had made the human annihilation possible. While the leader would have liked to treat this traitor with proper contempt, the involved ceremonies of Cylon courtesy demanded that he at least be polite.

"Welcome, Baltar," he said, controlling the vocal output of his helmet so that a human-sounding warmth underscored the words. "You have done well."

Baltar, who had sustained an emotionless appearance since being led to the Leader's pedestal, now suddenly spoke in anger, adding to his voice that strange inflection that humans termed sarcasm.

"I have done well, eh? What have *you* done? What of our bargain? My colony was to be spared."

Another unexpected and unreasonable outburst of emotion from a human. Imperious Leader should have been prepared for it, he knew, but he did not always correctly judge the erratic use of emotions that made humans so annoyingly unpredictable.

"The bargain was altered," the leader said, his third-brain instructing his voice box to put a humanlike sarcasm into the words. The sarcasm was a good approximation, and he felt quite satisfied with it.

"How can you change one side of a bargain?" Baltar said.

It was like a human to place what little logic he did have at his command into a framework of extreme selfishness. They could never see the scope of a larger plan unless they were directed toward it. Even then, their minds seemed unable to absorb such a plan's completeness. They could, it seemed, see parts but never wholes. No wonder they were not fit to govern a single portion of the universe. As he replied to Baltar, he continued to give his voice a human sound, so as not to confuse the stupid, traitorous man.

"Count Baltar, there is no other side. You have missed the entire point of the war."

"I don't know what you mean," Baltar said. His voice suddenly subdued, he cringed.

"What I mean is that there could be no dominion over the species so long as man remained a power with the universe. There are no shades of meaning when it comes to this. Man or the Alliance, the answer is obvious. Compromise is not at all acceptable."

A whining tone came into Baltar's voice when he spoke next:

"But you have what you want. The threat is gone, it no longer *exists*. I delivered my end of the bargain. On my world, my reputation is firm—whatever Count Baltar says he'll do, gets done by him and him only. I did what I was supposed to! My dominion was to be spared, you said it was to—"

"Dominion? There can be only one dominion, one power, one authority. There must be no exceptions."

"What are you, you think you're some kind of god?"

"Gods are one of the intellectual trivialities of your race."

"All right, forget I said that. But, believe me, I have no ambitions against you."

Imperious Leader blended a burst of laughter into the sarcasm of his voice-box mixture.

"You grow smaller as you stand there, Baltar. Could you think me so foolish as to trust a man who would see his own race destroyed?"

"Not *destroyed*—subjugated. Under me—"

"There can be no survivors. The Alliance is threatened even if one single human being remains alive on one of the colonies."

"Surely—surely, well, of course you don't mean me."

Urgent messages were being transmitted to him from his aides all through the chamber. He had spent too much time already with this pitiful human representative. And he fancied himself a *worthy* survivor!

"We thank you for your help, Baltar. Your time is at an end."

Two Cylon centurions materialized out of the shadows in which the leader had positioned them. Each took a fleshy arm and lifted Baltar off the floor.

"No!" Baltar shouted. "You can't! You still need me!"

"Need you. That is unlikely."

"I have—I have information. Please. My life for my information."

Always willing to bargain, Imperious Leader thought, this human would never stop desperately offering trades.

"What is your information?"

Baltar pulled away from the centurions and approached the pedestal. There was a surprising arrogance in his walk.

"My life?" Baltar said.

"Your life," the Leader said. An easy promise. Easy because he had no intention of keeping it.

Baltar looked to each side as if he suspected he could be overheard. By whom?

"At the spacedrome on Caprica . . . when your centurions were collecting and exterminating survivors, one of them gave me information."

"Oh? On what grounds?"

"That I save the man's life."

"Did you?"

"Of course not. I beheaded him myself."

"Oh. Interesting. Go on. What did he tell you?"

"Many humans escaped, he said."

"But how could that be?"

"They escaped in ships, anything they could find. A handful of survivors. And you haven't located them."

"Perhaps you are right. But they would have neither fuel nor food for a prolonged voyage."

"He told me they were heading for a rendezvous with a surviving battlestar."

"A battlestar!"

"Yes. He said it was the *Galactica*."

"That can't be! I will not allow it."

"I don't know what you can do about it."

"Make it my business to destroy those ships. And their precious *Galactica*. As I will destroy you now."

"But my information . . . you promised . . . you said—"

"Dispose of him."

The centurions seized Baltar and began to drag him out of the chamber.

"You can't do this to me!" Baltar shouted.

"I would remind you that this is exactly what you did to your informant."

As he awaited his centurion's return with the announcement that Baltar's head had been separated from his body, Imperious Leader contemplated the man's loathsomeness. By human standards, the trader was evil. To humans, evil was a relatively simple concept. A measure of premeditated malice, a dose or two of harmful action, some negative thoughts that did not conform to a standard that would change eventually anyway. The kind of trivial feelings that guided Baltar, traits like weakness and selfishness, were equated too easily with the idea of evil in human minds. To them, Imperious Leader would be evil, which certainly measured the absurdity of their view.

The centurion returned, and announced that the human traitor had been beheaded and his body had been disposed of—out a chute through which normally flowed Cylon garbage.

Imperious Leader ordered his network to root out and destroy the surviving humans, with special attention to the complete disintegration of the battlestar *Galactica*. As his centurions began sending out the message, the leader allowed himself a momentary surge of gratification. He was close to his goal now. With the annihilation of the humans, order could be returned to the universe, and he was the founder of that new universal order. Although he would not have admitted his feelings to be akin to Baltar's repulsively human selfishness, he could not help but acknowledge to himself that his place in Cylon history had been strengthened considerably by the imminent removal of the human pest.

Adama prayed that his rising hopes were not unreasonable as he oversaw the assembling of his ragtag fleet at the chosen coordinate points in space. Many of the survivor ships were decrepit, scarred vehicles, to be sure, but more of them had slipped through Cylon lines than he had expected. Reports showed that almost twenty-two thousand ships, representing every colony, color, and creed of the twelve worlds, had been dredged up as the result of the communications and physical searches initiated by his people. They might not exactly be suited for combat, but at least they were ships. They gave the human race, now reduced to a minuscule fraction of the population that had flourished in the twelve worlds, another chance. A chance to survive, a chance to—someday—defeat the Alliance.

As he watched reports come in on various screens, he was mildly amused by the signs on the battered sides of some of the rescued craft. *Trans-Stellar Space Service. Gemini Freight. Tauron Bus Lines.* The new fleet consisted of ships of every assortment, size, and shape. It might not look like much, but it was all he had.

"You look like the catlet that swallowed the underbird,"

Athena said, referring to a famous Caprican children's story. She smiled slyly. How long had she been standing there observing him?

"And you're rude for a subordinate whose sole claim to rudeness is that she's the commander's daughter."

She turned toward the starfield, and swept a hand across their immediate view of several of the odd-looking ships.

"That's quite an array of squadrons," she said. "Or are you even going to divide them into squadrons? You could put all the transportation vehicles into one, all the moving-van ships into another, all the sanitation—"

"That'll be enough, young lady."

"It's all just a roundabout way of asking you what you're planning."

Troubled by the question, he turned away from Athena. The move did him no good. Starbuck hovered nearby, slightly in front of a puzzled Colonel Tigh. In the shadows the newswoman, Serina, sat beside Apollo, their backs to the communications panel.

"All right," he said, "you all want some kind of an explanation from me. All right. I've got this idea."

"Idea?" Athena said, a bit too hopefully for her father's pleasure.

"It's just this. Long ago, I've no time concept of how long, and it's not important, there was an earlier civilization, a race from which we're descended. It's all in the secret history books, but I doubt if any of you have been privileged to inspect them."

They all shook their heads no.

"Well, our parent race left their home and set out to establish colonies throughout the universe. Many planets were settled but—because of dangers inherent in the individual planet or unpredictable disasters that wiped out colonies—only a few were successful. Finally, the twelve worlds were discovered, exploration showed them to be supremely habitable, and the remnants of all the other colonies were moved here. New colonies were established and, as you well know, they thrived. Now, those of us in this collection of motley ships are all that's left. We represent every known surviving colony, except one—"

"Except one?" Athena asked. "I don't understand what you mean. As far as I know, each of the twelve worlds had survivors and we've managed to rescue them."

"I'm not talking about the twelve worlds. No, I refer to a sister colony far out in the universe, perhaps not a colony at all, perhaps the planet from which our race originated. Whatever, it's only remembered through ancient writings. I'd show some to you but they, too, were destroyed by the Cylon assault."

"Okay," Athena said, "we all know something about this. It's been a part of our mythology for years—about an origin place called Earth, sometimes Garden of Earth, although that's never made much sense to me, it seems—"

"It may not be mythology, Athena."

"But it may be."

"Well, we'll see."

Adama was irked by his daughter's proddings. He had been excusing her recent shows of temperament on the grounds that she had been through so much misery since the beginning of the Cylon doublecross, but now he wondered if it was time to combine parental with military discipline and speak to her harshly.

"It's my intention," he resumed, speaking more slowly to test his own patience word by word, "to seek out that last remaining colony—call it Earth if you must. Whatever you call it, it may be the last outpost of humanity in the universe, perhaps a civilization like our own, perhaps with people just like us. We can ask their help in rebuilding and, perhaps, warn them of the Alliance and their goal of eradicating mankind."

"But, if the Alliance hasn't discovered them yet, maybe they're safe from attack. Maybe we shouldn't even—"

"Athena! It's the only solution we have. The Alliance is going to chase us across the universe. Lieutenant Starbuck, you have a question."

"Yes, Sir. If we're talking about this same colony, this mythological colony, well, I don't think anybody knows where it is. Even if we did, we barely have enough fuel to—"

"A very good point, Lieutenant. We have to find a fuel source, then. A fuel source and extended provisions for a long journey."

Colonel Tigh came forward.

"Commander, this is hardly a fleet of sturdy, well equipped soldiers, up to battling the universe. I mean, most of these people barely got away with their lives. They're emotionally and physically unprepared for the kind of journey you are proposing. . . ."

Apollo stood up and spoke.

"Sir, less than a third of these ships can make light-speed. It could take us generations to find Earth."

"Ah, but you're talking about it as if you believe in it, or at least in the possibility of it. It's a sign that it's worth seeking out. We'll find it because we have no choice. No choice. If we mark time in this corner of the universe, the Alliance'll find us. No, we'll travel only as fast as our slowest ship, we'll be only as strong as our weakest brother."

"Your rhetoric is attractive but I think we should fight."

Even Apollo was turning against him. Well, no matter. He had to persevere.

"We're the only surviving battlestar and our pilots are up to the task of protecting the whole fleet. Let's leave it at that. You may speak your mind at the next council."

"Thank you, sir."

Serina leaned forward and spoke in the style of her journalistic profession.

"I'm a bit vague on this business, star mythology was never my best subject." Which meant, of course, that she knew a great deal about it and was pretending ignorance in order to draw him out. "You say that this thirteenth colony, or parent world, is named Earth, and it may be somewhere out there in the universe, *still* populated and *still* amenable to receiving returning colonial inhabitants."

Adama turned back to the starfield, as if an easy answer to Serina's question was spelled out there in rusty letters by the decrepit vehicles. He felt like an ordinary seaman searching the horizon for a glimpse of sail.

"I think there is a real world called Earth and that it is out there and will welcome us," he said finally. "I believe it is there."

"Belief is a word associated more strongly with hope than fact," Serina said, adding a belated "Sir."

"Belief, hope," Adama said, "they're all we have, all we've ever had."

"Forgive my scepticism, Commander Adama, but you're asking us to join you on a religious quest."

"Perhaps."

"You can't go off on a religious quest when we—"

"I can," Adama said, "and I will."

He made a long survey of their puzzled faces.

"And you'll go."

When he saw that Serina was about to protest again, he said softly:

"There's no other choice."

FROM THE ADAMA JOURNALS:

I realized one thing about leadership during the period of exodus from the twelve worlds. A leader, no matter how benevolently he regards himself, has to be something of a tyrant. If he lets everyone in on every phase of his plan, allows them complete access to all information so they can see the overpowering odds against them, he takes the risk they'll become too discouraged to perform the little jobs that bring us forward through all the tedious phases. Human resilience is a marvelous quality, and we proved that during our time of reorganizing our society, repairing our damage, converting our ships to hyperspace power, building up the hopes of our people even while we reduced their food rations. I had faith in our resilience, but knew it worked best when the goals were limited. The emotions of people who are struggling with the aftermath of tragedy can be stretched to a breaking point if too much is demanded at once. So I had to remain a tyrant, remain aloof even from my friends and family. More than once my own resilience was put to task. No wonder tyrants so often turn mad.

CHAPTER FIVE

"I need sleep in the worst way," Starbuck moaned, as he and Boomer briskly made their way across a narrow walkway that hovered over a maze of tubing and pipes.

"Worst way, best way, *any* way," Boomer muttered. "I just want to get off this lousy duty detail."

Starbuck shrugged.

"I don't know. I get a kick outta being an investigator, makes me feel like a real detective. So I look at it this way. It isn't the worst duty in the fleet, asking a lot of questions. I hear they're gonna send some poor guys from Beta Section crawling around on the *outside* of some old skybus looking for a solium leak."

"Mmmm...how'd they miss us for that detail?"

"Beats me."

Like most fleet warriors, Starbuck hated the thought of a solium leak. A derivative of the fuel source, Tylium, the solium compound was less volatile but more insidious, since it was often difficult to detect until it was too late.

They left the walkway and entered the freighter's engine

room. Turning a corner, they came upon Captain Apollo, who was concentrating on an electronic measuring device as his crew pointed solium detecting wands in various directions.

"What have we here?" Starbuck said.

"I don't think I wanta know," Boomer replied.

Apollo looked up from the measuring device and glanced angrily at the two new arrivals. Starbuck's body tensed. Apollo's emotions were unpredictable these days, since his father had begun assembling the ragtag fleet.

"Would you two knock it off?" Apollo said. "I'm trying to listen for solium leaks."

Starbuck and Boomer looked quickly toward each other, then turned in unison, intending to retreat to the walkway.

"'Bye," Starbuck said.

"Halt," Apollo said.

The two men stopped in their tracks.

"Apollo," Starbuck said. "That stuff is dangerous. I don't want any part of it. I mean, these old ships shouldn't even be flying."

"There wasn't really any choice, was there? How many people did we have to leave behind for lack of ships, do you imagine?"

"Nobody knows."

"But you can be sure there were a lot, all left to be exterminated by those lousy Cylons. So—unless you want to volunteer permanent assignment on this tub, which incidentally shows every sign of adaptability to hyperspace conversion, you'll help survey each and every ship in the fleet for damage. And that means look for solium leaks. Or I'll be tempted to loan you out to Beta Company."

Without waiting for any response from Starbuck or Boomer, Apollo abruptly turned, picked up the measuring device, gestured toward his crew, and walked toward the ship's bulkhead.

When he was out of hearing range, Boomer whispered to Starbuck:

"Keep talking, old buddy, and you're going to get us in real trouble."

"Ah, he's got a fly up his exhaust tube. I don't know what's going on with everybody. They're all going felgercarb, if you ask me. Ten thousand light years from nowhere, our planet's shot to hell, we're running around looking for leaks in old buckets, our people are starving, and you're worrying about me getting us in trouble. What's the matter with you? What's the matter with everybody? I say we might as well live for the day. We haven't got many of them left!"

They followed Apollo through a bulkhead hatch into a passenger compartment. At least it was a passenger compartment now, whatever its original function might have been. Starbuck was at first struck by the thick feeling of the air, which seemed to resist inhalation. Small wonder. The room was packed with people—old, young, crippled, babes in arms. Some of them lay on the floor, clearly exhausted and spent. Others pressed up against packing crates. Still others had transformed the crates into their own private shelters. As the crowd took note of Apollo's presence, many of them reached toward him, their smudged fingers clutching and clawing at the young officer.

"Back," Apollo said. "Please, stay back."

The crowd looked as if they might jump onto Apollo, but were apparently checked by the move of Boomer and Starbuck to the captain's side.

"Where is the food?" a bedraggled and obviously desperate woman shouted. "What is it that's happening? We haven't had water in two days! Two days!"

"Please!" Apollo shouted. Starbuck had never heard Apollo's voice become so strident. "I'll be glad to help each and every one of you. But stay back. Starbuck, Boomer. . . ."

Starbuck drew his sidearm. He raised it toward the ceiling to display it for the threatening crowd.

"Put it away, Starbuck," Apollo said. "These people are already in battle shock."

"Yeah? Well, in another couple moments they'da been using you for a doormat, *Captain*."

"Where is the food?" an emaciated old man screamed. The phrase was quickly becoming a ritual to these suffering people, Starbuck noticed. "Why haven't we seen or heard from anyone in two days?"

"What the hell's going on?" another man said. "Have we been left behind?"

Apollo took a deep breath and gestured for silence. The crowd quieted down.

"You haven't been left behind," Apollo said in a level

voice. "There must be some problems in distribution. But it'll be corrected, I promise you that. Just be grateful you're alive and please give us a chance to adjust and find out what your needs are."

"We need food, that's what we need," the emaciated man said in a whining voice.

"And medicine," said one of the women. "There are wounded here, with us."

"That's one of the reasons we're here," Apollo said. "To check these things out, find out what your problems are."

"The problem is," said a professorial, middle-aged man with a beard, "the problem is we're all going to die."

Apollo sighed.

"No," he said, "no one is going to die. Now, it'll take a little while but we're just now finding out how many of us have survived—"

"Hardly the fittest," the professorial man said bitterly. Apollo chose to ignore the man's sarcasm.

"We need to know what your skill levels are," Apollo continued, "so that we can utilize them in helping each other. Boomer, get on the communicator and let Core Control know these people haven't had any food or water in two days."

Boomer nodded and moved to a clear space, where he flipped open his communicator.

"Now," Apollo said, "do any of you need immediate life-station aid?"

An old woman raised her hand. Apollo nodded in her direction, and she began to speak in an unfamiliar tongue.

"What's she saying?" Apollo asked Starbuck.

"I think it's some kind of Gemonese dialect. I'm not up on it, maybe Boomer can translate."

"Boomer's too busy just now. Does anyone here understand this woman's dialect?"

A tall woman, almost the height of Starbuck or Apollo, moved to the front of the crowd. Her clothes were in shreds, and Starbuck noted that a trim, small-breasted and slim-hipped figure was suggested in those parts of the woman's body that were on public display. Although her face was dirty and smudged, and her dark hair disheveled, he suspected that, cleaned up and groomed, this lady would be quite a looker. Most likely, she would be a great beauty, he thought.

"She says that her husband is feverish," the woman said laconically, in a deep voice that was almost sultry in spite of her messy appearance. She held her left arm at her side at what seemed to Starbuck a peculiar angle.

"There something wrong with your arm?" Starbuck asked.

She turned toward him. Her eyes were dark and it seemed to him that they glowed with emotional strength as she stared directly at him.

"There are others in greater need than I," she said.

"Get her out of here," growled a plump woman who had stationed herself to the right of Apollo. "She should be jettisoned with the dead."

A number of muttering voices assented to the woman's opinion. Starbuck could sense a danger in their nastiness, an anger that could easily rise to open hostility.

"You're right, Starbuck," Apollo said. "Her arm looks broken. Get her and the old man to the shuttle."

Starbuck helped the old man and his wife to their feet, then took the injured woman by her good arm. He was conscious of the many obscenities and insults being released around him. Their jeering seemed to be escalating to a danger point. He might have to draw his weapon again, in spite of what Apollo had ordered.

"Make daggit meat out of her," one woman shouted, and several voices assented. Starbuck did not look in their direction, although he kept a wary eye for suspicious movements in his immediate vicinity.

"Dirty," another woman said.

"Socialator," said a man.

"No place for refuse," muttered a voice that clearly belonged to the professorial bearded man.

A muscular man stepped up to Apollo as if he were spoiling for a fight.

"It's a sin to starve us," the man said, "while the bureaucrats and politicians luxuriate in their private sanctuaries."

"No one is in luxury," Apollo said, "I can promise you—"

"I've seen it," said the slighter man, who joined the muscular one in his confrontation with Apollo. "I saw it with my own eyes aboard the *Rising Star*, before I was cast out and reassigned here."

Boomer saved Apollo from answering by stepping to his side and announcing loudly, "Core Control is aware of the problem."

"Then I can tell these people that food and water is on the way?" Apollo said.

"They're aware of the problem!"

"What is it?" said the professorial man. "You're keeping something from us, aren't you?"

"Relief is on the way, I'm sure," Apollo said. "You have my word as a warrior."

Starbuck had finally made his way to the bulkhead hatchway, but hesitated there in case Apollo needed his help. The woman and the old couple waited with him, their bodies clearly tense with apprehension that violence could erupt at any moment.

"Your word as a warrior," said a plump woman. "You were the ones that brought us this death watch, *warrior!*"

Apollo looked back at Starbuck, motioned for him to get the woman and the old couple through the hatchway. He and Boomer began edging back to the opening as the space between them and the crowd narrowed.

"Corrupt," the professorial man hollered. "The entire Quorum was corrupt. We were betrayed. Betrayed . . . by all of you."

From the other side of the hatchway, Starbuck watched Apollo and Boomer get through the opening. Apparently just in time to save themselves from being trampled by the angry but frightened crowd. Boomer quickly shut the hatch and spun its wheels rapidly to shut off the compartment. Sounds of agony and anger could still be heard on the other side of the round portal.

"My Lord. . . ." Boomer muttered.

"You said it," Starbuck said.

Apollo's crew, who had remained in the engine room checking out solium leaks, gathered around, while Boomer told them what had happened in the passenger compartment. Apollo shook visibly. Starbuck moved to him.

"What happened? Why aren't these vehicles being supplied? I know we're low and Adama's cut rations, but we're not this—"

"I don't know!" Apollo hollered, his voice again a bit more strident than Starbuck was used to. "But something's gone wrong, and I've got to find out what."

When the pounding began on the passenger side of the hatchway, Apollo ordered everyone back to the shuttle. He and Boomer took the controls, while Starbuck remained with the young woman and the old couple. As soon as they had put some distance between themselves and the old freighter, Apollo switched on the shuttle's communicator, and spoke angrily into its mike.

"Alpha shuttle to Core Command."

"Core Command. Go ahead, Captain Apollo."

"Request clarification on food dispersal."

There was a crackling silence before the Core Command voice replied.

"No information available at this time."

Apollo exploded with anger.

"What're you talking about, no information available? God damn it, I just left a ship filled with starving people. They haven't seen a morsel of food in two days, and no water either. What in the twelve worlds is going on?"

Another long pause before the Core Command reply:

"I'm sorry, shuttle Alpha. Core Command has no information available at this time."

Apollo gave up and flipped off the communicator. Turning to Boomer, he said, "What is going on? What'd they tell you when you called in the food shortage?"

"Same thing they told you. A vague acknowledgement of the problem, you might say."

"Boomer, I'm getting a very uneasy feeling."

It seemed to Cassiopeia that her broken arm had felt better since the *Galactica's* officers had removed her from that seething crowd. In the cramped spaces of the passenger compartment, the arm had been jostled too often, pinched in between shifting bodies. Now it seemed filled with a comforting numbness. Her emotional panic had subsided as well. Knowing that so many of those poor despairing people were conscious of her previous position as a socialator, she had been afraid that some of them might have taken out their frustration on her. There were many hidden weapons among that crowd. One of them might have been used on her. She felt much more relaxed now as she helped Starbuck interview the old Gemonese couple. When he had finished with that interview, he turned to her and said:

"Now I'll need some data from you. That way the Life Center will be ready for you when we dock."

"Life Center?"

"Fancy name for sick bay. Don't fret it. Let's see. First I'll need your name and designation."

"My name is Cassiopeia."

"Lovely name."

"I think so."

"Designation."

"I am designated a socialator."

She saw the usual reaction in his eyes. She was used to it. Men from the other worlds, Capricans especially, had a good bit of doubt in them when it came to discussing socialation.

"It's an honorable profession," she said testily, "practiced with the blessing of the elders for over four thousand years."

She wondered if she should explain to him the years of preparation to which she had been submitted—the endless courses concerning social behavior, human knowledge—before her license was granted. She decided that, although there was kindness in this handsome young officer's eyes, a warm look that conveyed the potential for understanding, she had better not martial the arguments that defended her profession.

"I didn't mean to imply anything," Starbuck said. "I was just trying to figure out what all the excitement was about back on that barge."

She smiled.

"Those women were from the Otori sect among the Gemonese. They don't believe in physical contact between genders except when sanctified by the priests during the high worship of the sunstorm, which comes every seven years."

"No wonder those little buggers are such good card players."

"I beg your pardon?"

"Nothing."

He asked her several more routine questions before ending the interview.

"Well," he said, "they'll be waiting for you with this information when we dock. Are you in pain now? Can I give you something?"

"You've already been very kind."

Starbuck's smile was engaging. She would have hugged him, if she had had two good arms to use for it.

"What can I tell you, Cassiopeia?" he said. "It's my job. Also, I'm not of the Otori sect, right? And I've been getting these headaches." Obviously Starbuck knew of a socialator's abilities at curing mild illnesses with intricate massage techniques. "The pressure's getting to me, I suppose. I just need some kind of release."

"Make an appointment," she said, using her professional tone of voice.

"I just might do that. I might just—might—uh—"

His fumbling with the language made him all the more attractive to her. He looked like he might be acting the role of shy young officer. He had not seemed the type previously. Well, she thought, it would be fun exploring that particular line between reality and pretense.

In order to collect his thoughts, Starbuck made an excuse to go to the command cabin of the shuttle. The woman had intrigued him from the first. Discovering she was a socialator excited him even more. He had heard about socialators, and often wondered about their arcane—some said even metaphysical—abilities. If things settled down, and he could shake the weariness that his incessant duties had brought him, it might be fun to take the glamorous Cassiopeia out. Athena, of course, would be angry. Lately the commander's daughter had been laying claims of ownership on him, and he didn't like that. Let her be angry, a good lesson for her.

In the command cabin, Starbuck noticed that Apollo seemed unusually tense and angry. He was about to say something to the captain, when Apollo flipped on the communicator and broadcast to Core Command.

"This is Alpha Shuttle changing course to rendezvous starliner *Rising Star*. Shuttle will proceed on to *Galactica* with patients for Life Station."

He flipped the communicator off as angrily as he had switched it on.

"What're you up to?" Starbuck said.

Apollo's look threatened discipline for insubordination if Starbuck continued the familiarity. They had always been easy with each other before. What had gotten into Apollo? He was beginning to act like a tin-god version of his father.

"If you don't mind my asking, *Sir*," Starbuck added.

Apollo waited a moment before answering.

"I'm stopping at the *Rising Star*. I think I can find out what's at the bottom of this conspiracy of silence there."

Reacting to the rage in the captain's eyes, Starbuck decided not to ask what he meant by conspiracy of silence.

After Tigh brought him the news that there had been several reports of near-riots due to the lack of available food, Adama sat for a long time, looking out the starfield at his scattered, vulnerable-looking ragtag fleet. The Cylons would tear those poor ships apart if they ever detected the camouflage field.

"Father?" said a voice behind him. Athena. "Are you all right?"

For a moment he did not want to talk to her, but her sad, pleading eyes forced the words out of him.

"I can't say I'm all right, no. If anybody said to me he was all right just now, I'd set him up for a psychiatric examination, special treatment—"

"Doesn't sound like the warrior I'm used to. What happened to the joy of living to fight another day?"

"I took a tour belowdecks. The commander appearing to cheer up the passengers, you might call it. You should've seen their faces. Desperate, looking for a chance to live. And here I am, the commander, the authority figure. I could make the choices, I could say who's to live, who's to die, pass out priorities like chits in a lottery. One woman, with a baby in one arm, grabbed at me with the other. I didn't know what to say, I didn't—"

"Father, don't."

"No, I have to say it, Athena. I don't want this anymore, don't want what they so felicitously call the responsibility of command. Let someone else do it, let someone else take up the burden. . . ."

Adama turned in his chair. Athena sat next to him, guided his head to her shoulder. She felt odd in this comforting position, as if she had become possessed for a moment by the spirit of her mother, Ila.

"Easy, father," she whispered. "Listen. If it hadn't been

for you, we'd all be gone now. Instead, many are saved. It's extraordinary. Look out on that field of stars. It's the most beautiful sight I've ever seen. Look at our ships. If you look at them technically, sure they're old, rusty, beat up, battered. But they contain life. Life searching for a new world, a place to be and grow. Happiness, a future."

Adama started to protest, wanted desperately to say it was time for him to pass leadership to someone else—but, for a moment, he was caught by the view outside. He saw it as Athena had described, and it was awesomely beautiful.

Apollo left Starbuck to pilot the shuttle back to the *Galactica* and took Boomer with him onto the *Rising Star*. Lieutenant Jolly, who had been alerted to Apollo's arrival, joined them in a dimly lit corridor that connected the liner's two baggage areas. Apollo was astounded at the information that the chubby officer provided.

"Contaminated?" he said incredulously. "That's impossible. Weren't the provisions checked before they were boarded?"

"For radiation, yes," Jolly said, "but there was no time to check for Pluton poisoning."

"You mean all this food is worthless?" Boomer said.

"We can't be sure of that," Apollo said. "Not yet. Pluton breaks down the structure of the food. Jolly, have your crews go through every container. Chances are some of the supplies were shielded enough from the bombs to be saved."

Jolly did not look particularly confident.

"This is the third ship I've checked so far," he said. "It isn't looking good."

"Salvage anything you can," Apollo ordered. "Even scraps will help."

"What do we do with the rest?"

Apollo found it difficult to speak the words of his reply: "Jettison it. And keep the lid on the problem. If people find out we haven't any food we're going to have a mutiny on our hands. C'mon, Boomer, something I want to check out up in elite class."

Apollo charged up the iron step ladder as if in response to a full alert.

Serina came around a corner in a hallway and bumped into the briskly walking man. As they backed away from each other, Serina started to laugh at the awkwardness of their situation, but Apollo's cold look made her think better of it. She changed the laugh to a smile, and then waited for his response. He just continued to look at her, his opaque blue eyes showing no emotion. Serina was as impressed with the look of the man now as she had been when they had first encountered each other back on Caprica. With his obviously strong body and broad shoulders, his light brown hair so carefully groomed that its strands might be arranged by the book, his ruggedly attractive face whose hint of cynicism suggested vast experience in so young a man, he appeared to be just the type you could rely on in an emergency, and these days she anticipated emergencies on a regular basis. In spite of his impressive look, however, there was a definite note of arrogance, a drawing back from that which shouldn't be touched, hinted at by his stiff bearing and in the way one corner of his thin-lipped mouth turned down.

She held out a hand, which he took with a definite lack of eagerness for the social amenities. She wondered if she dared ask him for help.

"My name is Serina, Captain Apollo," she said amiably.

"I remember your name," he said brusquely.

"Come down off your epaulettes, Captain. I need to talk to you."

"Look, Miss Serina, I'm very busy now, I've got to—"

"Far be it from me to interfere with your duties. Goodbye, Captain."

She whirled around and started to walk away from Apollo.

"Wait a minute," Apollo said, then turned to the young, black officer who was standing slightly behind him.

"Boomer, why don't you go on up to elite class and see if there's anything going on we should be concerned about."

Serina, recalling the ugly plushness she had observed on her single visit to elite class, considered telling Apollo he wouldn't like what he would find there, but decided the captain would see it for himself soon enough. After the black officer had left them, Apollo turned to her and said:

"Well then, what can I do for you?"

In spite of the cool politeness, he sounded quite irritated with her.

"Please come with me," she said. "It won't take long."

She led him down a series of hallways which normally housed the lowest-class passengers on the *Rising Star*. People were crowded into its narrow cubicles.

"I'd've thought a celebrity like you'd do a little better than this," Apollo said. "A neat little compartment of your own on the elite levels."

"I was offered that, from several men whose approaches were quite subtle. Anyway, I had no interest in pulling space. I took what I could get fairly."

"I believe you."

She was startled by the warm sincerity of his comment. She might like this captain, after all, even if he did have a ramrod up his spine.

"I want you to help me with the little boy," Serina said.

"Little boy? The one I saw on Caprica?"

"Yes. Boxey's his name. I found him in the rubble during the bombings."

"What's wrong with him?" Apollo asked.

"I'm afraid it isn't good. A mild form of shock. He hasn't eaten or slept since the bombing."

"You have food?"

"I managed to get some from Sire Uri, on the upper level. Boxey won't eat it."

"I'll have him dispatched to the Life Station right away."

"I don't think that's going to be the answer. I don't know what to do. The poor kid's blocked out all memory, can't tell me anything about his family or where he comes from. All he ever talks about is this little daggit that got killed while they were running through the streets. He doesn't know it's dead, thinks it's just lost. I . . . uh . . . maybe you might be able to help. . . ."

"Me? If he won't eat for *you*, I don't know what *I* can do."

"Well, if you remember, he seemed to spark a little when you talked to him on Caprica. Frankly, I got the feeling you're pretty good with children, Captain."

Serina didn't understand the brief sad look that crossed Apollo's face, but she began to see that the aloof young captain was more complicated than she had thought.

"I grew up with a kid brother," Apollo said. "Well, let's take a look at your little Boxey."

Serina led him down a long companionway in which refugees had been crammed into many improvised living quarters. Some of the little niches were already decorated with simple makeshift remnants, a couple even had curtains up hiding blank walls.

They stopped by a niche which had a curtain drawn across its entranceway. A dim night light inside showed through the thin material of the drapery. He glanced at Serina, who told him to go inside. Entering, he found the young boy lying on a cot and staring at the ceiling.

"Excuse me," Apollo said. "Hope I'm not interrupting anything." The boy's eyes widened as he recognized his visitor. "I'm in charge of finding young men to try out as future fighter pilots. Your name is Boxey, correct?"

"Uh huh. . . ."

Apollo nodded. He moved to the edge of the bed and crouched down beside it. The boy, in fear or awe, shifted backward to the wall side of his cot.

"Good," Apollo said. "I've been looking all over for you. You know, you should've made contact with the commander. We're very short on pilots."

The boy looked quizzical. Apollo could remember teasing Zac and obtaining a similar look in response.

"I'm too little to be a pilot," Boxey said.

"Oh sure, right now. But how long do you think it takes to become a full Colonial warrior?"

"I don't know."

"You nave to start when you're very small, or you won't get these until you have gray hair."

Apollo pointed to the Captain's bars on his shoulder. Interested, Boxey lifted his head to stare at the shiny emblems.

"You like them?" Apollo asked.

Boxey seemed about to respond enthusiastically, but the interest vanished as quickly as it had come, and he put his head back on his pillow.

"I want Muffit," the child said.

Tears came to Serina's eyes, and she wondered if she should back out of the small quarters, stay out of sight in the hallway until the captain was through or had given up.

"Well, I don't know," Apollo said. "Not much room for a daggit in a fighter plane."

"He's gone. He ran away."

"Oh? Well, maybe we can find one of Muffit's friends."

"There are no daggits. I asked."

Apollo glanced back at Serina. His face seemed less severe in the dim light. She didn't know what to say.

"Well," Apollo said to Boxey, "tell you what. Here, you take one of these—" He removed one of the bars from his shoulder and placed it above the pocket of the boy's tunic. "—you take this until I furnish you the proper emblem. Now, as Colonial Warrior First Level, you are entitled to the first daggit that comes along."

He rose and started for the door, where he hesitated, then said:

"But *only* on the condition you get your rest, eat all of your primaries, and stop chasing girls. Good night, officer."

He saluted and went out. Serina followed but could not resist one peek backward. She saw Boxey looking down at the bar that Apollo had pinned on him. In the corridor, Apollo waited for her.

"Thank you," she said. "See, I was right—you are good with kids. You and your brother must be very close."

"We were."

"I'm sorry! The war?"

"I suppose...."

"Look, if you'd rather not involve yourself with—"

"Don't be silly. I've already lost the big one, I can stand a few little ones to win."

"That's not a little one in there, Captain. You win that one, you've accomplished something."

"Sure, cheered up a six-year-old. I'm afraid that's not—"

"I'm afraid it is, whether you want to admit it or not."

A hint of smile appeared again on Apollo's face. A potentially handsome smile, Serina was careful to note.

"I'm sorry, but I do have to go now," Apollo said. "Have to check out elite level."

"I hope your reaction to it is similar to mine, Captain."

"I don't understand."

"You will."

He gave her a half-salute and strode down the companionway. Serina noted, with a wry interest, that the captain no longer seemed so aloof and detached in her eyes.

Apollo found an elevator that went directly to the elite level of the *Rising Star*. As soon as its doors closed in front of

him, devices were activated that had originally been designed
to prepare the vacationer for his stay in the elite quarters of a
luxury spaceliner. Subtle perfumes drifted out of the air
vents; they suggested food or sex depending on which
direction the elevator rider was facing. A bizarre style of
music—quiet, soothing, intricately melodic—emerged from
speakers positioned strategically all around the elevator car.
In an odd, subliminal way the music seemed to suggest
romantic joys to come. Apollo recognized the insipid melody
as a series of variations on a Leon chant. That was likely,
since Sire Uri was a Leo. What struck Apollo as odd about
the music was that the song was originally an agricultural
chant celebrating the wonders of the harvest. The elevator
version had changed the simple tune into a ridiculously
complex and unrhythmic love melody.

A golden light switched on suddenly above the doorway
to signal that the elevator was stopping at the primary elite
level. The perfumes faded and the music diminished as the
doors slid open. Apollo's eyes hurt from the amount of gilt
ornamentation that he now faced. As he stepped into the
reception area, he noticed with annoyance that an absurd gilt
sign spelled CLUB ELITE over the doorway leading to the
level's inner sanctums. Apollo had traveled on a luxury liner
a couple of times, when there were no sensible accommodations available, and he did not recall from either of those trips
anything approaching the ugly embellishments that decorated the reception area.

As Apollo's eyes became accustomed to the ornate glare,
he was startled by Boomer's voice resounding through the
small chamber.

"Officer! I will ask you only once more to step aside."

Boomer was addressing a stocky muscular guard whose
broad body blocked the closed entranceway to the inner
quarters.

"Sir," the guard said in a bored voice, as if he was used to
discouraging other passengers of the liner from gate-crashing
the luxury quarters, "this is a private accommodation
secured by Sire Uri and his party."

"I don't care if it's—"

"I might remind you, sir, that Sire Uri is a newly elected
member of the fleet council. He has ordered me to see that he
is in no way disturbed by intruders."

"How's this for an intrusion, daggit-meat?"

Boomer's "intrusion" was his sidearm, whose barrel was now pointing at the guard's left nostril. The guard looked surprised, but not really scared. Boomer might be causing more trouble than was necessary, Apollo thought, might be better to proceed a bit closer to the book.

"What's going on, Boomer?" he said, striding forward.

"Fella here doesn't seem to want to let us in the club area."

"Is that true, soldier?"

"Well, uh, yes sir. Sire Uri said—"

"Do you recognize me, soldier?"

"Yes, Captain Apollo."

"Do you know I have complete authority to check out all levels of all ships by fleet order?"

"Uh, yes sir."

"Are you going to let us through that door?"

"Yes, sir!"

Apollo smiled at Boomer, as the guard obsequiously ushered them through the doorway. Sometimes there were advantages to being the commander's son, after all.

As they walked down a corridor just as over-decorated as the club lobby, Boomer muttered, "When I think of those starving people, I—"

"Don't even say it, Boomer. I hate this just as much as you do."

The liner's grand ballroom had been transmogrified into what looked, to Apollo, suspiciously like a throne room. A series of tapestries depicting what he recognized as a famous hunting cycle from the planet Tauron hung along one wall. Other walls displayed paintings, sculptures, holoviews that Apollo was certain were confiscated from all over the twelve worlds. Uri and his cohorts must have grabbed every art work they could rescue from the dying planets, looting museums and galleries while citizens died around them. Before the Cylon invasion, Uri had been famous throughout the colonies as a political manipulator of some skill.

For a moment it was difficult to locate Uri amid the impressive art work, the luxurious furniture, and the milling crowd, most of whom appeared to be elder statesmen and their courtesans. Almost everyone in the room was gathered around arrangements of food, shoveling victuals into their mouths with an obscene eagerness. Uri lounged behind one of the largest food tables, almost obscured by a high pile of exotically colored fruit. He was still as handsome as Apollo remembered him and did not seem to have aged much at all. There was a suggestion of jowliness, a bit of a bulge at his waistband—likely results of the present orgy—but overall Uri still looked every bit the aristocratic politician who had been extremely popular all over the planet Leo. Beside him, with her arms around his neck, there was a scantily clad young woman whose vapid beauty was marred only by the food stains around her mouth.

Apollo drew his sidearm and gestured to Boomer to do the same. As the revelers noticed the guns, the sounds of merriment diminished. When Apollo and Boomer walked slowly toward Sire Uri, glaze-eyed people along their route drew back. Apollo stopped at Uri's table. The man looked up at him with heavy-lidded eyes.

"I trust you have an explanation for this intrusion?" he said.

"Thass right," said the girl beside him.

Apollo pushed her away from the Sire and motioned for Uri to stand up. Uri was about an inch taller than Apollo and he tried to take advantage of the height difference by assuming an imperious tone of voice:

"What is this all about, young man?"

Apollo stared scornfully at the handsome politician.

"Would you like to make a statement before I arrest you, Sire Uri?"

Uri gestured with his right hand, signalling all activity still proceeding to cease. Even the musician stopped playing abruptly.

"I'm glad you know my name, sir," Sire Uri said. "At least you'll know from where the blade fell."

"Drop the cheap rhetoric, Sire Uri. You're going to follow me to my shuttle."

"I'll do nothing of the sort, young man. You've no jurisdiction aboard the *Rising Star*."

"I have all the jurisdiction I need. I can take this garbage scow and appropriate it for the fleet if I so wish. Better yet, if you choose not to accompany me back to the command ship, I'll just turn the six levels of starving passengers beneath you loose. You can take your chances with them."

Apollo gestured toward the overladen food table, and Uri understood his message.

"Captain," he said, "I'll grant you all this may seem a, well, a bit *excessive*. Blame it on overenthusiasm."

"Excessive? Overenthusiasm? All this? I'd say obscene and—"

"Wait just one moment, young man. I and my friends were merely enjoying a small, well deserved celebration, you might call it our prayer of gratitude for deliverance. We've a right to—"

"You have no right, no privilege of the Lord, for this kind of—of *celebration!* In case it's eluded you, Councillor, some hundred people have died since our *deliverance* from the Cylons."

"I was not aware of any cases of starvation, Captain."

"Maybe not. It may even be that hunger hasn't taken a life. Not *yet* anyway. But it's only a matter of time if we don't strictly follow the rationing plan my father's sent out to all fleet ships. If—"

"Your father?"

"Yes."

"Ah, then you're Commander Adama's son. Captain Apollo, I believe. I didn't recognize you, my deepest apologies. No wonder then."

"I don't follow you, Sire Uri."

He glanced toward the immediate audience and drew himself taller. Obviously what he was going to say next would be played to the crowd.

"I say, Captain, that it is no wonder that you are making this ill-timed power play." He turned toward the audience. "You see, my friends, this young man is an emissary from his father, our honored commander. When he mentions appropriating this ship, he is quite serious, and we are not allowed to argue with the commander's son, after all."

"What're you saying?"

"I am saying, Captain, that you will jump at any excuse to appropriate ships. To siphon off fuel for the *Galactica*, perhaps. I suspect that's the reason you're throwing your weight around, and not out of any compassion for hungry passengers. I recognize a political ploy when I see it, and you can just tell Adama that—"

"Can it, Sire Uri. With all due respect. Boomer, notify Core Command that we've located some stores which we will distribute as far as they go."

Uri's face suddenly turned red with anger.

"This is a violation of proper procedure, young man. And I'll not allow it."

"You don't have that choice. I remind you you're under arrest."

Uri took a deep breath before speaking again:

"Every morsel of this food is *mine*. I had it brought from my own estate, and it belongs to me and my guests. The law has not yet been written to confiscate personal property without a presidential order."

Some of the guests clearly agreed with Uri's aristocratic views, although Apollo could see that others were looking somewhat embarrassed and ashamed. The drunken young woman at Uri's side snuggled closer to him and made a dramatically meaningful hand gesture in Apollo's direction. He wished he could arrest her and all the revelers who endorsed Uri's view.

"Does your wife share your feelings about denying your food to others?" Apollo asked, with a meaningful glance toward Uri's strumpet.

"My wife?" Uri said weakly.

"Siress Uri. I don't see her."

Uri could not maintain eye contact with Apollo and he suddenly looked toward the thickly carpeted floor. Apollo remembered Siress Uri as a plump gentle woman, whose main job in life had been discovering ways to rescue her impulsive husband from potentially dangerous situations. She had been kind to him and Zac when they visited her during their childhood.

"No, Siress Uri is gone," Uri said. "Unfortunately she did not arrive at the *Rising Star* in time to be rescued with the rest of us."

Apollo did not for one moment believe the sob that Uri placed into his voice when he spoke of her.

"My sympathies," Apollo said. "I share your bereavement. Siress Uri was an outstanding woman."

Uri's head remained bowed. Dutifully, it seemed.

"Yes," he whispered.

"I'm sure she'd be *moved* by your period of mourning, and the style in which you choose to honor her memory. Boomer?"

"Yes, Cap'n?"

"Have Jolly send a team up here to collect and distribute

this food throughout the ship."

"Sir, shouldn't we check with Core Command?"

"Now!"

He grabbed Uri by the arm and rushed him out of the room. The young woman remained attached to the politician's arm for a few steps before falling into a drunken, glutted stupor onto the thick, red carpet.

While they awaited Jolly and his men, Boomer whispered to Apollo.

"Without being critical, Captain—is there a chance you overplayed our hand a tad, considering Sire Uri is on the new council?"

"This isn't a card game, Boomer, not one of yours and Starbuck's two-bit cons. Those people down there are starving, damn it!"

"Take it easy, Cap. I'm on your side."

"Are you sure?"

"Captain—"

"Sorry, Boomer. I'm easily irritated these days. You must've noticed."

"Well, now you mention it, yeah."

The elevator arrived and Jolly's large form seemed to fill the entire doorway.

"Let's get to it," Apollo said. "Collect every scrap of food you can find here and get it to the people."

The look of hatred from Sire Uri as two of Jolly's men took him into the elevator sent a chill up and down Apollo's spine.

Working gently, Dr. Paye positioned Cassiopeia's broken arm inside a transparent cylindrical tubing which was connected to a larger, more impressive set of medical machinery. The arm felt numb now, and none of the doctor's touching of it gave her any pain. With the arm in place, Paye drew out what looked like a trio of gunbarrels from inside a cavity of one of the machines. After each gunbarrel had been pointed at a different area of her arm within the tube, the doctor pressed a series of buttons and faint, laserlike beams came out of the gunbarrels. After the beams had penetrated the transparent surface of the tubing, they were diffused, entering her arm at several points. The numbness immediately left her arm and sharp tingling sensations replaced it.

Abruptly, Paye pressed the buttons again, and the gunbarrels retracted back into the machine. As he removed her arm from the transparent tubing, Paye said:

"How does it feel?"

Cassiopeia stretched the arm, then folded it. Even the tingling sensation was fading now.

"Feels like it hadn't even been broken," she said.

"The bone has been fused whole," Paye said, in a friendly professional voice. "It's probably even stronger than before."

"It's wonderful. Damn wonderful. Thanks, doc."

"With equipment like this I'm just a mechanic. A talented mechanic, to be sure, but just a mechanic. Anything else I can do for you, Cassiopeia?"

The offer seemed to mean more than mere medical attention. As a socialator she was used to even such an oblique approach and it was easy for her to demur politely.

In the corridor outside the sick bay, Starbuck leaned laconically against a wall, still in his flight gear. She smiled, glad to see the brash young officer again. Then she frowned, realizing why he might be waiting for her.

"You're going to take me back, aren't you?" she said.

"It isn't easy to cop a ride around here," he said.

She turned away from him. She felt the blood drain out of her face.

"I dread returning to that ship."

She did not like to admit it, but she was afraid of the stupidity of the passengers aboard the *Rising Star*. She sympathized with their plight, their hunger and their disorientation, but on the other hand she didn't care to offer herself as a sacrifice for their frustrations. Starbuck seemed to understand, for he said, "Look, maybe I can check around, see if there's anyplace else you can stay. There're better ships, might even be space aboard the *Galactica*."

Well, if there was anything this young officer wasn't, it was shy.

"What's the matter?" Starbuck asked.

"I sense a price tag. Would you be doing this if I weren't a socialator?"

"I might. Then again, I might not."

"Please don't joke. I'm ... I'm a little weak. I mean I—"

"Okay, okay. Let's forget the little jokes for a while. Look, *really*, I just want to help you. Nothing personal."

"*Nothing* personal?"

"Well, *some*thing personal. But I'll still locate some quarters for you. And that's all. You can break my arm if I'm lying. 'Course it might be worth a broken arm—"

"All right, all right."

"It's a deal then?"

"I think you've made a terrible deal, but all right."

Starbuck smiled genially as he took Cassiopeia's arm, the one that had just been repaired at the Life Station, and led her down the corridor.

Adama, coming onto the bridge, discovered Colonel Tigh smiling broadly, clutching the latest reports to his chest as if they were love letters.

"What is it, Tigh?" Adama said.

"Long range patrols've reported in. Their scanners find no sign of pursuit from the Cylons. All vectors are looking good. The camouflage shielding that Apollo devised seems to be holding steady. Except for that one flyby some time ago, not a Cylon flight team has been anywhere near us."

"So long as we remain hidden in space like this, it's highly unlikely they'll find us. Pray the camouflage continues to hold, Tigh."

"I do that every waking minute, Sir. Finding us now would be disastrous. We're not able to mount any heavy battle, Sir, not right now."

"I'm aware of that, Tigh. Painfully aware."

"What do we do next?"

"That question I propose to leave to other voices."

Tigh looked shocked and angered simultaneously.

"You're going to go through with that resignation plan then?"

"I'm submitting it to the council this—"

"Commander, we'd better talk."

"Of course, old friend, but my mind is made up."

"With fuel and food running so low, you can't resign now. If we ever needed leadership—"

"The fleet is filled with good men. You included, Tigh. The council will decide."

"Commander—"

"Yes, Tigh?"

Tigh paused, obviously reluctant to speak his mind.

"Go ahead, old friend," Adama said. "Say it."

"If you resign now, it will look exactly the same as your act of pulling the *Galactica* out of battle with the Cylons. I'm sorry, but—"

"And I'm sorry you think that. Perhaps the two events are related. And perhaps they merely support my decision that it's time for me to step down."

"No, you can't!"

"I've made my decision."

"I can see that, damn it!"

"Will you accompany me to the council chamber?"

"I'd rather not, if you don't mind."

Adama started to say that he did mind, but instead whirled around and left the bridge. Behind him as he went out the hatchway, he heard a loud thump. Undoubtedly Colonel Tigh hitting something metallic with his fists. Adama did not look back to verify that speculation.

The newly-appointed council of elders, a temporary assemblage that would govern until a proper Quorum could be elected, started voicing their anger immediately before Adama could even finish his resignation speech. Some of them sprang to their feet, shouting:

"No! We won't have it!"

"Unacceptable."

"You can't resign. You especially!"

Councillor Anton silenced the surge of protests with a sweeping gesture. Anton had some time ago been an aide-de-camp to President Adar. A hawk-faced, emaciated, old-line politico from Scorpia, he was crafty, but Adama had always perceived him as trustworthy and intelligent.

"Adama," Anton said, rising to his feet, "you have led us wisely and well. That's why we can't accept your resignation. Things are too grave now."

"I disagree," bellowed Councillor Uri. Adama had known that, if there were to be any serious opposition to any sensible plan, it would originate with the representative of the Leon survivors. Tainted as he was with scandal, his people had nevertheless given him a vote of confidence to continue on the council.

"I think our dear Adama is best qualified to judge his own capacity to lead," Uri said.

Adama glanced at Apollo, who was sitting with the newswoman Serina in the gallery in front of the council table. His son appeared to be furious, and the pretty young woman had her hands on his arm, apparently to convince him to remain seated. Adama liked what he had seen of the Caprican newswoman, and liked the fact that she appeared to show interest in his son. Apollo, so unhappy over the deaths of Zac and his mother, needed such a compassionate friend. He turned his attention back to Uri.

"In all due respect," he was saying, "I'm not at all sure that the commander has led us all that wisely, all that well. I cannot in good conscience characterize our present predicament as the result of good planning."

"Uri, without Adama none of us would've survived the Cylon—" Anton shouted.

"That may be," Uri said, "but I place the blame for the chaos that we endure now squarely on the commander's shoulders. Poor judgment in choosing food and fuel lots now leave us on the brink of disaster."

"Councilman Uri," Anton said, "you have a lot of nerve casting accusations about food shortages when you have been brought up on charges of hoarding in the face of starvation."

"Are your hands so clean, Anton? What about—"

"Gentlemen," Adama interrupted. "Gentlemen, please. This squabbling is not in our best interests. Uri is not entirely incorrect about the state we are in now, nor is he unjustified in blaming me. The problem is, and has been, that there are too many of us. Too many people, too many ships. We would have had troubles even if so much of our food supply had not been contaminated, even if so many of our ships had not proved to be in such unstable condition. If we had time—ah, but that's the real source of our disturbances. We *must* obtain fuel and food, that's our only solution. Otherwise, we all perish—slowly and gradually, as our supplies run out. We have to convert our ships to hyperspace capability and leave behind those that can't be converted."

"That would mean crowding ourselves together even more," Uri said. "Conditions now are intolerable."

Adama resisted the opportunity to comment on Uri's own solution to the supposed intolerability of conditions.

"Yes, Uri, it would. That's why I've intended to propose

that we pool our stock of fuel and send the *Galactica* and the most capable ships of our improvised fleet on ahead in order to obtain fuel and supplies for the rest of us."

"Ships left behind?" Uri shouted. "Commander, just how many ships do you propose we send on this fool—on this foraging mission?"

"Captain Apollo has the hard figures on that, Councillor Uri."

Apollo stood and spoke brusquely, obviously holding in his temper.

"About one third of the present fleet. There's just that amount of fuel to spread around, and that's a bit of thin spreading, gentlemen."

"Thin spreading indeed!" Uri said. "I say this is just a ploy for you and your chosen people to escape the rest of us, leave us here, without fuel, to die slowly. That is—"

"Sir," Apollo interrupted. "As things stand, there's not sufficient fuel to get the entire fleet anywhere. We must let those few who can seek out a solution do so."

"You're your father's son all right," Uri sneered. "I'm not certain you're not deceiving us in tandem."

"That is uncalled for," Anton shouted. "You know better, Uri, you—"

"Ah, are you in league with them, too, Anton?"

"Gentlemen, please," Adama said. "Hear me out."

"You sound very authoritarian for a leader who's just resigned," Uri said.

"I am merely advising," Adama said.

"Tell us your *advice* then. I am anxious to hear it, Commander."

Adama cleared his voice to buy time. He wished he could make Uri disappear. It was bad enough having to cope with ignorant opposition in a meeting like this; it was worse to know your opponent was merely a boastful crook who would never listen to reason anyway.

"I propose," Adama said, "that we send our best ships to Carillon for the purpose of obtaining fuel and food."

"Carillon?" Uri asked, a curious sarcasm in his voice. "Why in the twelve worlds an outpost like Carillon?"

"Carillon was once the object of a mining expedition from our colonies. Rich sources of Tylium."

"But, if I recall correctly, it was abandoned as impractical to mine."

Uri was obviously prepared. His spies must have obtained Adama's plan before the meeting.

"It was abandoned," Adama said, "only because there was no local labor, and it was too far from the colonies to make shipping a very practical operation. However, the exigencies of commerce need not concern us now."

"I do not believe Carillon is a proper solution. The same problems do exist. Carillon is too far away. Too many disasters could occur to our ships and people left behind."

"It's the only solution, Uri."

"Is it? What about Borallus? It's closer, and we know everything we need is there. Food, water, fuel."

Many of the councillors clearly agreed with Uri's proposal. *How could they be so dim, so unaware*, Adama thought.

"And there's undoubtedly a Cylon task force there," Adama said. "It could be fatal to let down our camouflage shield and attempt landing on Borallus."

"*Possibly* fatal," Uri shouted. "To me it seems *surely* fatal to use Carillon as destination."

"Carillon is our only hope," Adama said. He noted, by a quick count of the nodding heads around the half-circle of the council table, that more than half of the group seemed to be on his side now. "Gentlemen, you must understand that the situation has reached a critical level much sooner than we'd anticipated. Rations have already been cut by two-thirds. We can't afford to squabble any longer. We must act, and we must be able to present our plan of action to our people unanimously."

"Unanimity means just being your echo," Uri said bitterly, but he sat down. He was the last holdout to the plan. When the final vote came, Uri voted for the plan only after the council had agreed to accept Adama's resignation as president, and after they had agreed that Uri's ship, the *Rising Star*, would be one of the vehicles chosen for the hyperspace jump to Carillon.

After the council meeting, Apollo felt relieved that a positive action would finally be taken, but unhappy that his father had chosen to resign. He also felt deep anger at the insult Uri had thrown his way during the meeting. The bastard was just getting back at Apollo for arresting him. A lot of good the arrest did, anyway. Uri had manipulated the situation to his advantage and become leader of the factions opposed to his father.

"You look so sad," Serina said softly. She had been standing silently at his side for some time.

"Forget it. I wanted to ask you, did you bring Boxey with you over here?"

"Just as you ordered, Captain. I stowed him away in that lovely compartment you provided for us. Thanks, by the way."

"Think nothing of it. Let's go get Boxey."

Apollo strode through the labyrinthine corridors with a fierce determination. Serina, although she was long-legged and near his height, had trouble keeping up with him.

"How's the boy doing?" Apollo asked just before they stopped in front of the door to Boxey's quarters.

"Still won't eat, doesn't sleep."

"I think we may have something that'll interest him."

"Right now?"

"Yes."

"But there's so much for you to do, preparing for the trip to Carillon and all. Shouldn't you be getting your rest?"

"I thought I might sleep better after we solve Boxey's problem."

"That's a tall order!"

"Watch me."

Boxey, lying on the lower level of a double bunk, appeared as listless as ever. Apollo ordered him to get up and come with them. The child asked if he had to. Apollo said it was orders, and the boy reluctantly took his proffered hand. They traced a circuitous route to an area of the ship that Apollo had only visited two or three times in his entire tour of duty aboard *Galactica*.

Stopping at a door marked Droid Maintenance Laboratory, Apollo said, "This is it." He smiled at the confusion on Serina's face as he ushered her and Boxey into the lab. Immediately in front of them was a row of droids, propped up against a wall, all of them obviously switched off. Some of them had been opened up and various wires dangled from the regions of their heads, chests, and legs.

"What are these?" Serina asked.

"Droids. Mechanical constructs designed to simulate human or animal—"

"I know what droids are. I thought they were banned."

"On Caprica they were. Capricans didn't believe in using mechanical substitutes for human effort. A noble philosophy but—"

"I don't know about philosophy but I do know, in the few experiences I've had with droids, I'm uncomfortable perceiving human traits in something that turns out not to be human at all."

"I think you're wrong but under the circumstances it's not a worthwhile discussion to pursue. Let me just say that droids have become a necessity for spacecraft. They can tuck themselves into niches that bulkier humans can't reach and they can perform minor repair jobs on the surface of the ship or in atmospheres we can't breathe."

A stocky, middle-aged man in a lab coat came through a door. There was a certain mechanical look to his movements and Serina wondered if he was a droid, too. The way his face lit up when he recognized Apollo proved him to be human, after all.

"Ah, Captain Apollo. Right on time. We've been expecting you. Is this the young officer who's been put in charge of the new project?"

Boxey, surprised at the attention from this stranger, started to hide behind Apollo's legs.

"Well, Dr. Wilker, I haven't had time to fully discuss the project with him. It's our hope he'll accept."

Boxey pulled on Apollo's leg. Apollo looked down at the befuddled young boy.

"I want to go back," Boxey whispered.

"Boxey, this is a military order. We have at least to hear the doctor out. Tell us more about the project, doctor."

Dr. Wilker assumed a professorial manner and addressed most of his next speech to Boxey.

"Well, you see, we'll soon be landing on various alien planets, no telling what we'll find there. It's important that we be safe. Ordinarily, we'd have trained daggits to stand watch at night when our people are asleep in their encampments, but we don't have any daggits. So, we've had to see what we could come up with. We'll call the first one, Muffit Two."

Boxey looked sideways at Apollo.

"What'd he say?"

Apollo shrugged.

"I didn't really get it all, Dr. Wilker. Maybe you'd better show us."

"Right. Oh, Lanzer."

The call to his assistant was as exaggerated a cue as any found in ancient melodrama. Lanzer, a young, bespectacled man, held what appeared to be a small bundle of fur in his arms. Apollo knew the short-haired fur was fake, implanted on the droid body, but he would have taken the construct for a real daggit if he hadn't known better. Lanzer put the daggit-droid down on the floor, and it immediately began to bark in a high-pitched, compellingly friendly tone. Moving to Boxey, it stuck out its tongue and began to pant. The wagging of its tail was natural and convincing, unless you looked up close and could see that the tail protruded through a square hole at the back of the droid.

"Naturally," Dr. Wilker said, "the first one will have to be looked after very carefully."

Boxey, incredulous, backed a couple of steps away from the eager daggit droid.

"That's not Muffit," Boxey said. "It's not even a real daggit."

"No," said Wilker softly, "but it can learn to be like a real one. It's very smart. If you'd help us, he'll even be smarter."

Boxey couldn't take his eyes off the daggit. The panting replica of an animal seemed to have a similar fascination for the boy. With the first hint of a smile in several days, Boxey took several careful steps backward from the daggit, who stopped panting and looked up quizzically. The boy started to turn and the daggit ran toward him. Looking back over his shoulder, Boxey started to cross the room. The droid, appearing quite content, stayed at the boy's heels.

"We used the image of Boxey you gave us to train the droid to respond to him," Wilker whispered to Apollo and Serina.

Boxey stopped walking and turned to look down at the daggit. Slowly he opened his arms. The droid moved forward, sat up on its hind legs and put its paws on the boy's chest. The trying-out period was over. Boxey hugged the daggit and smiled back at the three watching adults.

Apollo smiled toward Wilker, and said, "That's one I owe you, Doc."

"Any time," Wilker said.

As they followed Boxey and his new pet into the corridor, Serina whispered to Apollo:

"That's one I owe you, Apollo."

"Any time."

"You look quite smug, you know that?"

"If you say so."

"But I'll kiss you anyway."

FROM THE ADAMA JOURNALS:

One day, when there was a lull in the war and we were off
doing convoy duty for some ships carrying supplies to a
fueling station under construction, I noticed Starbuck
running down a corridor, muttering to himself and making
furious entries in a little notebook. Now, when it came to
military matters, Starbuck was the proverbial innocent
ensign—if you could take a peep at them, you'd've expected
his diapers to be as green as he was. But, when it came to
money matters, especially when the money could be wagered,
Starbuck had been born adult. In his first week on the
Galactica he had maneuvered so many people into so many
corners that everybody was walking around round-
shouldered. By this particular time I thought I was on to the
shrewd young man, so I decided to see what he was up to. I
figured if I could catch him in the act of some illegal
enterprise, I could apply a little discipline and get him to
confine his sinning to the proper designated areas.

He moved fast and I had a hard time tailing him, since it's
hard to be a very good shadow when you're the ship's
commander, but I could soon see he was making for the
medical section. Sure enough, when I caught up with him, he

was in an empty ward. A bunch of the medics were gathered around him, hollering dates at him, and passing him little slips of paper along with what appeared to be a good amount of money. Starbuck was very busy, somehow managing to write things in the notebook and take the money and the slips.

"What's going on here, ensign?" I hollered in my best authoritarian voice. "Some off-hours gambling?"

Starbuck began to look very sheepish, very much the green ensign.

"I'm sorry, skipper," he said in a soft voice. The diabolical louse knew I hated to be called skipper, but I ignored that.

"And what's the subject of your little swindle this time, Starbuck?"

All the medics began to look apprehensive and I thought Ensign Starbuck might sink through the metal floor.

"Well, sir, we're betting on—uh, we're betting on—"

"Out with it, ensign. I want to know what this is all about before I confiscate everything for the ship's pension fund."

"Sir, we're getting together this little bet on, well, on the day you'll die, sir."

I have to admit I was taken aback by that reply, and couldn't speak for a moment.

"You're—you're all betting on—on the date of my *death*?" He nodded. I sputtered a bit more on the subject, then demanded that Starbuck turn over the betting money to me. It began to dawn on me that the money in his hand was fake, the kind of lead cubit used by non-bettors in card games.

"Just as well I got caught," Starbuck said to the medics. "Skip's right; it's a swindle. The fix was in."

I felt a little unsettled in my stomach.

"Fix?" I said, choking a bit on the word.

"Yes," Starbuck smiled. "I was gonna win. *No* doubt."

"You were going to win? You know the date of my death?"

"Yep."

As he stood before me and smiled smugly, I felt like strangling him.

"All right, Starbuck. Tell me your winning bet. I'm especially interested in the part about the fix. When am I going to die?"

Smiling, he handed me a betting slip that he'd been holding.

"My prediction," he announced.

I opened it up. It said, "Never." Then Starbuck started laughing and handed me a neat pile of fake cubits.

"Never," he said.

I'd been suckered. Standing in the middle of an enormous empty sickbay ward, I was backed into a corner. I joined in the laughter and ignored the insubordinate character of the whole episode. Starbuck showed me all the slips. They all said, never. I never tried to catch Starbuck out again.

CHAPTER SIX

Starbuck stole a cigar from Boomer and slipped away from the work party to his special hideaway—by his ship in the *Galactica*'s launching bay. Fitting himself into a dark wall niche, he lit the cigar and leaned his head back against the metal wall. Almost immediately he felt himself dozing off and a cautious part of his mind wondered if he should do something about the cigar. Then he couldn't think straight. What cigar? he almost said aloud. Visions of a starving mob coming in and out of light initiated a dream that never developed into a full-fledged nightmare because the sound of Cassiopeia's voice startled him awake.

"Starbuck," she said, "what're you doing, crouched in that hole?"

He realized that the cigar was about to fall out of his hand, and he tightened his grip on it. Moving out of the niche, he put the cigar to his mouth and took a long puff. The smoke that lingered in his nostrils had a faintly narcotic feeling to it, the result no doubt of one of Boomer's extra special blends. Cassiopeia had bathed and put on fresh clothes—a one-piece

clinging outfit that threatened to become transparent in the
right light—since Starbuck had left her at the nurses'
quarters. By all conventional measurements of beauty, she
was quite stunning now, but Starbuck briefly wondered if he
did not prefer the look of her in her previous smudged and
disheveled state. There'd been a vulnerability about her then,
a need to be helped that he had enjoyed responding to. Now
she stood before him, tall and attractive and strong. Another
strong woman, like Athena. He always found himself
attracted to strong women, but there were times—moments
of false nostalgia—when he almost wished for one of the
weak, submissive maidens of intergalactic legend. A foolish
thought, maybe—he knew he would be bored by such a
maiden in less than a day, and the only real benefit obtained
for someone like Starbuck would be a much needed rest.

"How'd you find me?" he asked.

"Followed you partway. Lost you here, then I saw the
light of that sweet-smelling cigar. Can I have a puff?"

"Sure."

She took a heavy drag on the slim cigar and appeared to
savor its taste.

"Ooooh, thank you! That joystick's been efficiently
doctored."

"My friend's an expert at the chemical alteration of cell
composition."

"My compliments to the botanist, then."

She took a couple of steps backward and looked up at
Starbuck's ship. Jenny and the rest of Starbuck's flight crew
had done an excellent job of repair work on it, replacing the
parts that had been destroyed by his crash landing and
generally tuning up all its systems. As always, they had
superbly polished its surface and the pinpoints of light that
seemed to spring out from its high gloss gave the impression
that the viper ship was performing its own strange abstract
little dance. Cassiopeia stared at it a long time before
speaking again.

"It's somehow beautiful, suspended up there like it's in
permanent flight. A perfect machine, born to dance with joy,
curve in and out of constellations...."

"Nice way of putting it," Starbuck said, biting down on
the cigar.

Cassiopeia's eyebrows raised.

"But you don't buy it?"

"Too poetic, leaves out the way the metal stinks when there's a fuel foulup, the pain all over your skin when something shorts and starts sending sparks up your sleeves. Still, I get your drift, lady. I'd rather be in the cockpit of that junkheap and flying some boring duty than any other job I can think of."

A headache was developing in what felt like spreading lines behind Starbuck's right eye. He squinted his eye and rubbed at his right temple.

"You look overworked," Cassiopeia said, sympathetically.

"Me overworked? Nah. I overwork myself just to get away from overwork. Still, it's been something of a strain these last few days, the work and the starving people and...."

"And Captain Apollo? I noticed he's been pushing you guys like a martinet. I almost expected some kind of mutiny."

Starbuck laughed.

"Mutiny? I doubt that. Not against the captain anyway. Too much trouble around anyway without playing revolution. No, I feel for Apollo. He's going through hell."

"Well, you're all suffering, I don't see why he should be singled out for—"

"No, I didn't mean that. Didn't mean just the ordinary misery that's facing everybody. Apollo lost his brother in the Cylon attack and he's pretty broken up about it. That's where his irritability comes from."

"Oh, I didn't know...."

"Certain kinds of scuttlebutt we don't allow to filter down to the civilian levels."

"You guys protect each other. I like that. Back home, we always felt that spacer pilots thought too much of themselves, I'm glad to see—"

"Yeah? Well, it's no big deal—protecting each other, like you say. Protecting each other's part of the job. You got to protect a piece of a guy's private life just like he's gonna protect you when you got a pair of Cylon fighters blasting at your tail. Same thing really."

"Do you love me?"

The abruptness of the question startled Starbuck. He did want to make love to her, but he didn't want her to ask the question.

"What's the matter?" she said.

"Is that the way you go about it, changing the subject and aiming right at the old target?"

"No, it isn't. If we were back on my planet, and you were accepted by the proper segment of our society, and you had given me the signal that you loved me, even then I would not be able to ask the question. I don't want to love you as a socialator. I'm not one anymore, not really. I think the job's just a part of history now, I'm unemployed. I want to make love to you. That's all it is. Not as a socialator, not as a refugee. Just as me, okay?"

"I'll think about it."

They stood and stared at each other for a very long time. Finally, Cassiopeia said, "Have you thought about it?"

"I'm inclined favorably—"

"Do you ever take that smoldering weed out of your mouth?"

He removed the cigar and tossed it onto the launching bay floor. It landed lit-end first and sent sparks flying.

After they had kissed, Starbuck said, "If I'da known that was the prize, I'da prepared a speech."

"I've heard all the speeches."

"Would you mind if we didn't spend much more time in this launching bay?"

"Can you think of anyplace more pleasant?"

"Come to think of it, I can't think of anyplace pleasant in this whole fleet."

"What's in there?"

"That's the launching tube. You don't want to go in there."

Cassiopeia had already walked into the tube through a circular side opening. Her hand gestured toward him. He looked all around the launching bay, even up at the ceiling.

"Lord," he said, "I'll do anything you ask tomorrow. Just don't call an alert tonight."

Athena had a strong hunch something was wrong. Starbuck had not been where he was supposed to be. When

Starbuck was not in the proper place, he was up to something. That was an axiom among everyone who knew the brash young lieutenant. She had glimpsed him earlier, giving more than the usual attention to a bedraggled woman who, from a distance, appeared to be sexy in spite of her scraggly condition. As she strolled onto the bridge of the *Galactica* and saw that it was deserted except for the ever vigilant Colonel Tigh, she wondered if her weariness were not just making her overly suspicious of Starbuck.

"You seem tired," Tigh said. "Why don't you steal a nap?"

"There's just so much to do, preparing for this hyperspace jump, educating the people. Some of them think we're just skipping out—"

"No way you can help that, Athena. They won't really believe us until we bring them back the fuel and supplies."

"You're more confident than I feel."

"No point in not being confident, I always say."

"Have you seen Lieutenant Starbuck?"

"You always take a while getting to what's really on your mind."

"Have you seen him!"

"No. I don't think I—wait, I did see him on one of the monitors earlier, just before we shut down the flight deck. He was near his viper. I think he was checking it out."

"That'd make sense, I guess."

"That was a while ago. I'm sure he's long gone by now. Getting a good night's sleep before the jump. Like I say, you should do the same. There'll be enough work from now on for all of us."

She nodded. Touching her briefly on the arm, he said goodbye and left the bridge. As soon as he had disappeared out the hatchway, Athena strode to the launch control console and stared for a long time at its monitor screens. Then, with an almost casual movement of her hand, she reached down and flipped a switch. On one of the monitor screens, she watched lights go on all over the fighter bay. No people were in evidence anywhere. Her finger eased over to another switch marked "launch tubes." As the monitor lit up, Athena's face flushed crimson with anger as she recognized Starbuck and the tall woman she'd seen him with earlier.

"That little snake," she said aloud. Her finger quickly proceeded to another button. This one was marked, "STEAM PURGE."

She tried to laugh but could not as she watched the monitor screen in which the two stood amidst a rising cloud of steam. Starbuck screamed and, flinging the woman before him, vacated the launch tube in all expedient speed.

Athena switched the monitor off quickly, but sat staring at it for a long time. When she ran a check on the launching bay later, neither Starbuck or the woman was in evidence. In her mind she made promises which, even though she might never keep them, were delightful to contemplate.

When Marron had developed her interstellar drive centuries ago, replacing the earlier more cumbersome systems, there had been more than enough Tylium available on the discovered planets to keep all of the human spacecraft going, and the expense of extracting the fuel from its geological sources to convert it into its volatile liquid form seemed quite economical. However, human colony expansion followed by the thousand-year war had depleted the supply of the only fuel source that could power the highly complicated Marron drive. In the time preceding the Cylon ambush, the price of Tylium had skyrocketed to new levels due to the controls exerted by war profiteers like Count Baltar (who, Adama had perceived, always seemed to have sufficient amounts of the fuel to fulfill any request). There had been a question whether the Fleet might have to cut down severely on its Tylium use. In fact, Adama felt, the Tylium crisis had been at least partially responsible for the fussy politicians, anxious to cut a budget wherever even a small rip could be detected along a margin, rushing so eagerly into the Cylon peace trap.

Now that they, the *Galactica* and the few other ships able to make the jump through hyperspace, had arrived in the sector containing the planet Carillon, Adama devoutly hoped that the old rumors of this place as a prime black-market source of the elusive fuel base were true. If not, he had left behind thousands of people in thousands of ships who would futilely watch for their return.

Almost as soon as they had materialized in Carillon's solar system, the bridge scanner announced an obstacle for which they had not planned. Immediately the commander called in his three best fighter pilots—Boomer, Starbuck, and Apollo—to brief them on their unexpected mission.

"It appears," he told them, "that the skies around Carillon are heavily mined. They—"

"Mined?" Apollo said. "But who would set up such a—"

"For the moment, Captain, that's an irrelevant consideration. The point is that we cannot pass in order to get into position to accept supplies. Certainly the *Galactica* and our other larger ships can't make it through as things stand now. It's possible that a path through the mines can be found—I don't think the planet has been sealed off. The mines are clearly protective. We need to discover that path. And that will be the job of you three."

He paused to let the impact of the order sink in.

"All right, we don't have time for elaborate searches. You'll have to navigate by scanner and sweep everything out of your path with turbolasers. Any questions?"

"It's my bio-pulse line, Sir," Starbuck said. "Bad time for me to be cooped up in a cockpit. Would this be an appropriate time for me to take my sick leave?"

Adama smiled. The three pilots laughed nervously.

"It would," Adama said, "but request denied. I didn't arrive at you three to lead us through without a great deal of anguish." Apollo's eyes narrowed at his father's words. "You three control our fate. The rest of us will sit in anticipation of your skill."

"Or lack thereof," Starbuck said, and Adama nodded.

Apollo stayed behind after dismissal. Touching his father's arm, he said:

"Thanks."

"For what? For selecting you for a dangerous mission? Apollo, if I could've excused you, I would—"

"No, it's not that at all."

"What is it then?"

Apollo lowered his gaze to the bridge floor, a bit embarrassed.

"Well, father, it's just—well, lately I've been getting a lot of flak. That old clown Uri insulting me during council, accusing me of being in league with you to deceive everybody. I mean, I think I've proven myself, but there're still people around here who attribute my rise through the ranks as well executed nepotism. When I arrested Uri, he accused me of a political ploy, threatening to appropriate the *Rising Star* simply to collect fuel for the *Galactica*. And then there're the dissidents—"

"Stop it there. I shouldn't let you go on about it. There are many things we can't talk about, not in this place, at this time. Maybe later." He tried to say something more, but could just repeat, "maybe later."

"Sure, I'll work up a list of complaints."

"Apollo, if it's any consolation, there's one thing I've observed about this damn minefield."

"What?"

"Every mined satellite is firmly in orbit. No sign of a decaying orbit anywhere. The implication is strong that the minefield is maintained on a regular basis and that there has to be somebody down there on Carillon's surface."

"And it's a good chance they're mining Tylium, right?"

"Right. They've got to be doing something sinister to bother with all this protection."

"Thanks for mentioning that," Apollo said. He looked at his chronometer. "Well, I've got to hotfoot it now, and check on my ship."

As he watched Apollo stride out of the room, Adama felt pleased at the clues to a renewed confidence in his son. Perhaps all the new troubles had forced the memory of Zac's death to the back of his mind. Continuing troubles had a way of doing that. He wondered, too, if the improvement he perceived in Apollo was at all attributable to the charms of that lovely newswoman, Serina, or the way she had directed his attention to the troubled boy, Boxey.

Athena sprang into the room as if she'd been crouching by the doorway, awaiting Apollo's exit. She had a copy of the three pilots' orders clutched in her fist.

"Father," she said, "I can't believe you're doing this. Why couldn't you have listened to the others, gone to Borallus instead of this filthy, dangerous place?"

For a moment Adama felt terribly confused. It was difficult to shift his concentration from the satisfaction over his son's confidence to this new disturbance from his other child.

"What is it, Athena?"

"You're taking such an awful chance with their lives."

"Of course. They know that. They could back out without blame, you know that."

"Ah, damn, Starbuck's too much of a fool to back out of a dangerous mission."

Adama was beginning to understand the source of her rage.

"It's Starbuck you're worrying about, is it?"

Her shoulders sagged suddenly, as all the rage seemed to go out of her in a rush.

"It's not just that, Father. I'm worried about Apollo, too—you know that. And Boomer. It's just that—I don't know what it is."

"You love Starbuck and you're naturally—"

"I hate that . . ."

Another surprise. Adama took Athena in his arms and asked her what was wrong. Holding back her tears, she told him about her discovery of Starbuck and Cassiopeia making love in the launching tubes.

"Well, so you have to fight for your young man," Adama said. "That's not so hard. You're a fighter. I'm proud of your courage and your—"

"Oh, shut up, Father. That's not what I want to hear. I'm just, I don't know, very disturbed, and I don't know what to think. I used to think I could cure myself of Starbuck, get a pill out of sickbay or something and forget about him. But, I don't know, it's this war and the destruction of our home planets and this desperate voyage to a place where we don't know what we'll find. Everything's in a different perspective now. Hopeless. That's why I'm so frightened about this—this mission. Everything's been hopeless since—if they survive this, if any of us survive, what next? Will we find this Earth you claim isn't myth?"

"Perhaps not."

"I was thinking that. We could grow old waiting. I mean we may never have the chance, the chance to—to—"

"To form permanent relationships, have children, and a home?"

"Yes."

"You know, I think it's a bit premature for you to be worrying about your old age. I, on the other hand, ought to give a great deal of thought to this voyage. When we reassemble the fleet and my resignation as president of the council takes effect finally, then I—"

"Get that idea right out of your head. You're not going to resign. You have to lead them. You're all that's left."

"We're recycling an old argument, which is not to the point right now."

Athena hugged her father. She had not done that so spontaneously in some time, and he was happy to feel the tension between them alleviate.

"Thanks for consoling me," she said.

"Just returning the favor. Remember when you had to console your old Dad."

"Well, I'm sorry if I spoke out of turn."

"You're allowed it."

After Athena had left, Adama sat alone for a long time, thinking about the conversations with Apollo and Athena, satisfied that—whatever their arguments with him—at least they were on his side.

As Starbuck waited for launch signal, his ship vibrated under him, as eager to get into action as he was. In his mind he went over Tigh's final briefing. All they had been able to discern through the scanners was that there were at least three types of mines in the field. There was the normal explosive type, which could blast to smithereens any ship that came into contact with it, plus any other craft within a kilometer's radius. A second kind seemed more instrument than weapon. It had electronic equipment all over its surface, and nobody aboard the *Galactica* had ever seen any mine like it, if indeed it was a mine. The third type created the most trouble. Rather than exploding, it sent off flashes of light whose intensity was so concentrated they would blind anyone unlucky enough to set it off. Because of that danger, the three pilots had to fly the mission with their cockpits darkened and treated with a chemical to ward off the ray.

Fine, Starbuck thought, if that had been the only kind of mine. But the chemical protection that opaqued the cockpit made it necessary for them to fly blind against *all* the mines, relying on their scanners to locate targets. In combat Starbuck liked this kind of seat-of-the-pants flying, but not in a suicidal mine-detecting mission.

Tigh's voice came over the communicator, asking his pilots if they were ready.

"Ready," Boomer's sturdy voice said.

"I'm ready," came the cool sound of Apollo. "What about you, Starbuck?"

"I'm not ready. But let's get it over with anyway."

A short tense pause, then the launch light came on and the three ships catapulted into space. Forming a neat triangular formation, they headed for the minefield. In the short interval of time it took to reach the field, Starbuck said a silent prayer to the goddess Luck, wishing her continued good health and a return of the favor.

"I'm going in for preliminary scouting," Apollo said.

"Good luck," said Boomer and Starbuck simultaneously.

"Don't jinx me with good wishes," Apollo said, laughter in his voice. "All right, I'm going to make a sweep by the nearest thingama—my God!"

"Apollo!" Starbuck yelled. "What's wrong?"

There was an agonizing wait for an answer.

"I found out what the mysterious mines were. They're not mines at all really. They're electronic jammers. Soon as I got near that one, everything in this plane started going haywire, including the controls. I was able to wrest back command of the controls and jerk the plane out of its range, otherwise I think I'd have been sucked in and then, I don't know, probably then it explodes. Come in carefully, you guys."

Starbuck flew in slowly, keeping most of his attention on the scanner, so he could avoid the jamming mines. Boomer came in directly behind him.

"Hey Boomer," Starbuck said, "don't slipstream me."

"Shows how much you know. There is no slipstream capability in spacecraft which—"

"I know, I know. We got to stop you memorizing those manuals in your bunk. I was just using a figure of speech and you give me academy lectures. I mean, get out on your own."

"Just trying to cash in on your luck, bucko."

"My luck has decidedly changed lately."

On the scanner one of the light mines was activated near the form of Apollo's fighter.

"You all right, Apollo?" Starbuck said.

"I'm fine. They were right about darkening the cockpit, though. I'd be blind now. Though I feel like I'm blind as it is. I can't see much. My scanner's doing an erratic dance. And it's getting hot, very hot. I'm veering off. Anybody make out anything else on their scanner about this field?"

"Negative," Starbuck said. "My scanner's burning up."

"Mine's gone," Boomer said.

"I was afraid of that. The jamming's playing havoc with our instruments. We shoulda stayed in bed."

"A little late for that, I'd say," Starbuck said. "What do we do?"

"Only one thing I can think of, fellas, and it's not exactly the best academy procedure. Seems to me we've gone by the book as long as it's feasible. Our only chance is to haul off, hold positions and blast away."

"You mean run a path right through the minefield?" Starbuck said. "With our scanners out of whack and our cockpits dark?"

"Does it sound difficult to you, Starbuck?"

"Oh, no. Duck soup. The nuts. Easy as pie."

"What if we miss a mine?" Boomer said.

"One of us'll be the first to know it. You with me?"

"I'm with you," Boomer said.

"I'm with you, too," Starbuck said.

"Let's fly!" Apollo said.

On the bridge of the *Galactica*, Adama and Tigh listened to the communications among the three ships avidly. When Apollo proposed running a path through the minefield, Tigh looked panicked.

"Shall I tell them to abort the mission, sir?" he asked Adama.

"We can't. Apollo has full authority."

"But we've got to stop him. This is too reckless a—"

"Colonel, there's no way we can stop him. Not only is it essential that we get our ships through the minefield, Apollo has a great deal to prove."

"What does he prove by killing himself?"

Adama shrugged, resigning from the argument. The truth was too painful to admit. Apollo might just like to kill himself in the middle of a bold heroic exploit; it would at least prove to others that he was not, after all, the vassal to his father's tyrant-king, doing Adama's bidding in a vast plot to deceive everybody.

Everybody watched the massive screen at the top of the console silently as the three sleek, delta-winged ships angled through the minefield, which was now brightly lit by two activated light-mines. The three pilots were firing everything they had, and with stunning accuracy. Mine after mine exploded and disappeared. Suddenly, when it became clear that Apollo's foolhardy plan was going to work, a cheer went up among the bridge crew.

"I don't know what to say, Commander," Tigh said. "They're clearing the path."

"Now that's precision flying," Athena said from her post, smiling at her father. It was one of his phrases, and she meant it affectionately. Starbuck's voice came over the communicator:

"I can't see a blessed thing. Are we hitting anything?"

"Be hanged if I know," Apollo said. "But it's cooling off. I do believe we made it."

"Yaaahooo!" screamed Boomer.

Then all their voices chattered together, and the exuberance of their three young heroes buoyed up the spirits of everyone on the *Galactica*.

Since the fleet of human survivors had disappeared, activity aboard the Cylon base ships had declined, leaving Imperious Leader more time for speculation about the minor failures within his otherwise enormously successful plan. He knew there could not be many human ships left, yet where were they? If the Cylon culture had had any inclination toward proverbs, they might have felt they were looking for a needle in a haystack—although haystacks were nonexistent on Cylon worlds, where grotesque livestock were fed blocks of nutritive substances through an osmotic process, and where needles had no point, literally and figuratively.

Perhaps the humans had worked up some kind of force-field camouflage. Imperious Leader's spy network had discovered clues that they had such a capability, and he had ordered his experts to develop anti-camouflage devices. He had not had a transmission from them since.

The leader was not so much disturbed by the technology causing the humans' disappearance as by the fact that they continued to keep out of sight. Baltar might have said it was the famous human resourcefulness, implying that resource-fulness had been a key human trait throughout their history. A human, Baltar had once said, was never so confident as when he had his back against the wall. A pompous outcry of arrogance, of course, no more than could be expected from the smug human traitor, but still a troublesome concept. The image, especially, bothered the leader. A Cylon arranged matters so that his back was never against a wall. He either plunged forward to his death or emerged victorious. There was little middle ground. But humans were always finding middle grounds. Curious.

A message came along the network from an executive officer. Some explosions had been registered near Carillon. Evidently some mines set in the protective field around the planet had been set off or had malfunctioned. On occasion that minefield caught and eliminated space pirates who had heard rumors about Carillon. Whether the humans had anything to do with the present series of explosions was debatable. However, the Leader ordered intense surveil-lance, because of the importance of the Tylium mining complex there. In all the years of the war the humans had not discovered that Carillon was a prime source of fuel supply for their enemy. Nevertheless, a sneak trip to Carillon might be exactly what the devious Adama might be attempting now.

This war with the humans must end for once and for all, the Leader thought. It had gone on too long, used up too much of Cylon resources. He wished to get back to the proper business of his leadership—to seek out the cracks and flaws in the unity and organization of his own race, to make the concepts of peace and order the synonyms they should be. Even now, in some Cylon worlds, the human practice of monogamy had been communicated to certain sectors of the population, and they were busy practicing it. Monogamy went against the basic concepts of the network of Cylon civilization, where it was vital that every Cylon attempt and complete as many forms or degrees of contact as possible. Monogamy contained in its disagreeable structure too many forms and degrees of limited contact, a state Imperious Leader could not abide, and he vowed to severely punish those Cylons practicing it when he could afford to devote attention to domestic matters again.

He ordered his executive officers to keep him well-informed with any clue that might suggest the invisible fleet's whereabouts. There would be no more middle grounds—not with the surviving humans.

After preliminary scanning by a scouting patrol of Red squadron planes, the livery ships were cleared to land. It was considered essential to provide the animals with some grazing and eating room. The livery ship officers had reported an increased listlessness in their animals, one which seemed to be caused by something more than just the limited rations available to feed them.

The farming ships landed soon after, and took immediate advantage of Carillon's fertile soil, whose texture and mineral content indicated a fine medium for the planting of accelerated-growth foodstuffs. At the same time, the farmer-technicians collected as much grazing material from the Carillon surface as they could, and transplanted it to the meadows inside the livery ships.

While Carillon was proving exceptionally fruitful for livestock and farming, it didn't impress some of its human visitors. Especially Boomer and Starbuck, who had been dispatched to the dark side of the planet to investigate mining possibilities.

"I'll be sure to come here on my next rest-and-recuperation leave," Boomer commented. "I just adore monotonous landscapes."

"Yes, it is lovely," Starbuck said. "Can't imagine why it isn't overpopulated."

A pilot on a viper flyby informed them that his scanners read life forms in an area a short distance from where Boomer and Starbuck were driving in their landram. Boomer broadcast the specified time check to the main expeditionary force, and announced they would investigate the life-form report. Starbuck accelerated the landram and headed for the area the pilot had indicated.

"If this place is so bloomin' rich in resources, how come it was abandoned in the first place?" Boomer asked.

Starbuck shrugged.

"Legend has it the mining and colonization groups both got spooked and pulled out. Probably that's just a story, though. Looks to me like the planet was just too drab. In those days sources of supply were plentiful, plus it's off the normal trade routes, so I suppose Carillon was just written off as a bad investment."

"Then why's the old man think it's such a good investment now?"

"It's the *only* investment, Boomer, that's what he'd tell you."

"Yeah, he does have a penchant for finality, the commander does."

"Yes, well—hey, will you look at that? That glow over that hill. What could it be?"

"I don't know, but it's what we're sent out here to investigate."

Starbuck coaxed extra speed out of the landram as they headed toward the aurora framing the hill ahead of them.

Not far from Boomer and Starbuck, the main body of the *Galactica*'s survey team were coordinating their detection equipment to search for the fabled lost Carillon Tylium mine. From the point of view of a quartet of rather large insectoids who were spying on the *Galactica*'s force from a nearby mountain, the humans themselves looked like small insects— organized and disciplined small insects. Each of these spies was about five feet tall, with large bulbous eyes near the top of oval heads, long thin trunks, and four arms, all of which were busy with either two-triggered weapons or several-lensed cameras.

One of the insectoids took aim at the formidable target of Lieutenant Jolly, but another one pushed the barrel of the weapon down. Seetol, a leader of the race called the Ovions by the few humans unlucky enough to encounter them, had for the moment decided not to kill any of the invaders. At least, not until she reported back to her queen. She gestured her soldiers back, took the camera from the Ovion who held it, and in the soft, monosyllabic language of her race ordered them away from the spying post. At a nod from Seetol another Ovion used all four of her hands to turn in different directions and at different speeds a series of four wheels concealed underneath a rock. With a just audible whine, an opening appeared in the ground and the Ovions disappeared into it.

Riding on a pod whose soft leaves sheltered them totally, the four Ovions progressed through a long, descending, subterranean passageway to a cell where the pod opened and they stepped out of it. The tunnel they now traveled through was walled with cell-like panels from which amber light glowed. They emerged from the passageway into an immense underground cavern. The giant, many-celled chamber went deeper into the ground than Seetol's keen eyes could see, and ascended almost as high. There were countless levels, each one ringed with compartments shaped like honeycombs. Within the compartments Ovion workers poked at walls, extracted nuggets of amber-colored ore, and placed them in small, many-wheeled vehicles which other workers continually drew in and out of the compartments and sent on through dark intervening corridors. To an outsider, this large-chambered mine might have looked quite nightmarish—but to Seetol, something of an aesthete among her people, it had an artistic coherence that excited her each time she stepped into it. Today, however, there was little time for aesthetic satisfaction; she had to continue her mission.

She crossed a natural bridge that stretched across the wide chamber. At the guarded archway to Lotay's chamber, Seetol's four arms provided the proper ritual password and she was admitted to her queen's presence.

The luxury of Lotay's throne room contrasted strongly with the austerity of the mine. Finely woven, elaborately patterned cloth decorated the walls and ceiling. Lotay herself lounged on a cushioned floor, surrounded by her bejewelled retinue of slaves. One slave played a gentle tune utilizing the Ovion three-note scale artistically, discovering intriguing variants on her restricted melodic theme. A pair of other slaves were filing down the fine spikes that dotted the surface

of Lotay's limbs. Another slave held a long tube from which
the queen occasionally drew a liquid substance whose residue
she blew out her mouth as smoke. When Lotay acknowl-
edged Seetol, she requested her report.

"They have come," Seetol said, her voice soft and
pleasant.

Lotay's even more musical voice replied:

"Don't disturb them. It will only stir them up. They'll be
perfectly harmless unless angered or frightened."

"My thought exactly, highness."

"Naturally."

Seetol bowed and withdrew, leaving Lotay to draw and
puff on the long tube.

Apollo felt extremely comfortable at the controls of the
landram he had commandeered for his own particular search
of the Carillon surface. He liked the feel of a landram as it
rode the air currents with a surprising smoothness, adjusting
to surface peculiarities with barely noticeable shifts to right
and left, up and down.

He also felt comfortable with the presence of Serina
beside him in the co-driver seat. He had been impressed with
the way she had picked up the skills of driving a landram
without ever having been inside one before. In the back seat
of the landram, Boxey played quietly with Muffit Two.

"That was some show you and your buddies performed up
there," Serina said suddenly. "You seemed to be trying to
prove something. I wondered if it had anything to do with
your brother."

The comment evaporated the feeling of being comfortable.

"I get it," he said irritably, "you're saying I'm being
reckless to make up for leaving Zac behind."

"Or proving your courage for his ghost."

"How did you find out so much about Zac and me?"

"Asked around."

"I don't appreciate that."

"Sorry. I was a newswoman on Caprica, remember? I
can't get out of the habit. Change the subject, why don't you?
Or I will. Tell me about the agriculture project. I was

especially impressed with it. How long before things start to grow?"

"Oh, say, morning. I think we'll see quite a few sprouts and stuff by morning. Then, by the end of day tomorrow, we'll have a whole crop of fresh food—which, you must admit, will be a welcome substitute for the comrations. They'll taste better. And you be sure to eat them, you hear, Boxey?"

"I guess so."

In spite of Muffit Two, the boy had still been showing signs of moodiness.

"Say, Boxey," Apollo said, "time for your part of the mission. What I want you to do is keep your eye on that readout. If the indicator gets up into this colored area, it means we're right on top of a rich Tylium deposit."

"Yes, sir."

The job assignment seemed to pick up the boy's spirits.

"You sure you don't mind working with such a green crew?" Serina said.

"I chose you, didn't I?"

"I'd think, with your connections, you'd do better, that you'd—I'm sorry, didn't mean to touch a sore spot. You're upset your father resigned the presidency, correct?"

"Stop being a newswoman, and let's concentrate on the mission. We've got to get a lot done in a short time. We don't dare stop on any one planet for too long."

"Why'd we have to leave home at all?" Boxey asked. "Why'd those people want to hurt us?"

"I'm not sure, Boxey. Some say it has to do with very complicated things, political things. Others say the Cylons just like war, and will attack anybody who interferes with their part of space. I don't know—sometimes I think it just boils down to who's different. There're always life forms who cannot accept anything they don't understand. Some humans are like that too; they can't accept anything different."

"What do you mean different?"

Apollo sighed, not knowing how to explain complex matters to a child. He remembered years ago, trying to have complicated conversations with Zac, who was then much older than Boxey was now, and then discovering that the answer Zac sought for was much simpler than Apollo expected. Other times, Apollo's answers were too simple and Zac prodded him until he had not only extracted the more complex ideas but successfully argued against them. But what should he tell a six-year-old whose main concern was the welfare of an animal about the subject of prejudice?

"Well, Boxey, just about anything at all can make one species different from another. The shape of your eyes, the number of limbs, the color of the outer layer of your skin, even thoughts and ideas. Maybe our enemies just aren't equipped to deal with the difference."

"You mean they're stupid."

"Yeah, in a way. I mean, in some ways they've got it all over us, in certain matters of science and technology, in certain methods of fighting the war. But, yeah, they're stupid, too. It's stupid to kill what you don't understand."

"Why don't we just kill them back?"

In Boxey's belligerent question, Apollo could hear, almost like a ghost-echo, the sound of Zac's voice. Zac sometimes showed a positively bloodthirsty desire for violent solutions. In that sort of mood he would never listen to the calmer voices of his brother or his father. For that matter, there were times when Adama's humanistic theories of war proved too much for Apollo, who still had sharp pangs of doubt about the *Galactica*'s leaving the scene of battle.

"Boxey, if we just killed mindlessly, the way the Cylons seem to do, then we'd be changing what we are. We'd become like them. Although we're quite skilled at war, we are not basically a warlike race, at least I don't believe we are. We were pushed into this war, had no other choice. In fact, perhaps what we're doing now, searching for someplace else, away from our enemies, is the better thing to do. Fighting them on their own terms has not certainly—"

"What if they come after us?"

Why did Boxey have to ask the hard questions?

"Then we might have to defend ourselves."

"You mean kill them?"

"Possibly."

"Then we'd be like them."

Apollo smiled.

"You know, Boxey, I think you're getting glimpses of just how complicated life is. Yes, we don't believe in war—but the opposite of war isn't necessarily peace. No, what we want is freedom. Just that, freedom. The right to be left alone. It's a right we humans have always tried to protect and preserve. But there's always a chance someone will come along and spoil everything—"

He could see in the boy's questioning eyes that Boxey was not following this part of the discussion.

"So you kill them?" Boxey said.

"No. What it is, you try to establish, well, penalties, something that'll make spoiling others' way of life unrewarding."

"You kill them."

"Boxey, you've a way of reducing everything to very simple terms."

"Well, I'm only a kid."

"Right. Sometimes I forget you're only six."

"Almost seven."

"Almost seven. I don't know, though. Maybe you're right. No matter how you slice it, what words you use, in the end we're talking about life and death. Life is precious. No one has the right to tamper with another's life, without the risk of forfeiting his own. Ah, I sound like one of the classes in war games I used to teach back at the academy—and I think getting a bit deep for a boy your age."

"Why? You can die at any age, can't you?"

"Yes, Boxey, you can. Keep an eye on the readout, okay?"

"Sure. C'mon, Muffy, looka that."

Muffit Two barked and nuzzled closer to the boy.

Starbuck stood at the rim of the hill and stared down at the evidence of genuine life forms that had been registering on the scanners. He called to Boomer, who was just climbing out of the landram.

"Boomer...."

"Yeah, what is it now?"

"You aren't going to believe this, Boomer."

"Feeling is believing. I just busted a finger on—"

"No, I mean *really*...."

Boomer looked down. His mouth fell open.

"I don't believe it!"

In contrast to the drab landscape around them, the carnival of color and light and glass in the meadow in front of them was a dazzling spectacle. Surrounding glass-walled spherical buildings was a meticulously landscaped garden of greenery and exotic plants. Waterfalls slipped gracefully between what seemed an artistic arrangement of rocks. Sounds of laughter drifted upward. Songs were being played and sung in the distance. A few people, talking gaily, emerged from a building and began to chase each other, with obvious amorous intentions, through the neatly sculptured garden paths.

Starbuck looked over at Boomer, who appeared just as confused as he was.

"What is it?" Boomer asked.

"I don't know," said Starbuck. Drawing his sidearm, he started to make his way along the narrow pathway that zigzagged down the hill leading to the bizarre complex of spherical buildings and lush gardens.

"You sure you need that?" Boomer said, pointing to Starbuck's sidearm.

"Whenever I'm not sure, that's when I need it."

Nobody in the gardens seemed to notice the two men. If anything, the happy noises of celebration and song grew louder as they reached the garden. They stood at the beginning of a path for a long time, just watching the myriad colors and shifting lights that kept changing the appearance of the garden and the buildings.

"It sure is pretty," Starbuck said, some awe in his voice. "And it sure sounds friendly."

Starbuck started town the path, Boomer following, staying close. As they came to a fork in the path, a sudden scream made both of them jump. Starbuck whirled around, his sidearm pointed in the direction of the scream.

A woman stood trembling in the center of the path. Her wide staring eyes only emphasized the look of beauty in her face. Starbuck was impressed with her voluptuous figure, round in all the best places. She wore a red gown that clung appropriately.

"Don't shoot!" she said. "What do you want?"

Starbuck, red-faced, glanced down at the weapon in his

hand, made a show of putting it in its holster.

"I mean no harm," he said.

"I usually go on the assumption that men with guns just might mean harm," the woman said.

"You're from Taura," Starbuck said.

"Yes," the woman said, obviously surprised at the shift in topic, "I'm a Taurus. How'd you know that?"

"The dialect. Always can tell. What are you doing here?"

"What am *I* doing here? What are *you* doing here? Why are Colonial Warriors sneaking around a resort with their weapons drawn? Everything here is perfectly legal."

Starbuck and Boomer, both just as bewildered as the woman, exchanged mystified looks.

"Isn't it?" the woman said.

"Would you mind telling us how you got here?" Starbuck said, trying to sound as official as he could under the circumstances.

"On the bus."

The incongruity of her answer startled both men.

"Must've been sniffing plant vapors," Boomer commented.

"Um, would you tell us about this bus?" Starbuck asked.

"Sure. It was all handled through my travel agent. This place is *fabulous*! I just can't believe they can give you all this for so little money." She opened a red-sequined purse that had been dangling from her wrist. "Look, I won over a thousand cubits."

Some of the cubits spilled over the edge of the purse onto the path. The woman made no effort to retrieve them. Starbuck, always responsive to the glow of gold, became excited.

"You won those cubits *here*?"

"In there, sure." The woman pointed toward the complex of varicolored glass buildings. "Look, they said it was all legal so if it isn't you'd better take on the whole star system, because everyone is doing it. I'd like to stand here and discuss all this with you, but I'm late for a moonlight cruise. Two moons, how can you go wrong? And talk about meeting people, the brochures weren't kidding about *that*. I never had it so good. See you in church, fellas."

The woman giggled and hurried off down the path.

Boomer stared after her, while Starbuck picked up the fallen cubits.

"I don't get it," Boomer said. "How cut off can they be? She didn't act like she'd even heard about the war."

"Yeah," Starbuck said thoughtfully. "I wonder if they have. Something else is peculiar about all this. If it's such a big deal, like she said, how come we haven't heard about this place?"

"I suppose *you* know *every* gambling den in our star systems."

"Well?"

"You're right. If there's a game going on, you know about it."

Starbuck resumed walking along the path, heading toward the nearest lavish sphere.

"But this isn't back-room cards!" he said. "This is the biggest splash I've seen outside of Orion."

"But who'd want to set up a gambling resort on an outpost planet? Why put something like this together and keep it a secret?"

"That puzzles me, too. If you don't tell anyone about a place like this, you don't do any business."

As they made their way through the verdant garden and into the lobby of the spherical building, they could see no evidence of security guards to interfere with them. In fact, all they could see were groups of people having a ball. And not only people, as they found when they looked close. There seemed to be representatives of every sentient and civilized extraterrestrial race so far discovered in the universe. Except, of course, for Cylons—although even their unlikely presence wouldn't have surprised Starbuck. The Cylon sense of order and austerity would not have permitted them to participate in gambling and the various wonderful forms of self-indulgence that were evident in this resort. Across a massive archway, in several languages, were variations of the phrase, *Festival of Paradise*, apparently the name of the resort.

"Shall we investigate further?" Boomer asked.

"By all means, Boom-Boom, by all possible means."

Accustomed to seeing aliens only on occasion, Starbuck and Boomer eyed with some fascination the various examples of inhuman and humanoid life. There were tentacled lizards, furry octopods, a grotesque sexpartite set of connected individuals from a species that the two men had heard of only in galactic legend, bulky, hard-surfaced oddities that could be mistaken for rocks if they hadn't spoken and moved—creatures of all varieties and shapes. However, the majority was humanoid, sometimes oddly so. As Starbuck and Boomer entered a magnificent casino, a feline cocktail waitress, modestly attired in a clinging dress revealing her four shapely breasts, asked them if they'd like anything to drink. When they declined, she smiled and walked away, her furry tail removing a dirty glass from a gilt railing. Starbuck could not take his eyes off her.

"Did you see that tail that—" he said to Boomer.

"Sure did."

At a nearby gaming table, one of hundreds spread through the ornate cavernous room, a scream of victory went up. Checking it out, Starbuck saw a chubby humanoid raking in cubits with a horselike paw. Another winner's cry erupted at an adjacent table.

"The odds must be incredible here," Starbuck said. "People are winning fortunes. Look!"

After further investigation, Boomer spotted rows of food tables, on which delectable items were being snatched at greedily by the gameplayers.

"They're obviously well fed here," he said. "Let's get hold of whoever's in charge and see about getting some food back to the fleet."

"Hold it, sky-pirate. Slow down. The last thing these people may want to find is a battlestar sitting on their front doorstep."

"Then you think this setup is illegal?"

"Is a Cylon nauseating? Yeah, I think it's illegal. It wasn't exactly listed in the Colonial Guidebook of places to go, things to do."

"And we're standing here in full uniform. They may not be too happy when they notice that. Let's take off—"

"Wait, wait. Let's not look a gift horse in the mouth, especially when it's dressed in gold. I've never seen a crooked gambling den that didn't depend on military pay vouchers to keep their doors open. Let's see what this guy has to say."

A human pit boss came toward them, his mouth spread in a wide smile.

"Welcome, gentlemen," he said. "Is that an emblem of the Colonial Fleet I see?"

Boomer looked scared, but Starbuck answered confidently:

"That's what it is, all right."

"I didn't realize they were in the area."

"As a matter of fact, we're kind of here on our own."

"Little out of the way, aren't you?"

"Secret mission," Boomer said, getting into the spirit of the deception.

Starbuck slapped him on the back and said jokingly:

"He likes to be dramatic. Just a reconnaissance flight. See that the armistice is being observed."

They all three stood around silently for a long moment. Was the pit boss's grin directed at their naive lie, Starbuck wondered, or was it just a reflection of the genuine hospitality of the casino?

"How worthy," the pit boss said. Starbuck couldn't tell whether or not the man intended the observation sarcastically. "And how fortunate to have you with us. Consider yourselves guests of the establishment. Food and drink on the house."

The pit boss snapped his spidery fingers and Starbuck and Boomer found their hands full of food and drink, supplied by short simian waiters who moved like lightning through the crowd. Starbuck took a sip from his glass. The drink turned out to be a Sagitarian straight-arrow. He took a bite of the pastry in his other hand, an Aquarian ambrosia cake.

"These are my favorites, my favorite drink, my favorite dessert," Starbuck said. "How did you know what to give me?"

"*They* knew," the pit boss said, pointing to the simian waiters who were now supplying a creature who looked like a sculpture of plastic, slightly melted. "They're primitive types, the waiters, but they're mildly telepathic, at least in matters of food and drink. Enjoy yourselves."

The pit boss smiled and walked off. Starbuck stuffed

some more ambrosia cake into his mouth. Moist crumbs clung to his lips.

"Well," Boomer said sardonically, "how do you feel now, sport? Here we have the run of this place while our people are out there starving and scrabbling for crops and grazing land."

"What did you expect me to do, ask the guy for enough food for a ragtag fleet when he thinks we're just a couple of straggler pilots on a reconnaissance flight?"

"Well, maybe we should just tell the guy the truth."

"Sure, he looks a swell sort, an honest john. Boomer, until we know who these people are, just keep in mind that it'd only take one informer to have the whole Cylon war machine on its way."

"So what do we do? We've got to find ways to get fuel and food back to the ships."

"First thing, we'll try to find out who's behind this place. How many cubits you have with you?"

"Cubits? Starbuck, you disgust me, you know that? People in our fleet are half-starved and you're going to gamble?"

"You expect me to be a miniature Commander Adama, you got another think coming. Besides, this time it's in the line of duty. We've got to start asking some questions, digging out some information—but carefully, *very* carefully."

Boomer seemed reluctant to hand Starbuck the money.

"Well, all right, but you'd better make this last. That's all there is."

Boomer dropped three cubits into Starbuck's outstretched hand.

"Boomer my man, cubits don't mean much just now, no matter how you measure it."

Starbuck's active eyes sought the source of the best action. He decided on the Hi-Lo table, since Hi-Lo was a game at which he could make a quick turnover of his limited funds before seeking out a big-stakes game. Three people, all humans, sat around the table. An open chair beckoned. Starbuck sat beside an attractive woman who, he thought, might have been an absolute stunner if she would drop just a few pounds from her pleasingly plump figure. The other players were men, both cheerful, both quite obese. As he sat, the woman, obviously liking what she saw, gave Starbuck the eye.

"Well!" she said. "The fleet's in. Sit down, *Lieutenant*. You've come to a lucky table."

"That right?"

"Yep. Not sure what I mean. Whether it's lucky because I've been cleaning up, or because you chose to sit here."

Starbuck assumed his best appealing grin, and signaled to be dealt in. The nonhuman dealer, with a friendly smile, began tossing out the next round of cards with an elegant flick of his triple-jointed, gray-green wrist.

Apollo ran a check on the other branches of the survey team. Ensign Greenbean got on the line and reported a disturbance.

"What is it, Greenbean?" Apollo said.

"It's Jolly, sir. We seem to have lost him."

"How could you *lose* anybody his size?"

"Beats me, sir, but he's lost."

"Send out a search party and report back to me."

"Roger."

Apollo leaned back against the bucket seat.

"The man probably just wandered off," Serina said.

"Maybe."

He was about to say more when the Tylium detector started beeping. The beeping caused Boxey's daggit-droid to bark.

"Quiet, Muffit. I see it, Captain...Tylium!"

Apollo slowed the landram and checked the indicator. It seemed to display a Tylium lode, all right, a large one. He brought the vehicle to a slow stop. As soon as it stopped, Muffit leaped out the window.

"Muffit!" Boxey cried. "Wait, I'll bring him back."

Before anybody could stop him, Boxey had followed the daggit-droid out the landram window.

"Should we go after him?" Serina asked, her voice nervous.

"He's in sight for the moment. Let him run free a little."

"You're right, I may be keeping too tight a leash on the

boy. Thank you, by the way."

"For what?"

"For saving his life."

"You're getting things a little out of proportion. Anyway, maybe I should be thanking you."

"Now it's my turn to ask for what?"

"Well, you've helped me to—"

He stopped talking, leaned forward to squint out the window on Serina's side.

"What is it?" she said.

"Boxey. He was there a moment ago."

"Maybe he just ran over a hill."

"Perhaps, but we'd better give a look. C'mon."

Serina became frightened by the agitated way Apollo scrambled out of the landram and onto the Carillon surface.

Seetol emerged from her ground concealment and, in one rapid move, swept Boxey and Muffit into her four-armed grasp. Before the boy could scream or the animal could emit one of his disgusting sounds, Seetol had carried them back to the camouflaged ground entrance and onto a pod which she immediately activated to descend into the ground to the Tylium mine below. In the corridor leading to the queen's chamber, the boy struggled fiercely. As Seetol tried to improve her hold on him, the animal leaped out of her arms and ran a short way down the corridor.

"Muffy!" the boy cried. "Darn you daggit. Come back here."

Immediately the animal obeyed. Seetol, unused to domesticated animals or their robot substitutes, was impressed with Muffit's quick obedience. She picked it up again, and both animal and boy were serene until they had been carried into Lotay's throne room, where Muffit again scrambled out of Seetol's arms, this time to run to the throne. It barked furiously.

A slave seemed to want to kill it, but the queen was too amused. The sharp spikes upon her body had faded to a soft yellow, as they always did when she was pleased. Boxey squirmed out of Seetol's arms and ran to his animal. The other human in the room took a couple of steps forward, and Boxey looked up at him.

"Lieutenant Jolly!" Boxey cried. "What're you doing here?"

"I'm not paying a social call, youngster," Jolly said. He glanced toward Lotay lounging on her throne. "I left all my calling cards in my formal jumpsuit, your highness."

Lotay did not understand the sarcastic humor in the fat man's remarks. Seetol was about to scoop up Boxey again, but Lotay gestured her away, saying:

"Leave him."

Muffy licking his face, Boxey looked up at the queen from a crouch. Lotay raised herself from her throne. The spikes on her body got brighter as she pointed to the child, the fat flyer, and the droid.

"A curious group," she said. "But they will do quite nicely. Seetol, arrange that they be taken care of and prepare for the others as soon as possible."

Seetol nodded approval and walked to the captured humans. Jolly edged over to Boxey and put his arm around the boy. Seetol was amused by the fat human's obvious fear. She observed even her own race with a cynical eye. She had always liked what she was, but not who she was—or, for that matter, who anybody else was. Even her love for her queen felt incomplete, no matter how much worship she attempted. It could not be complete unless the queen would love her back, a possibility not even within the scope of Ovion reasoning. Seetol, her four arms suggesting a quartet of elegant gestures, guided Boxey and Jolly out the entrance, Muffit trotting happily behind. On the throne, Lotay began to laugh mysteriously. Seetol never knew the meaning of her queen's laughter.

Apollo and Serina searched the immediate area around their vehicle to no avail. Serina held back tears, muttered to herself that she should never have let the child get away from her. Back at the landram, Apollo got on the communicator to Greenbean, who reported no sign yet of Jolly.

"What is it?" Serina said. "What's happening on this planet?"

"Don't panic. We'll find him."

Apollo wished he could be as certain as he sounded. For a moment all he wanted to do was fold this beautiful, auburn-haired, green-eyed woman in his arms and soothe her, tell her everything would be all right. The trouble was, he couldn't feel that everything was going to be all right.

"This planet is eerie. With this darkness and the two moons it's—what is it, Apollo?"

Apollo had drawn his sidearm and pointed it toward an area beyond the landram. Serina followed his look, then screamed. There were two Ovion warriors emerging from a hole in the ground, a hole that had not been there a second ago. Their two-triggered weapons were aimed at Apollo and Serina.

FROM THE ADAMA JOURNALS:

My father told me as a sort of valedictory when he handed me command of the *Galactica* that the best advice he could give me was that, when everything appeared to be in place and everything was placid, it was time to consider what was absent. The questioning of the apparent reality, and the ability to add the absent to the visible, was a prime requisite for any commander. I didn't think much of the advice at the time. Later, when I had to study a star map and plot out dangers before sending in attack craft, I knew exactly what the old man meant. When I dealt with apparently docile friendly creatures, I learned it was imperative to listen for what was *not* being said. At the time when peace was a most tempting reality, it was necessary for me to question the absence of the most important parties to the agreement. I can't even look at a painting without wondering what the artist eliminated from the original landscape or model. It seems that, except at that rare point when an act or set of events reaches a definite conclusion, I'm always at odds with what I see, with the apparent reality, and am nervously looking for something to fill in the parts I can't yet see.

CHAPTER SEVEN

The two Ovion soldiers forced Apollo and Serina down long,
sloping, labyrinthine corridors. After the suffocating
closeness of the pod in which they had traveled to these
underground levels, the blasts of cold, damp air seemed
refreshing. When they emerged into the massive main
chamber of the mine, Apollo caught his breath in surprise.
Serina, too, was astonished by the seemingly limitless heights
and depths of the main chamber, and at the furiously active
work going on in all its cells.

"What is it?" she asked Apollo.

"Incredible! May be the largest underground Tylium
mine anywhere. Father was right about there being Tylium
here. There's enough here just in sight to fuel all our ships,
run them half across the universe. But—"

"But what?"

"I don't know exactly. For something like this to exist
here without us knowing that it had been reactivated, it's,
well, bizarre. Who uses all this energy, and for what?"

An Ovion gave them a shove, guiding them toward the
bridge that crossed the large chamber.

"Where could Boxey be?" Serina said. "I'm so worried about him."

"I know. If they've done anything to him, I'll—"

"Don't say it. I'm scared enough already."

The guards stopped at Lotay's throne room and beckoned the two humans inward. Apollo and Serina entered the queen's chamber.

At first Lotay didn't notice them—or, in queenly fashion, waited an imperial minute to recognize them. In the meantime Serina was fascinated by the colorful layers of cloth that decorated the room, the scurrying slaves performing all kinds of odd duties, the musicians playing some tune that didn't sound at all musical but rather more like an out-of-whack generator. Finally, the queen looked up from her perch upon a high pile of cushions.

"You are Captain Apollo?" she asked. Her voice, although low-pitched, had a scratchy sound to it. Both Apollo and Serina would have been astonished if they had known that, to the Ovions, Lotay's voice was considered ethereally musical.

"I am," Apollo responded.

"Welcome to Carillon. I assume you are impressed."

"Outraged might be the better word. Where is the boy?"

The creature formed what was recognizable to the humans as a smile, but it looked peculiar on her insectoid face.

"Would you care to join him, Captain?"

"You bet I would, and if anything's happened to him, you'll answer to the Colonies!"

Lotay smiled again, nodded her oversized head noncommittally and rose from her plush cushions. Serina, already accustomed to the uniform shortness of the Ovions she had seen thus far, was astonished by the queen's height. She towered over the other Ovions. With a walk that was definitely queenlike, Lotay led the way out of the royal chamber. Serina noted that their guards fell easily into step behind them as she and Apollo followed the queen out. As they made their way down the narrow corridor, Serina leaned toward Apollo and whispered, "Did that spooky smile of hers mean she knows the colonies don't exist anymore?"

"I don't know," Apollo whispered back.

Lotay led them into a small chamber and brought them to

a halt. She gestured toward one of the guards who sealed off the entranceway. Immediately, they could feel the floor beneath them move.

"What's happening?" Serina asked.

"Must be their version of an elevator, except it moves sideways as well as up."

When the moving chamber had stopped, Lotay ordered the guard to open the door. Apollo and Serina, exchanging wary looks, allowed themselves to be guided through the doorway. They were not at all prepared for what confronted them now, a large banquet room teeming with movement, reverberating with loud discordant music. Some Ovions near them danced, their four arms twisting in rather graceful gestures. There was a troop of jugglers. Serina had never imagined what intricate juggling a quartet of arms could accomplish. Banquet tables, enormous and overflowing, displayed succulent-looking food that seemed to represent the best of the twelve-world cuisines. It smelled wonderful and reminded her of how hungry she had been for so long.

"Captain!"

Starbuck came toward Apollo, his hands held out in welcome. Other eaters turned around to look. Jolly held a drumstick of something clutched tightly in his chubby fingers.

"Boxey!" Serina called and was answered immediately. The boy jumped off Boomer's knees and ran to Serina, embraced her.

"Good fortune is smiling on us," Starbuck said, lifting in toast a flat, blue, hexagonally shaped fruit.

"It's like nothing we could've dreamed of," Jolly declared, the signs of his joy foodstained all over his tunic. "They've got everything we need and plenty of it."

"And they're happy to share," Boomer said.

"It sounds like paradise," Serina said, her voice not as sure as her words. Her hugging of Boxey was composed of equal parts of joy and protection.

"Yes, it does," Apollo said, his wary eyes inspecting the lavishness of the room.

Lotay stepped forward and addressed her human guests.

"We are a communal order from birth. We all work. We all share. There is no competition, no jealousy, no conflict. Only peace and order."

"Perpetual happiness," Apollo observed. He wasn't sure whether Lotay perceived the irony of his inflection.

"Happiness is the goal of an immature order. All pursue it. Few have it. None can sustain it. The Ovion is content. It is better."

Serina could see a doubt in Apollo's eyes that was a match for her own feelings.

"It seems to work for you," she said to the queen.

"For millenniums it has been so. Now, join us. Be our guests. Be well fed, well entertained. What you need, merely ask for it. Be content."

"She's not just a-kidding," Starbuck said. "You think this banquet is something, wait'll you get a look at the casino a couple levels above."

"Casino?" Apollo said.

"Yep. I'm on my way back there as soon as I get sustenance."

"Lieutenant Starbuck, there're people *starving* back on the—"

"I know, I know, Captain. Ease off. These people're assembling food for us right now. And fuel. Our problems're solved."

"It sounds good, Starbuck, but—"

"But nothing, Captain. C'mon, have you ever tried this orange wine? Take a sip."

"I'll pass for the moment."

Lotay, watching their conversation, smiled at the humans benignly. To Apollo and Serina, the queen's smile seemed to contain just as much mystery as ever. There seemed to be more meaning in it than she was willing to exhibit. Apollo had sensed a tone of command in her invocations to enjoyment. Serina was not sure what she sensed, but whatever it was, was cloying. She desperately wanted to return aboveground, to be in the comforting, though spare, confines of the *Galactica*.

The executive officers around Imperious Leader's pedestal transmitted nothing but trivialities through their communications webs. At first-brain level a Cylon hated inactivity. By the time he achieved a second-brain, the Cylon hated confusion. Third-brain Cylons despised both inactivity and confusion, but even more they hated triviality. The centurion officer that he had dispatched to the planet Carillon to rendezvous with their Ovion allies and to check out the rumors about human ships in that sector had not yet reported in. The leader felt disused, as if he might decay if nothing important happened soon.

His mind was burdened with inconsequentialities that he did not even have to correlate. He kept finding himself making random connections which, though accurate, were meaningless.

He remembered a conversation he had once had with a human captive. The man had been a scientist, a short, somewhat plump fellow who fancied long sideburns to counter his thinning hair. Suspecting the man might be a fit conversationalist for a Cylon, the leader had made some attempts in that direction. While they talked theory and technology, their communication level remained higher than that of the average interaction between Cylon and human. However, the scientist had grown lethargic after several days, and had begun to provide answers in a monotone.

When the Leader asked the reason for the scientist's change in mood, the man tried to explain the concept of boredom to the Cylon. It was a concept that was so loathsome to the leader that he refused to accept it. He became quite incensed with rage. The man copied the Cylon's mood and spoke back angrily, defending boredom as a common, even acceptable, human trait. Nobody liked to be bored, the man said stridently, but it was a necessary part of human life that often led to the kind of contemplation which eventually resulted in revolutionary insights. Boredom could even be beneficial for humanity, the man said. The leader commented that, since starting the discussion of boredom, the man seemed much less bored, therefore talking about boredom must not be boring. The man screamed that he was more bored than ever, that the Leader and all the rest of the Cylons were such smug hypocrites with such infinitesimal variance in attitude or personality that any sensible human could not *help* but be bored after a few days in their company. Although the leader did not believe in boredom as a useful or even genuine state, he resented the man's claim of boredom in Cylon company, and he banished the scientist from his presence forever. He had probably put the man to death, although that was a piece of information that he would not have bothered to preserve in any of his brains.

Now he wondered if such accumulations of trivial data as that under which he presently suffered were roughly comparable to what that scientist had called boredom. He did not have to consider this offensive proposition for long, since some important new information suddenly came through. The centurion on Carillon had finally transmitted a message. He had entrenched himself in an underground cavern of the planet, and was in communication with their Ovion allies. They had told him that the humans definitely had arrived in the Carillon sector. Some of them were already in Ovion sway, others hovered in orbit around the planet on the battlestar *Galactica* and a few other ships. Their fighter ships had destroyed large sections of the minefield which the Cylons, by treaty arrangement with the Ovions, had encircled the planet to protect the secret fuel supply which had been at Cylon disposal ever since they had originally enslaved the Ovions and transported them to the uninhabited planet. The leader, satisfied to be back in real action again, transmitted the order that a large fleet of Cylon fighters on the planet Borallus be put in readiness to travel to Carillon sector. Then he relaxed, satisfied that what he felt now—the waves of important information—was not in any way the quality humanity endured under the name of boredom.

In the viewer by Adama's desk, the image of the planet Carillon appeared benign. The figures on the report in his hand confirmed the wisdom of his decision to come here. Not only could they replenish food and supplies easily, but they would obtain enough Tylium to power the entire ragtag fleet for some time. Activating his private comline, he began recording his log.

"The Ovion people have extended to the survivors of the colonies every measure of goodness and support we might have hoped for. It is now possible to foresee the entire fleet able to resume our voyage soon, within a—"

There was a knock on the door. Adama shut off the comline and hollered, "Come in."

Colonel Tigh entered the room, looking troubled. Tigh was always finding something to worry about, especially if the worriment could be written up in a report.

"Nothing can be as bad as you look, Tigh. What's happened?"

"It's this report, sir, from the surface."

"It's a very optimistic report, Colonel."

"Too optimistic. Uri has everyone in the fleet breaking in the bulkheads to get down to the surface, and none of them're volunteering for work details either."

Adama had a mental picture of Uri addressing the weary people left aboard the *Galactica*. The councillor had a way of using his maturely handsome looks with a political sense of strategy. With the food stores so desperately low, it was no wonder they would respond to Uri's suggestions.

"Well," he said, "perhaps Uri has a point. Perhaps we could allow some of our people to visit the surface. In small numbers, an orderly rotation. What's wrong, Tigh?"

Tigh cleared his throat before speaking again:

"I'm afraid it's too late for cautious plans, sir. Uri's already authorized visitor permits to half our population."

"Half the population! Countermand those orders immediately."

"I'm afraid we can't. As a member of the council, Uri has the right to make certain nonmilitary decisions. If you'd stayed on as president, well—"

"Don't rub it in, Colonel." The commander sighed. "Okay, do what you can to stem the tides. How are the work parties coming?"

"Very well. Livestock're being well fed and the first agricultural growths have sprouted."

"All right, Colonel, carry on."

Adama considered what Tigh had told him. Uri could not be allowed so much political license, and it was dangerous to send so many people down to the surface. Contingency plans would have to be devised. As he picked up the electronic recording stylus to begin making notes, there was another knock on his cabin door. He shouted, "Come in!" It was Athena.

"Request permission to travel planetside," she said.

"Why are you asking me?" Adama asked. "I thought Sire Uri was handing out permits like friendship gifts."

Athena reacted with surprise to her father's hostility, but said, "I wouldn't go down there with his blessing on a bet,

Father. And I won't go if you say no."

He was about to reject her request, but something sad in her eyes made him say, "It's all right. You might as well go. You need the relaxation more than most, you've been working so—"

"It's not relaxation I'm after."

"Oh? Starbuck again, is it?"

"Maybe."

"I know he's down there, and that he discovered that casino. With Starbuck, a casino must have seemed his rightful gift from the gods. I thought you were mad at him."

"I am."

"But—I think I can guess. That woman you caught him with. She's in one of Uri's visitor parties, isn't she?"

"Maybe."

"Well, give her hell."

"Is that to be interpreted as an order, Sir?"

"Give 'em both hell, ensign."

"Yes, Sir!"

He smiled at the brisk way she turned on her heels and exited the room.

As he took up the stylus again, his communicator buzzed. It was Tigh.

"Fuel has begun to arrive by tanker-shuttles from the Ovion Tylium mines, Sir."

"I detect disturbance in your voice, Colonel."

"Well, the supplies are smaller than Captain Apollo arranged for. The Ovion leader sent up some sort of flimsy excuse that they weren't prepared for such a large order just now. Yet, from the reports we've had from Apollo and the others, that excuse doesn't seem justified."

"I see. Well, stay on top of it, Colonel."

The moment Tigh had signed off, Adama raised the stylus and began writing furiously into the recording log. He felt the need for precautionary measures even more. Extraordinary measures.

When he had finished outlining his contingency procedures, he buzzed Tigh.

"Yes, Sir?"

"Prepare my shuttle. I'm going down to the surface. I want to see this paradise for myself."

"Sir, are you sure—"

"Are you suggesting I should get permission from Sire Uri?"

"No, Sir! The shuttle will be ready."

Adama swivelled around in his chair, pleased at the tingling sensation in his fingers, the feeling of blood pulsing through his veins. He had not felt this ready for action in some time.

FROM THE ADAMA JOURNALS:

I used to imagine paradise when I was a kid. While I don't
remember very many details of my image of the place, I know
there were a lot of toy airplanes and most everything was
blue. My more adult visions of paradise put me in the center
with all I wished for available on call. Athena says she
imagines paradise as her very own battlestar to command.
Tigh's is one where no paper exists. Our paradises tend to be
solipsistic dreams in which there is either more of everything
we think we love and need, or we are awarded gifts of all
that's usually denied us. Seems to me the point is that, in all
our paradises, we don't pay heed to the slaves who are the rest
of the population in our ideal imaginary lands. A paradise,
which should suggest expansion of human potential, is
usually a reduction, generally to the state of inertia. People
lounge in paradise a lot more than they do in life, or even
want to do. The Carillon paradise was in reality a trap, as
false as the peace offer of the Cylons or the pleasant words of
Count Baltar. We humans have an unfortunate tendency to
welcome traps if we can find some way to call them paradises.
Be content, the Ovion queen Lotay said. And we can be

content if we don't have to think of the slaves or the inertia, so long as there are plenty of toy airplanes and everything is blue.

CHAPTER EIGHT

Adama had visited Tylium mines before, but the Ovion one resembled no other mining operation he'd ever seen, especially when one viewed it from the mammoth underground cavern and contemplated the seemingly infinite depths. Its network of cells was an amazing phenomenon to anyone familiar only with deep-sunk tunnels and shafts. Adama felt uneasy. The workers, live beings after all, moved like machines. The Ovion guards stood too near them as if overseeing every action. It all had the smell of slave labor about it, and he didn't like it.

During the tour, Lotay's soft but raspy voice had supplied the kind of statistics that generally awed visiting committees. She finished off by describing her operation as the most efficient Tylium mine anywhere.

"It's a testimony to communal order," Councillor Uri said obsequiously.

"Thank you," Lotay replied. "Now allow me to show you some of the finer points of Ovion existence."

She led them to the banquet room, where the enormous feast had been replenished. The councillors crowded the table like men starved for some time—which, of course, they were.

Although Adama had also suffered the rigors of privation, he was not quite so eager to accept Ovion hospitality, and he held back from the banquet. The vigorous music being played on a host of stringed instruments agitated his nerves.

"This is too much to expect," Uri said, slivers of food dripping from the corners of his mouth.

"We have plenty," Lotay said. "We wish to aid you. As many of your people who desire it are invited to be our guests."

Uri, triumphant, whirled on Adama.

"And you, Commander, wanted to deny our people such a kind and generous invitation?"

Adama felt uncomfortable under the man's piercing gaze. For the moment all the cards were in Uri's hand, and Adama could only reply, "I suggested only a small rotation and not a mass descent upon—"

"But I thought time was our greatest consideration," Uri interrupted, talking in between sips of a purplish liquid. "The more people we bring down here at once, the sooner we can be on our way, get back to the others. You know, I think it might be wise to consider, once all the ships are refueled and converted to hyperspace, bringing them *all* here to enjoy the hospitality of this planet. Perhaps, with a little work we could even settle here. That's the best idea I've had in a long time, I must consider it."

Uri's proposal, clearly a political one, drew a murmured approval from the other members of the council on the tour, even from Anton, who was usually not quick to agree to anything. Adama decided not to reply to the challenge in Uri's voice. It was never wise to argue with a politician well on his way to inebriation. And, back on the sober decks of the *Galactica*, the others would see that his proposal was nonsensical.

Adama turned to Lotay and said, "May I ask how our request for Tylium is being received?"

"We have already prepared and processed the first shipment for you, have we not?" Lotay said, her voice sounding much too political for Adama's comfort. Trying to interpret a possibly calculated move of an alien seemed too much to ask of himself after just enduring Uri's insidious strategies.

"Yes, we boarded the first load of liquid Tylium," he said. "However, I understand there's to be a delay in obtaining more."

The pinched lower part of the queen's face managed a quite humanlike pout.

"Our processing procedures are antiquated," she said. "It takes time to process the ore, and we were not prepared for such a large order. You did come upon us as something of a surprise, after all. Generally, we are not called upon to process the ore into a liquid state for an *entire* space fleet."

"Oh? What purpose do you usually process it for? Or should I ask *whom* you process it for."

"Our records are not for the perusal of our clients, Commander. We are industrious, but we are also small, and we have every reason to fear any intruder, especially those who blast their way through our protective layers. However, we appreciate the scope of your order, and are also appreciative of the profits for us in a transaction of this nature. But we must take time and you must have patience."

Lotay's smile, intended to be ingratiating, was so false it gave Adama a pain in the pit of his stomach.

"I think we press our luck, Commander," Uri said, his fingers working frantically at what seemed to be a piece of bluish meat. "Let us not be rude in the face of *such* hospitality."

"Please enjoy yourselves," Lotay said. "Be our guests. Be well fed, entertained. Be content."

The queen slinked backward toward the arched entranceway, giving the appearance more of a loyal slave than a regent. Adama stopped her movement by saying:

"You aren't joining us?"

She glanced back at the food table without much interest. A vague smile crossed her face.

"No. I am afraid not."

With a graceful bow, she swept out of the room.

"Well," Uri said, edging toward the commander while peeling a lumpy lavender fruit, "I don't think there can be any doubt as to our decision. It will take time to obtain the Tylium. We will give every person an opportunity to share in our bounty down here on Carillon."

"But Uri—"

"Yes."

All the members of the council were looking at Adama with intense interest.

"Never mind."

Adama sensed their unanimity of opinion. They all nodded their agreement with Uri while stuffing their mouths with all manner of foodstuffs. A nauseous feeling growing in his stomach, Adama couldn't force himself to go near the banquet, and he sat instead in a plushly upholstered chair by the doorway. He could not look at the men crowded around the food table. They were his fellow humans but, at least for a moment, they looked to him more like insects than any of the Ovions did.

Joining her queen in the corridor outside the banquet rooms, Seetol fell in step with her as she set a brisk pace down the passageway to the concealed pod elevator. The tiny spikes along the queen's body now glowed in a bright yellow, as they always did during those rare moments when Lotay felt high excitement. Before descending to the throne-room level, she surveyed the tunnel in front of the elevator, clearly making sure there were no spying humans. Beckoning to Seetol to accompany her, she entered the elevator and went down to the throne room. As the queen walked out of the elevator in front of her, Seetol felt a surge of desire for her.

Lotay approached the throne but, instead of sitting on it, dropped to a most graceful and regal curtsy in front of it. Seetol became aware of the tall Cylon centurion sitting on the throne.

"By your command," Lotay said. It annoyed Seetol to watch her beloved queen act so subserviently to a Cylon. Seetol hated these helmeted arrogant creatures even more than humans and resented their hold over the Ovions. Worse, she was afraid of them.

"Many of the humans are here now, but their commander has only allowed a few of his warriors to land. The rest stand alert on the battlestar."

"That will change as they grow secure in your hospitality. After all, who has more experience dining with humans than you?"

"You are most gracious, centurion," Lotay said. "We live to serve you."

"And serve us you will. Our leader intends to eradicate every human left in this sector of space. Except, of course, those useful to your people."

"As you wish."

"As soon as we can lull the human forces and can ambush the battlestar, we will. Our leader appreciates your cooperation and pledges to continue his protection of the Ovions as part of our glorious Alliance."

"We are pleased, centurion."

Lotay bowed and nudged Seetol to bow with her. Even though the act disgusted her, Seetol obeyed her queen's bidding.

When Greenbean reported in that the *Galactica*'s agricultural project on Carillon was now being harvested, Apollo realized that he had lost all sense of time. No wonder his father had seemed testy with him when he had shuttled up to the *Galactica* to provide reports on all the activities of the humans on Carillon, including the rest and recuperation in the casino and food rooms. His father had, Tigh told Apollo, been particularly disturbed by his own visit to the Ovion mine and the recreation area. Adama had not seemed interested in the statistics, nor in Apollo's overall conclusion that their mission was not only proceeding ahead of schedule, it was overwhelmingly successful. When Adama said he felt disturbed by something he could not put his finger on, Apollo told him that he had felt the same way at first, but the obvious happiness of their people during their visits to the surface had quelled his apprehensions. Adama said that was exactly what was wrong, exactly what he couldn't put his finger on. The discussion with his father had left Apollo feeling even more disoriented.

Tonight he would forget all that, he decided, tonight he would snatch pieces of the fun that everybody else had been enjoying for the better part of two Carillon days. Serina had agreed to accompany him to the casino, and who knew to what else, and he was going to enjoy himself for a change. Only the lure of the lovely Caprican newswoman could have coaxed him into his dress blues for any occasion, and he felt quite joyful as they entered the casino. Serina, holding onto his arm, had changed to a long-skirted, flowing, lavender dress, and she looked gorgeous, so much so that even the more fanatical of the gamblers glanced up from their games to take a look at her. Those people who were not engaged in the gambling activities could not get their fill of the substances on the food tables. The gambling itself was more raucous and joyous than any betting or playing activities Apollo had ever seen before. He got the impression that everyone was winning. Perhaps Starbuck's luck was rubbing off on everybody.

"It's a circus," Serina said, "a wonderland."

"That it is," Apollo said, "but at least it's giving a lot of people the kind of relief break they needed so desperately."

"I'm glad that you've found time to take a break for yourself. I've never seen anybody push himself as much as you have."

"All in the line of duty, ma'am."

"I'm happy to see you cheerful, and I'm so glad to see them all happy. That woman there at the table—"

She pointed to a middle-aged matronly woman who was so involved in dice play that her blond wig was on the verge of falling off her head.

"What about her?"

"I watched her husband die in her arms only a few days ago. Don't look at me so strangely. I'll try to have fun. It's not easy making the transfer. I'm exhausted. So much has happened, I think it's all catching up with me."

"I could take you to the guest quarters the Ovions've assigned us."

Was the young captain finally making his move, Serina wondered. She didn't know whether she hoped so or not. Not long ago she had believed that she could not accept an emotional relationship with a man, at least not until the human suffering had stopped. She looked around her. Nobody seemed to be suffering. She was not sure what was holding her back. Some little detail out of place, some color that was wrong in the room, something. She told herself to relax, she wasn't even officially a newswoman any more and did not have to act like one.

"Let's stay here for a while," she said to Apollo, who nodded without any apparent disappointment. "I'm going to have fun, too. I want to sit right here at one of the tables."

Apollo smiled.

"Why don't we win a fortune?"

"Why don't we, my captain?"

They took a seat at a roulette table and bought some chips from the green-skinned, scaly humanoid who was the croupier.

In a far corner of the casino, near an entertainment lounge, Starbuck was riding a winning streak that was like nothing he had experienced since the day his gambling dad had flipped his first pack of cards into his eager, waiting fingers. A tall pile of golden cubits stood in front of him as he tossed another winning hand back onto the center of the table. Touching the cubit pile, he hollered ecstatically, "Let 'em ride again."

He won another pot and leaned back in his chair. The chatter of the throng watching his streak nearly drowned out the raucous music coming from the lounge. He glanced up at the gallery and directly into the staring eyes of Athena, who stood by the empty chair next to him.

"This seat taken?" she asked.

"Uhhh, well...." he said, squirming in his own chair. Cassiopeia had been sitting beside him until just a few moments ago and had abruptly gone off, saying she'd just gotten a good idea. Since he had no idea what constituted a good idea for the Gemonese socialator, he had no idea when, or even whether, she would be returning.

Athena slid into the chair and leaned toward him, saying, "I think I owe you an apology."

"You do?"

"I haven't had the nerve to tell you until now. You know how I've always told you it was wrong for a commander's daughter to get involved with a combat warrior."

"I vaguely recall you saying that."

"Come on, this paradise is the perfect opportunity for us all to be honest with each other. Let loose even the psychological inhibitions. I hurt you, admit it."

Starbuck, feeling it would be better to go along with her until he could figure out what she was getting at, nodded and tried to work some pain into his face. Athena went on eagerly.

"Didn't you say that I was the only woman you'd ever really cared about?"

So that was it! Jealousy. She knew about Cassiopeia

then. But what exactly did she know?

Athena's look hardened as she said, "Well, did you say that?"

"Oh. Oh, sure. It's just that, with all the misery and everything, I've shut all those feelings out. To avoid the pain, you see."

Her eyes narrowed.

"I don't believe you. Look, I'll forget your little peccadillo with the socialator."

Starbuck's eyes widened in surprise.

"It was you. You turned on the bloody steam! I should—"

"Should what? Didn't you deserve it?"

"No, of course I didn't deserve it."

"Oh, you can hop into a launching tube with any socialator that comes along."

"That's pretty bigoted. You know better. A socialator's not a common—"

"I don't care if she's an uncommon anything. All right, I'm not the—not the warmest person around, especially when there's work to be done. For that matter, I practically forced you into that socialator's arms."

"She had interesting arms."

"Starbuck!"

He cursed himself for letting that remark slip. He didn't really want to hurt Athena, but that socialator comment had been unthinking and a bit callous. He was not used to callousness from Athena.

"All right, I'm sorry, but we're not going to work this out with a simple—"

"I believe you're occupying my seat," said Cassiopeia, who now stood behind the chair Athena had coopted.

No! Starbuck thought, what miserable timing. He could feel the sweat begin to pour out of his skin. This was worse than angling toward a tilted deck for a crash landing! He hardly noticed that he had just won another pot. Perhaps if he crawled under the table....

Athena turned slowly, with a studied deliberation, toward Cassiopeia.

"Your chair?" she said elegantly.

"Maturity doesn't become you, child," Cassiopeia said, then turned toward the redfaced Starbuck. She held up her hand. In her long thin fingers dangled a glistening golden key.

"Good news, flyboy! I got us the Royal Suite!"

In space-fleet parlance, such a turn of events was known politely as the moment that the Cylon hit the fan. Athena appeared livid with rage. She looked from the victoriously grinning Cassiopeia to the pained face of Starbuck. The lieutenant decided he should look pious, but he had no idea how even to feign that, it was so far from his normal behavior. He swallowed hard and figured his best maneuver was to say nothing. Athena and Cassiopeia were both fighters, let them work out a solution. He sat back in the chair, taking a brief moment to signal the dealer to let his current bet ride.

Athena, with a sly smile, reached up and snatched the key from Cassiopeia's fingers.

"Thank you!" Athena said. "*We* do appreciate it!"

She looked toward Starbuck and took his arm, trying to nudge him from his chair.

"Let's get out of here," Athena said. "To the Royal Suite, Starbuck!"

He looked up at Cassiopeia, then back at Athena. A weak grin broke up the panic in his face.

"Uh," he said, "look, I'm right in the middle of a hot streak here."

"Honey," Cassiopeia said, "your streak isn't that godforsaken gold-dust pile on the table. Your streak is here, with me, and you've just gone cold."

"That's right, you tell him!" Athena said.

"Hey!" Starbuck said.

"Forget it, *Lieutenant*," Cassiopeia said, "even an ex-socialator has a notion of when to bow out."

"Smart lady," Athena said.

"Don't get overconfident, child," Cassiopeia said. "I didn't say I'd quit for good."

"You little—"

"Don't say it. I've heard it somewhere anyway."

Cassiopeia angrily pushed her way through the crowd.

"About the Royal Suite," Athena said.

"Yeah," Starbuck said.

"Forget it!"

She threw the key down on the card table, pushed the chair over, and followed in Cassiopeia's wake. Starbuck let out a long-held breath and started collecting his cubits, while the dealer pushed his newest winnings toward him. Boomer tapped him on the shoulder, and said:

"We'd better talk."

There was an urgency in Boomer's voice that Starbuck could not ignore.

Boomer led Starbuck away from the gambling tables and into the casino's entertainment lounge. As they swivelled and sidestepped their way through the crowded room, Starbuck's attention was gradually drawn to the stage, where a trio of humanoid female singers was currently performing a song that bore no relation to any kind of music he'd ever heard. They sang in a high-pitched and raucous fashion, but not without a certain sweetness in a deeper timbre undercutting the melody. Starbuck was quite charmed by their act and could not take his eyes off them even when he and Boomer had been seated at a table along a side wall.

"What do you know about the entertainment?" Starbuck asked.

Boomer glanced toward the stage, said in a bored voice, "Tucanas."

"That the name of the group or their species?"

"They come from the planet Tucan."

"Never heard of it. Interesting sound, though, and sort of attractive in an odd way."

"Very odd."

"What do you mean by that?"

"Look closely."

Starbuck looked closely. He saw suddenly what Boomer meant. Each of the Tucan women had two mouths, and all of the mouths were engaged in the song. No wonder they were capable of such a bizarre sound!

"Hard for any of those damn Ovions to overhear us or read lips in here," Boomer said.

"Lips?" Starbuck said. "Oh, you mean, *our* lips. Look, are you sure you aren't jamming your scanner, imagining things? Why would anybody wanta read our lips?"

"I'm not sure, but somebody's up to something around this place."

Starbuck dumped a lot of cubits onto the table, inserted

one in a small pedestal at the center. A cup materialized full of brownish liquid.

"Where'd you get all those cubits?" Boomer asked.

"Gambling! You can't lose. The cards are falling my way."

"That's what I'm talking about. Everybody's winning."

"Boomer, one thing this place isn't, is crooked."

"You ever been in a place where you can't lose your money?"

"No, but then I've never been *here* either. Say, will you listen to those singers?"

"Starbuck, nobody else I know of's ever been here before either. I know this place is a little out of the way, but—"

"A little out of the way? We almost starved to death getting here!"

"Yeah, because of fuel problems, because we spent a lot of time under light-speed. Look, half the people here are from our home planets—Caprica, Tauron, Sagitaria. They were transported here before the Cylon invasion even. They don't even know about it. No communication's been going in or out. I tried to tell one of these clowns what'd happened. He thought I was joking."

"Understandable. Not a very credible story when you're sitting in a joint like this."

"And another thing. We've never heard of this so-called resort, never even encountered Ovions before, right? I took a quick poll. Nobody got a word of publicity about the most efficient gambling den in this place."

"Maybe it's like a secret club."

"Nothing's that secret. How is it they all come here but never came back home and told everybody about it?"

"Would you tell everybody you found a gold mine? I mean, who knows how long they're gonna keep this up? It may be some kind of introductory offer. Hey, those girls are great!"

"Forget the girls. Talk to me. What information've you picked up around here?"

Starbuck continued to stare at the singers in spite of Boomer's protests.

"Like what?" Starbuck said.

"Like why everyone eats so much in this place maybe?"

"Why not? The food's practically free, and *sensational*, like—hey, would you listen to that! They're incredible!"

One of the singers had moved downstage for what sounded like a riff solo, while the others provided a complex harmony. Starbuck was beginning to be surprised that it took only six mouths to perform such musical wonders. Then he noticed that the soloist was only using her upper mouth at that moment in order to carry the viciously sweet melody.

"We could make a fortune if we could put those girls on the star circuit," Starbuck yelled. "I mean big money, Boomer."

Boomer raised frustrated eyebrows.

"I really don't believe you. Every creature in the universe may be out to exterminate us and you want to hire a vocal group!"

"Have a little vision, will ya? Who knows how much longer this stupid war's gonna last—I mean, the way things are, it might be over now and we just don't know about it. Whatever, eventually we're no longer of any use to anybody and get mustered out and dumped. Then what'll we be? Antiquated, burned-out star fighters."

"Seems to me optimistic to plan on being burned out. Stop counting your pension money, bucko! We may be lucky if we last till tomorrow morning."

"Now what're you talking about?"

"People disappearing."

"Who?"

"I'm not sure, but I've picked up some talk, some strange stuff about guests who just drop out of sight."

"The tour you mean? Boomer, it's a big place and they have some kind of tour a lot of people go on before leaving for home."

"Home? What home? I just told you, nobody ever heard of anybody going home! And what home're they gonna go to now? What—"

"You ask too many questions."

"And you're not acting yourself. Something's gotten to you, Starbuck. I'm telling you. Something's not right around here."

"Well, *they* are. Listen to them."

The trio was building to their big finish. The two Tucanas singing harmony hit a sustained chord, while the soloist's voice rose and rose and rose. Then, just at the final beat, the singer's lower mouth came open and emitted a low resounding note that not only put a sensational capper on the piece of music but smashed the glass in Starbuck's hand to pieces. The audience broke into tumultuous applause. Flabbergasted, Starbuck rose from his seat, shouting:

"I gotta talk to 'em."

Boomer started pounding the surface of the table, hollering:

"I don't believe it! I don't believe it!"

Starbuck rushed toward the stage, trying to catch the attention of the Tucana singers.

The unpleasant sweetness of the air, the slightly repulsive richness of the food, and the raucous noise of the casino all affected Apollo, while Serina seemed to revel in it.

"I've spent too much of my life on my career," she said. "Fought too many petty battles with too many venal people just to get a picture centered right, a news item reported correctly. I don't know how to relax. I'm trying to learn. Will you help me?"

"I've got some ideas," Apollo said. "Let's try the garden."

"You're on, Captain."

The centerpiece of the casino garden was a fountain from which purple wine seemed to emerge as tiny waterfalls from between foliage. People scooped out portions of the liquid into golden goblets with broad handles. They then held the goblets over the tiny fires that encircled the fountain. The result, as Apollo and Serina soon found out, was a tantalizing concoction which seemed to mix hot and cold in delicious bursts of taste. The *Galactica*'s crew, who had been among the first to sample the mixture, had nicknamed it "grog." It was not only delicious, it seemed to have some aphrodisiac effect, as the couples who sneaked off into the surrounding foliage indicated.

After taking a sip, Apollo found it difficult not to suggest a little trip into the trees to Serina. He was jarred out of his romantic mood, by the ugly voice of Sire Uri who, a few feet away, was talking with one of the other council members—Lobe, the representative from Piscera.

"I had a long talk with their queen, what's her name, Lorry or something," Uri was saying. "Long talk. She's very kind, generous, even attractive if you can adjust your thinking to one of these insect creatures being at all attractive. She said she was happy we seemed to like it here so."

"I'll say," Lobe said. "Uri, have you seen the guest accommodations? They're as opulent as a king's palace and endless. Endless. If this planet could fly, it could see us to our destination in true style."

"And why need it fly?"

Uri kissed a pretty young woman at his side. Apollo thought it was a different pretty young woman than the one who had clung to him at the time of the arrest. A shudder ran up Apollo's spine as he listened to the two councillors and their drunken rhetoric. Uri continued.

"Precisely my point, Lobe. Precisely what I talked to the queen about. My God, look, if a man were to fantasize an environment for his complete fulfillment, he could not have done better. There's the food, all the necessities to feed our people, and the Ovions can produce it in mass quantities. And, with the Ovions, we have the support of a culture quite content to be subservient to our needs. When I asked the queen if we could stay here, she said they would be happy to welcome us, except for one thing."

"What, Sire Uri?"

"She said they are a peaceable race, and they fear our weaponry. Justifiably so, it appears to me. Justifiably so. What would you think if a superior race came down out of the skies and threatened us with superior weaponry? I mean, you can see their point. And, anyway, here we are so far away from the Cylons as not to pose a threat to them. At least we ought not to pose a threat, and would not, if we calmed the Ovions' fears by giving up our weaponry, our awesome war machines."

It was not that Uri had spoken so preposterously that surprised Apollo, it was that people all around him were nodding assent to the idea.

"Do you realize what you're saying, Sire Uri?" Apollo said, stepping forward into the center of the councilor's group. Serina stayed at the edge of the group, sipping at her grog and trying to focus her eyes on the scene before her.

"Ahhh," Uri said, "our young warrior-hero, or should I say savior? The son of our godlike commander. Captain, I was just pointing out that this planet offers us a marvelous opportunity."

"Sounds to me like an opportunity to be murdered for good and all by the Cylons."

"If they even bothered with us, which they would not."

"Sire Uri, they destroyed our worlds!"

"They attacked us, I would remind you, because we were a threat to their order. Here, isolated from them, we pose no threat. Especially if we disposed of our ships and weapons. What do you think of my proposal, young warrior?"

"I'd hope it's the grog."

Uri raised his goblet in a toast.

"Well," he said, "perhaps tonight it is the grog, but tomorrow. . . ."

Apollo whirled and walked out of the center of the circle. Taking Serina's arm, he led her along a garden path back toward the casino. Looking back, it seemed to Serina that Sire Uri stared after her somewhat lecherously.

"Don't let *him* ruin this wonderful glow," Serina said, a bit woozily. "No one would take that proposal seriously."

"Maybe not. A lot of those people were nodding right along with what he said."

"I'm about to nod out."

"In that case, would you like to hear my proposal? It's a bit more personal."

"Captain, I've been considering it for long before you ever got around to asking it. But I'm not sure about it. Not while my head is spinning, anyway. Would you mind if we discussed this again after we visit the guest quarters?"

"Which brings me right back to my proposal. I wanted to take you there."

"This time I want to go there to make sure Boxey is all right. And after that, let's hear no proposals you can't live up to when the grog wears off."

A sign in the casino elevator informed them that all guest accommodations were on the first three levels going down. Serina touched the plate for level two, where she had deposited a sleepy Boxey earlier in the evening.

"I wonder what's on these other levels further down," Serina said, pointing to the array of buttons on the panel.

"Want to have a look?" Apollo said.

"Why not? I'm a snoop from way back, you know. Let's start at the bottom and work our way up."

She touched the plate for the bottom level. Immediately a

soft voice floated down at them from the ceiling.

"I'm sorry, but you have indicated an incorrect stop. Guest accommodations are limited to the first three levels. All others are for kitchen, mining, and support personnel only. Thank you."

Serina smiled.

"Off limits, I think they say in your profession, Captain," she said.

"Curious," Apollo muttered.

The elevator came to a stop at level two. A quick check of Boxey's room showed that the boy was sleeping quite peacefully. His arm was curled around Muffit Two, who maintained a droid alertness, even giving Apollo and Serina a fast once-over when they entered the room. Apollo pulled Serina to a dark corner and kissed her. At first her response to the kiss was tentative but, in a moment, she returned his kiss.

"About my proposal...." Apollo said.

"Let's dispose with ritual. My room is next door. Mmmm... whatever's in that grog, I'm considering taking it with me when we leave this place."

Arm in arm, they left Boxey's room. Muffit Two's head settled back on a pillow, its eyes staying open, keeping a steady watch on the doorway.

FROM THE ADAMA JOURNALS:

I've tried many times to make entries in this journal about
Baltar's treason, but somehow I can't deal with the subject
without seeing the man's puffy egotistical face floating before
me, ghostlike, and feeling excruciating waves of hatred go
through my body. I become tense and can't think of words.
Trying to put his treason into words would give it a set of
perimeters whose very limitations would diminish the pure
and unalterably selfish evil of the act. And I'm not about to
rationalize a treason of such dimensions. The acts of aliens
like the Cylons or Ovions are at least understandable to me as
manifestations of ideas that belong to different, perhaps
ultimately incomprehensible, cultures. With Baltar I can
understand the ideas he spouted, and I can even imagine the
awesome selfishness that led him to sell out his own people
for rewards that seem trivial in perspective—but that doesn't
bring me any closer to a clear conception of the man himself.
It's all I can do to make the ghost-face of him fade away. In
his evil he is alien to me, more alien than any multi-limbed or
multi-eyed creature from a different part of the universe.

CHAPTER NINE

On the Cylon base ship, Imperious Leader contemplated the latest report from his centurion on Carillon. The plan was proceeding efficiently; more and more humans were falling prey to the lure of Ovion contentment. Lotay had managed to doctor the food of several of the human leaders (except, unfortunately, for Adama) with a drug that helped her to sway their minds toward foolish decisions. She had been successful, she said, with planting the idea of unilateral disarmament into several councilors' minds. Also, she had been successful in holding back on the shipments of Tylium to the fleet in the skies above the planet, supplying them enough of the liquid form of the fuel to lull any suspicions they might have developed. The leader wondered if the wily Adama could really be fooled so easily. All signs pointed to that conclusion, but one fact that had emerged in the leader's many battles with Adama was the man's unpredictability. If a conclusion about him seemed obvious, then it must be questioned.

Nevertheless, the time to act was now.

He sent out the order that the Supreme Star Force stationed at Borallus be immediately launched and set on a

course for Carillon with the mission of annihilating human
survivors and their spacecraft. This time Adama's forces
would be rendered impotent, even if a few humans did
manage one of their miraculous escapes.

Another message came to the leader a few moments later.
The rest of the human fleet, the ships left behind by Adama
that were traveling toward Carillon at a slow speed, had been
located. A malfunction in their camouflage had given their
coordinates away. The leader resisted an impulse to send out
a force to destroy this group of wretched and battered
remnants of the human fleet. The better strategy was, clearly,
merely to maintain surveillance on these ships. They were
powerless and indefensible, obviously low on Tylium and
supplies. No, the logical move was to save their destruction
for later. Adama was no doubt in contact with the ships he
had left behind. Attacking them now might alert a rescue
fleet, and that could not be allowed. Yes, the waiting game
seemed best for now. It was a strategy he had learned from
humans.

Cylon victory was certain, the Leader told himself. The
Supreme Star Force's larger numbers would easily over-
whelm the weakened human fleet, he told himself. The ships
left behind could be toyed with and blasted to pieces, he told
himself. He would have Adama's head as a victory token, he
told himself. Nevertheless, a certain uneasiness, an uncharacteristic tension, troubled his thoughts.

On the bridge of the *Galactica*, Adama paced his usual
path along the starfield. Frequently he made a fist out of his
right hand, pounded it into the palm of his left.

"Those fools," he muttered once, "give them something to
eat and all judgment flies out of their minds. It's almost as if
the food itself had muddled their minds. Is there any way I
can stop this council meeting they're planning, Tigh?"

"Nothing in the regs gives you any authority with the
council except in regard to military matters. In military
matters you can countermand—"

"Unilateral disarmament is *not* a military matter?"

"Traditionally such decisions have been in civilian hands,
sir. Many believe that it's proper and logical, even—"

"I know, I know. I've a firm grasp on the theories behind
the separation of military and civilian responsibility. I even

approve of it. In theory at least. It's just that this group of muddleheads seem possessed. Tigh, I just want to go into the council room and knock heads."

Tigh smiled slyly, said:

"May I remind you, sir, in all due respect, that if you had not resigned as president of the council you would have the privilege of going into that council room and knocking heads."

"I am all too aware of that, Colonel. All too painfully aware."

In the meeting room, the councilors eyed Adama's entrance with apprehensive caution. To Adama they looked curious, as if they had been physically transformed into total strangers.

Before taking his seat, which had been placed to one side to denote his present lack of status on the council, Adama said, "What, may I ask, is the purpose of this special council?"

Anton, the new president, gestured at the chair and replied.

"Adama, please respect the order of business until called upon by this chair."

Adama sat, his anger growing. Even Anton, who had once been his ally, seemed odd now. The emaciated old councilor called the meeting to order.

"It is the growing consensus of every man, woman, and child in this body that to set forth into uncharted space is madness," Anton said.

"Hear, hear," said the rest of the councilors, almost in unison. The muttered agreement sounded like a chant, orchestrated of course by Councillor Uri.

"The question is," Anton continued, "what do we do about the Cylons. Obviously to remain here is to run the risk of discovery. Councilor Uri has a measure to propose. Uri?"

Uri rose to his feet, surveyed the council with a smile that displayed his smugness for all.

"My brothers," he said unctuously. "A hasty attempt to outrun the Cylons spawned in the midnight of desperation seems foolhardy in the light of day."

Midnight of desperation, indeed! Adama thought. How quickly these oily politicians could reduce the circumstances of a tragedy to a cliché. Did Uri not remember the suffering, the panic, the Cylon fighters killing our people and reducing our cities to rubble? Did he not even remember the joy, however momentary, he must have felt when, safe in the plush compartments of his own luxury liner, he knew he was still alive, one of the few survivors? Or were men like Uri empty of all feeling, alive only to satisfy some instinctual greed or lust that moved them through their shabby existences like transistors inside a droid? Perhaps, Adama thought, he was just seeking rational excuses for what was in reality madness.

"I propose," Uri continued, with a significant glance toward Adama, "that, instead of rushing off on a doomed mythical quest, we now attempt to appeal for justice and mercy."

Adama could hold back his rage no longer. He rose to his feet, shouting:

"Justice from the Cylons? Mercy? Did you actually say *that*? Are you so far gone—"

"Gently, my dear Adama, gently," Uri said. His voice had dropped to almost a whisper. What really disturbed Adama was that the other councilors had appeared annoyed with him when he spoke and then had nodded at Uri's soothing imprecation. "Commander, I know your opposition to us and I understand it. From the military point of view—the militaristic point of view, I might say—gestures toward peace almost always appear senseless. But you miss the total picture, I think. The spoils of enslaving us so far from their base of power hardly seems worth the effort for the Cylons."

"Enslaving? Base of power?" Adama, still unable to control the anger in his voice, shouted. "Gentlemen, it's you who do not understand. The kind of reason you're trying to employ might be sensible if we were dealing with other humans, with any species whose system of values was analogous to our own. But these are the Cylons, gentlemen! They said they would not stop until every human had been *exterminated*. Not even enslaved, *exterminated*. We have not even had the privilege of dealing with their leaders openly. All we know of them is by inference and observation. Why should they change their own methods? For that matter, why should they believe we are now willing to accept that which we always found unacceptable? To live under Cylon rule? We have always been just as adamant about that as they have been in their avowed desire to exterminate us."

Many of the brows around the council table gradually began to frown. Perhaps, Adama thought, he was getting through the muddle.

"Commander," Uri said, with an obvious sense of theatrical timing, "the Ovion queen Lotay has observed the Cylons up close, and in much more peaceable circumstances. Her race has been at peace with the Cylons for a millennium, and she assures me that victory is the Cylons' only goal. It is a matter of satisfying their codes of order. If any individual enemy or group of enemies still roam the universe, then they feel it their duty to eradicate them—to wipe out the flaw in their sense of order, so to speak. By destroying our arms to prove we are willing to live in peace, the flaw would be removed and they wouldn't—"

"*Destroy* our only means of defense!"

"Or attack. May I remind my brothers that we once were at peace with the Cylons. We didn't have conflict with them until we intervened in their relations with other nations."

Adama struggled to keep from coming to blows with Uri. He wondered briefly whether, if Adama sprung upon him suddenly, the man would refuse to fight back.

"Yes," Adama said, "you are right. We didn't come into conflict with the Cylons until we defended our neighbors whom the Cylons wished to enslave. And, until we helped the Hasaris to get back their nation, taken by force by the Cylons."

"Correct," Uri said. "And you merely prove my point. If we mind our own business, there is every reason to believe the Cylons will leave us alone."

Again the other councilors, satisfied with Uri's rhetorical flourish, murmured approval. Adama could see there was no point in trying to get through to them with anything resembling logic. He had made his contingency plans. It was now time to put them into effect. He addressed the council in a quiet but tense voice.

"Gentlemen, if we have come to this table to turn our backs on the principles of human reason and compassion, the principles of our fathers and the Lords of Kobol, from whom all colonies evolved, you do so with my utter contempt."

He turned and strode quickly from the room. After he had left, many of the councilors squirmed in their seats. Uri turned to them and spoke.

"Warriors are always the last to recognize the inevitability of change. The commander has always been fond of telling us we have no choice, which always means to endorse his ideas slavishly. Fortunately, we have a choice, life or death."

"I submit that an issue this grave should be decided by the people," Councilor Lobe said.

"The military will be difficult to convince," Anton said. "How do you propose we present so delicate a matter?"

After an uneasy pause, Uri said:

"At a celebration. People are always easier to deal with at a celebration. I propose we hold a celebration to decorate those three brave young men who, at the risk of their lives, opened the Carillon minefield for us. Without them, we'd still be on the other side, starving. One of the pilots was Adama's son, Captain Apollo, correct?"

Some members of the council cheered their support of Uri, happy that some solution had been found. Others applauded, impressed at Uri's clever stratagem of including Apollo in the celebration.

"A brilliant suggestion, Uri," Anton said, "just the tonic our people need at this moment. Some old-fashioned, honest-to-goodness heroes."

"Exactly what I was thinking," Uri said, his smile a bit more malicious than usual.

Starbuck had spent a great deal of time trying to convince the lead singer of the Tucana group that he could hurl them from this dinky little engagement in an outworld casino into a full-fledged, big-time career. The singer had not responded to Starbuck's pleadings. She had merely sat nervously, a fat cigar in her lower mouth, looking around the casino as if she expected to see spies everywhere. Starbuck had gone as far as to offer them a seventy-thirty split, with him picking up transportation costs. But the singer had merely said she did not think it would work out, and that she couldn't talk about it anyway. When he had tried to press her on the subject, she had only become more nervous. Leaving her dressing room, he noticed that her apparent fear of spies was justified. An Ovion jumped behind a nearby stage curtain.

The next day, as Starbuck sprawled in his room in the guest quarters, his head throbbing with a hangover, Boomer rushed into the room and sat on the bed so heavily that the bounce sent waves of pain through Starbuck's head.

"Out of the bunk, Starbuck. Captain Apollo's sent out a muster call, and he asked especially for you."

"Boomer, I been lying here thinking, about what you said last night. I'm beginning to agree with you. Something's going on around here."

"Well, whatever it is'll have to wait. We're going to have to go back to the *Galactica*."

"What for?"

"Our dress uniforms."

"Dress uniforms? Look, Boomer, I hate dress uniforms and I've got a head that won't go through one of those tight collars. I'll pass. I'm not getting into any fancy—"

"Starbuck, one does not accept our people's highest military honor, the golden cluster, in a battlesuit."

Boomer's information made Starbuck sit up. Too soon, as it happened, for his head seemed to explode. No matter. He was too amazed.

"A star cluster? You're kidding!"

"You got it. For that matter, me too. All three of us who went into that minefield blind. Apollo, too."

Starbuck smiled.

"Hey," he said, "that's all right. Doesn't some kind of pay raise go with that?"

Boomer laughed, while shaking his head in disbelief.

"Hopeless," he muttered, "*absolutely* hopeless."

Serina walked Apollo to the shuttle that was to take him back to the *Galactica* to get ready for the awarding of the star cluster and to respond to a request from his father for a meeting. Boxey and Muffit Two trailed along behind them.

"It was a wonderful night," she whispered to Apollo.

"For me, too," he said. "And thanks for letting me get all of that stuff out of my system about Zac. I feel better. It'll take a while for the guilt to evaporate, as you suggest, but at least I feel better about myself."

"You should. You're very valuable, Captain Apollo. A walking lode of Tylium, one might say."

"And just as dangerous?"

"Well, it depends on what state you're in, doesn't it, just like Tylium?"

"You may have a point there."

At the shuttle gangway, he kissed her goodbye, to the

obvious delight of the young lieutenants, Starbuck and Boomer, who awaited him at the vehicle's airlock. After Apollo had entered the shuttle and the gangway had retracted and she had been ordered back to a safe area, Serina held Boxey's hand and watched the shuttle take off. Walking back to the casino entrance, she felt quite pleasant, content that some order seemed to be edging its way back into her life. Into all their lives, if what some people said was true. In front of her, Boxey frolicked with Muffy. The boy was steadily improving, too.

An Ovion stood in the casino entranceway. When she saw Serina approach, she started to back into the building. Serina called to her to wait, and the Ovion waited, dutifully.

"Your name is Seetol, right?" Serina said. "You conducted us on that brief tour of the mining facility."

"That is correct," Seetol said. "How may I serve you?"

"Oh, you might just satisfy a former newswoman's curiosity."

"Newswoman?"

Serina had extreme difficulty explaining to the alien what a newswoman was. Seetol seemed to think reporting the acti.ities of others a bit sinful, however newsworthy.

"I was fascinated," Serina said, "by the, well, the *order* of your society and I certainly couldn't help but be impressed by your industry, your complete dedication. I've never seen anything like it. I mean, one gets the impression that those people in the mines work until they simply drop."

She wondered if she was sounding too naïve. Seetol's answer, however, was noncommittal.

"We know no other way."

"Well then," Serina said, edging close to her real question, "what of family institutions? I somehow sense that something is missing." Seetol appeared a bit ruffled. All of her four arms were in motion expansively as she spoke.

"We are very complete."

"What about males?"

"Males. . . ."

Seetol seemed unable to cope with the subject.

"Well, I don't mean to pry," Serina said, even though prying was exactly her intention, "but the Ovions are a *female* culture. Obviously. Surely there must be males someplace. You do have need of them, you haven't found the key to parthogenesis, have you? Perhaps you keep the males at home—"

"We don't keep them at all."

Seetol's high pitched voice had become quite toneless.

"I beg your pardon?"

The Ovion looked up at Serina with her spherical insectoid eyes and said, "You are correct. Males have their place until they have served their purpose. And then, in our society, they have no place. I am sorry. Have I said something wrong?"

"No, not at all. I guess there are, well, value systems in your order worth looking into."

Serina walked away from Seetol, wondering if the alien had meant that the males were simply disposed of. Sometimes having a newswoman's instincts had its drawbacks.

Apollo was surprised to see only a token crew manning the bridge of the *Galactica*. His father engaged in a routine check of equipment with Colonel Tigh, turned to greet his son warmly. Apollo felt happy that he could be comfortable with his father again.

"Tigh was just briefing me on current operations," Adama said. "He wants to be at the celebration planetside. I offered to relieve him for the night. Strictly as a favor."

"You don't feel like seeing your son getting a star cluster then?" Apollo asked, puzzled.

Adama smiled.

"It's well deserved, Apollo. But there's more to this, this award ceremony than just honoring you and Starbuck and Boomer. My presence would somehow verify Uri's strategy, and that's all this ceremony is, just one of his ploys."

"Ploy? That seems strange—saluting his greatest rival's son as a ploy."

"It's exactly what it is, though. He'll propose destroying our arms at the celebration. He's hoping for a cascade of emotion that'll do the damage before anyone realizes what they've done."

Apollo cursed his own stupidity—of course, anything that Uri had set up should have been suspect from the beginning. After observing Uri the previous night by the grog fountain, Apollo should have known the man was plotting something.

"But you can stop him!" Apollo said to Adama.

"Not any more, I'm afraid. Haven't you heard the talk? The scuttlebutt? I'm the villain, at least to most of the population, who are willing to believe anything the handsome Uri tells them. I got us into this predicament, you see."

"How could anyone believe that. Certainly not the majority...."

"The majority, at least for the present, are with Uri. You must remember, Apollo, what they've been through."

"I'm compassionate, Father. I inherited that from you. But this isn't the time, it's—Father, you've got to speak out, to the people."

Adama took a deep breath before responding to Apollo's plea.

"I'm retired, Apollo. Except for running this ship and certain phases of the total operation, I'm—"

"I don't believe you're saying that! This isn't you. What's happened? Help me understand."

It was all he could do for Adama to maintain an aloof official stance, when he wanted to embrace his son.

"You'll understand, son. In time, you'll understand."

Apollo started to speak, then thought better of it, and walked away from the bridge.

Tigh came to Adama's side.

"That wasn't easy for you, not telling him," Tigh said. "Perhaps—"

"No. I need him down there at the ceremony. If I told him, he'd insist on staying at my side. The gamble is mine. If I win, we all win."

"But if you're wrong, Uri will have your head on a platter."

Adama looked out at the starfield. He felt confidence returning to him for the first time since he had assembled the ragtag fleet.

"I am not wrong," he said. "The Cylons lured me into their malicious deception once." His eyes narrowed, and he looked like the old Adama of galactic legend. "Never again!"

He turned to Tigh, his eyes glowing with eagerness to act.

"Report. The livestock."

"All being lifted off the surface of the planet now. No interference."

"Report. The agricultural project."

"Everything harvested, sir. The project will be completed soon."

"Report. The fuel."

"Another token load just arrived. Barely. Darn near exploded when the pilot set it down on the deck a bit too heavily. Other loads seem ready to be launched from the surface, but the Ovions're stalling."

"Don't make them suspicious. But get as much Tylium from them as you can."

"Aye aye, sir."

"Hop to it, Colonel!"

Tigh was already in action. As usual. Around them, the crew seemed to respond to the commander's newfound and boisterous energy. Adama remembered some story from his childhood about a sleeping giant awakening.

Apollo, waiting with Serina for the guest elevator to take them to the casino, could not stop thinking of his father's refusal to bring his case to the people. Something had to be done about Uri, or they would suddenly discover that the shrewd politician had eased himself into a position of absolute power.

"Write me a poem!" Serina said suddenly, clearly to break him out of his mood.

"I couldn't," Apollo said, stirred out of his reverie. "You don't know what you're asking."

"Oh, I do. It would mean a lot to me."

She leaned toward him and kissed his cheek, muttering, "I'll do better in private."

Apollo was about to suggest something even more specific for their later privacy, when he was distracted by a passing man who wore the dress uniform of the *Galactica*. The man, whose collar was clearly too large for his neck and whose sleeves seemed to hang down past his knuckles, seemed a shade too old for combat duty. Apollo's scrutiny was so obvious that the man noticed. He turned away uncomfortably and headed for the nearest corridor, as if to escape.

"What is it?" Serina asked.

"That man's insignia is Blue Squadron. I thought I knew everyone in it. Don't recall ever seeing him before."

"Maybe he transferred in from one of the other units."

"I know most of them also. And did you see the fit of the uniform?"

"Well, how often do you guys get to wear your dress blues? He probably bought it when he was a couple of sizes larger and hasn't worn it for years."

"I hadn't thought of that."

"In any case, the guest of honor fits into his uniform quite neatly—and looks delicious, I might add."

He squeezed her hand. But, in spite of her glowing smile, he could not get the sight of the officer in the oversized uniform out of his head.

The Ovions, as anxious to serve as ever, had rearranged the whole casino for the award ceremony. Colored lights had been arranged in flowerlike patterns to add to the festive atmosphere. Acrobats and entertainers of many species performed their acts at one end of the massive room. The men in full military dress uniform completed the decorative picture.

Starbuck could not get his shoulders to relax. As he and Boomer waited by the podium for the celebration to begin, he couldn't stop fidgeting. Boomer appeared to be equally uncomfortable.

"Have I ever told you how lovely I think you are in a dress uniform?" Boomer said, in a strained attempt to be cheerful.

"Just get me out of here," Starbuck said irritably. "Starfighters don't mix with all this pomp and—"

"Careful. Guests of honor don't curse. It's not etiquette."

Sire Uri, looking every inch the man in control, swaggered up to them.

"I don't see Captain Apollo. I trust he's well. . . ."

"Business aboard the *Galactica*," Starbuck said. "He'll be along."

Uri regarded the roomful of people, which was dominated by the *Galactica*'s dress blues.

"From all the uniforms, I'd deduce that most of our warriors are here," Uri said. "Other than your captain, of course."

"Well, Sire Uri," Starbuck said, "I'm always a big draw."

Uri, not certain how to take Starbuck's sarcasm, strode away, seeking another detail to attend to. Boomer pulled at Starbuck's sleeve.

"Don't spoil the crease," Starbuck said. "What is it?"

"Those three guys over there, watching the acrobats, can you tell me who they are?"

Starbuck studied the three men, all of whom wore ill-fitting Colonial fleet uniforms.

"Nope, Boomer. Darned if I know. Sure have lousy tailors, or else all the fun and games down here's tiring them out."

"Starbuck, you should know them."

"Why in hell should I know them?"

"They're wearing insignia from our squadron."

Starbuck peered at the oddly attired trio. Suddenly he started walking toward them, shouting back to Boomer, "Don't let them start the festivities without me."

One of the three men saw Starbuck coming, and he pointed to him for the benefit of the other two. Immediately the three began to walk toward the elevators. Starbuck picked up his pace, trying to close in on them.

Getting off the elevator, Apollo was bumped roughly by a man in a *Galactica* uniform. He was about to dress the violator down but the elevator doors closed in his face. There had been something odd about the man and his companions. Shrugging his shoulders, he turned to Boxey and said:

"The Ovions've really fixed up this place attractively, haven't they?"

"I don't like them," the boy said laconically.

Serina whispered to Apollo, "Boxey's a little miffed because some Ovion tried to prevent him from bringing Muffit to the celebration."

"I see he won the dispute."

Apollo gestured toward the daggit-droid in the boy's arms.

"Of course he did," Serina said. "He's in training to be an officer of the *Galactica*, isn't he?"

Starbuck came running up to Apollo, saying, "Captain, those men that just got on the elevator. . . ."

"Yes, I have a strong tactile impression of one of them, but what's it all about?"

"Something's going on around here, and I don't like the feel of it at all," Starbuck said. "I think those three were imposters. Somebody else wearing our uniforms, or duplicates of our uniforms. Can we talk?"

"Of course. Serina, will you excuse me?"

"Sure, but not for long, okay? I'll take Boxey and get something to eat."

Muffit Two sprang out of the boy's arms and ran into the main room of the casino, Boxey running after him.

"Gotta go," Serina said. "But you two, don't be long. You don't want to miss your own honors ceremony."

As she walked off, Starbuck took Apollo to a quiet corner.

"Now what is this about imposters," Apollo said, remembering the man in the ill-fitting uniform he had spotted near the elevator.

"I don't know," Starbuck said. "I've been running into people all night who aren't from our unit. But they're in our unit's clothes."

'Yes, I saw one myself. We'd better find out what's going on."

The elevator door slid open and the two men rushed into it.

It took a long time for Cassiopeia to find a dark place where she could get away from the crowd of people. A dark place for her dark mood. When she had arrived at the casino, Starbuck had been distant with her, and she did not care for the young lieutenant's mercurial moods. Then the wretched and lecherous Sire Uri had made about twenty indiscreet proposals to her, following her around while she denied him his every wish until he finally gave up, muttering that no damn socialator should dare to insult him like that. Finally, the festive atmosphere had depressed her more, and she knew she needed to sulk for a while, work some of the sadness out of her system.

What she found was a plush chair which had been placed behind an ornate screen. She flopped down onto it and shut her eyes. The darkness did not enclose her as it should have, as it usually did when she employed the meditation techniques she had acquired in her training as a socialator. Too many other scenes intruded.

Her winning of the highest academic honors and the awarding of the golden fringe which she was allowed to wear along the neck and hem lines of her street-robe. The award required Gemonese males to treat her with a special dignity.

Her selection as a socialator officer and its accompanying privilege of teaching the young.

Her long intermittent love affair with a Gemonese artist, his kindness to her, the way she had felt when he had not turned up among the refugees.

Her one disastrous night with Starbuck, the only man who had treated her with an extra kindness in a long time. Why couldn't he—

An Ovion, apparently stepping out of the wall, interrupted her thoughts. Before she could say anything, the alien had placed one of her four hands on Cassiopeia's mouth and started dragging her to a concealed pod-elevator in the wall.

Serina responded to Sire Uri's gesture to approach the podium. He asked her where Captain Apollo was.

"He'll be here in a moment," she said, "I'm sure."

Uri looked toward Boomer, the only one of the three awardees on the platform.

"I suggest you find your two friends and tell them we're going to begin," Uri said. "With or without them."

Boomer snapped to and jumped off the podium, a weak smile on his face.

"I would like to speak with you later," Uri whispered to Serina. "*Alone.*"

"Drown yourself in the grog fountain," Serina said sweetly and moved off.

Seetol could not figure out why she was disturbed about the operation that seemed to be progressing in the casino and within the several levels of the Ovion colony. The Colonial warriors, most of them, had been assembled for the award celebration. They would be easy targets when the proper time came. Her troops were successfully abducting humans who wandered away from the main body and taking them to the lower levels. Everything she had been ordered to see to had been done. Still, she felt troubled.

The Cylon centurion walked arrogantly into the throne

room and both she and her queen automatically bowed.

"By your command," Lotay said.

"Speak," said the centurion.

"The humans are in full attendance."

"How many warriors?"

"We have counted more than two hundred."

"My reports indicate that number as very near the full complement. A very good effort, Lotay."

The centurion's condescending compliment sent a shiver of distaste through Seetol's body, agitating all four of her limbs.

"We are, but to serve," Lotay said in her soft deep voice.

"You have served well. See that the humans remain entertained until the end."

"How will we know—"

"When the *Galactica* is destroyed, the night will be as bright as a thousand suns, for a quick moment, then there will be darkness. Eternal darkness for the humans. And their remnants will be yours, for your lower chambers."

"We are very grateful, centurion."

"As you should be."

Lotay and Seetol bowed and backed out of the throne room.

Imperious Leader sensed that the time for action had finally arrived. His centurion on Carillon had reported that the human warriors were collected in one spot. The battlestar *Galactica* and the rest of its fleet were being operated by token crews. They could not launch counterattack craft, nor could they adequately fight back with their artillery. An attack could be initiated now, both against the ships in the sky and the trapped humans on the ground. He ordered the Supreme Star Force out of the ambush screen, where they had hid themselves upon arrival in Carillon Sector, and toward the planet. At the same time, he activated another force to head for the ships that Adama had left behind. They could be wiped out in one sweep of fighters, they were so weak. Then all humanity, except those whom the Ovions claimed for the pods in their lowest levels, would be finally annihilated.

The leader allowed himself a moment of satisfaction, the kind of joy he felt when conducting such a multi-faceted campaign. He would be both relieved and happy to rid himself of the human pest. He had been fighting them so long he had begun to think like them. He was glad there would be no more of that.

Apollo and Starbuck could find no trace of the three strange men in *Galactica* uniforms on the guest accommodation levels.

"They've got to be down here *someplace*," Starbuck muttered in frustration. "If they aren't here, they must've reached another level."

"The other levels aren't accessible to humans."

"They are to Ovions. Maybe somebody gave them a free trip. You know, I've been wondering: just how inaccessible are the other levels?"

"That speculation's crossed my mind, too. Shall we try?"

"After you, Captain."

They returned to the elevator. Inside the car, Apollo drew his weapon, aimed it at the control panel and fired. The thin red beam pierced the metal of the panel and, in a near-perfect circle, a section of the control panel above the selection touchplates was severed, falling to the floor. Inside the panel, several wires were cut by the beam from Apollo's sidearm.

Staring at the dangling wires, Starbuck commented, "You realize that's private property."

Apollo smiled.

"I think we owe it to them to try to put it back together," he said. "Any suggestions?"

"Yes, sir. I'd suggest you try tapping those little critters there together."

Apollo connected a pair of the wires. As soon as they touched, the elevator car came to life again and began moving downward.

"You're a gambler," Apollo said. "Pick a level."

"I say we take a look at what's farthest from the guest rooms."

"Agreed."

Apollo pressed the touchplate for the lowest level. No soft forbidding voice intruded and criticized this time.

Her abductor carried Cassiopeia down several levels to a dark, cavernous chamber. She struggled all the way, and the

Ovion had to call in reinforcements in a high-pitched but ominous voice. The group of Ovions flung her onto a massive table and, before she could squirm off, a large canopylike cover came rapidly down from the ceiling and sealed off her escape. Tubing leading into the canopy started pumping in a dark reddish gas. Cassiopeia tried to hold her breath but, looking down at her arm, she saw that the gas penetrated her skin. Her mind told her to scream, but her body was beginning to feel extremely comfortable, extremely content. As the tension rushed out of her, she looked out the transparent canopy. The Ovions were opening what appeared to be large pods. In a trio of other pods three men in *Galactica* dress uniform were nestled snugly, calm expressions on their faces. Cassiopeia smiled at them and managed a weak wave. She was dimly aware of some human voices moaning in the distance.

Moaning was the first sound Apollo noticed as he and Starbuck stepped in the oppressive atmosphere of the lower level corridor. Drawing his sidearm, he gestured to Starbuck to follow him in the direction of the sound.

"You're the leader," Starbuck whispered.

Right after they turned into a corridor, they heard a chattering noise behind them. Recognizing the sound as the Ovion language, Apollo whirled around ready to fire. However, the Ovions were gathered around the elevator, examining the damage Apollo and Starbuck had caused, and arguing among themselves. Their queen, Lotay, swept up and examined the damaged car control. Her excited chatter sent the other Ovions scurrying in all directions.

"They're gonna be looking for us," Apollo whispered. "Let's move."

As he started running forward, he thought he heard the sound of a daggit barking ahead of him.

Serina finally located Boxey on the other side of the massive casino. He was, as usual, chasing after Muffit Two. The daggit-droid was sniffing around a decorated screen that blocked off a small part of the room. As if picking up a trail, Muffit scampered behind the screen.

"Come back here, you daggit!" Boxey hollered, and ran after the pet.

Serina smiled. It was time to herd in Boxey and Muffy, get them both something to eat. She went behind the screen, and saw an overturned chair. And nothing else. Boxey and his daggit were not there.

All right, don't panic, she told herself, somehow they got back into the casino. She rushed back into the main room. On the podium, Sire Uri had made some excuses for the missing guests of honor and was launching into a speech about rebirth, about wiping the slate clean of animosities, of displaying peace to their former foes.

People were applauding. There was a madness in the room, she thought. Where was Boxey? Where was Apollo? Why were there so many Ovions slowly gathering, as if in ranks, near the exits of the casino?

She started walking fast, looking for somebody she could trust, and finding no one.

Apollo and Starbuck leaned against a corridor wall, out of breath.

"I'm beginning to think you're right," Apollo said.

"About what?"

"Your suspicions. About something being wrong here."

"But what? What's the connection between the casino and the luxury quarters, and all of this?"

"I suggest we get out of here, then figure that one out."

Ovion chattering plus the sound of barking up ahead brought Apollo away from the wall. He began to run down the corridor toward the sounds, Starbuck following close behind. The agitated growling of the daggit-droid was the equivalent of a guidance system. They turned a corner and saw Muffit Two, snapping at an Ovion who seemed puzzled by the animal android. The Ovion kept reaching for Muffit with one of her four arms, and then springing back when the daggit leaped toward her, steel teeth gleaming. Boxey came out of a nearby corridor, hollering, "Muffit? Muffit?" The Ovion moved toward the boy, drawing a small but sharp-looking, thin-bladed knife from her belt. Boxey cowered backward as the Ovion raised the weapon.

"Run, Boxey!" Apollo shouted.

The boy ran toward Apollo. The Ovion whirled around. Starbuck emerged into the dim light and sent a beam of laser fire through the alien, who seemed to collapse inward as she fell to the ground.

"Let's get out of here," Apollo said, sweeping Boxey into his arms.

"The elevator," Starbuck shouted.

"Muffy!" Boxey yelled. The daggit yelped and followed after them. They stopped at the corridor archway leading to the lobby in front of the elevator bank. Apollo peered around the corner.

"Oh, God, no!" he muttered, springing back against the wall.

"What?" Starbuck whispered.

"There's a crowd of Cylons collecting there. A whole brigade, it looks like."

"Cylons! But how'd they get—"

"They must be able to key a path through the minefield. Either that or. . . ."

"Or what, Apollo?"

"Or the *Galactica*'s under attack. Damn it, that's why the award ceremony. To get us down here while the Cylons sneak-attacked us. Father's up there with just a skeleton crew. He's probably—"

Muffit Two, peeking out of the archway, began to bark. Apollo looked. Several Cylons were looking toward the archway, light beaming out from their helmets. When they saw Muffit and Apollo looking out, an officer pointed toward them, and a platoon started running their way.

"Let's get out of here!" Apollo screamed, and they broke into a run. The daggit-droid held ground for a moment, yelping at the Cylons, then scampered after the retreating humans.

The leaves of the pod were gently wrapped around Cassiopeia's body. They felt soft and velvety. Ovions picked up the pod and carried her out of the chamber. She began to feel dizzy. The feeling of peace seemed to be wearing off. The pod leaves were wrapped too tightly about her. She could not move her arms or legs. Her entire body was becoming numb. She opened her mouth to scream, but no sound could be forced out.

They arrived at another large cavern. Lying around its floor, filling almost the entire surface, were many pods, each with tubing leading to machinery at the far end of the room.

Most of the pods contained human beings, but some of them contained red and gray clumps of matter which, if you squinted at them and filled in missing areas, were recognizable as human shapes. Recognizable human shapes and they seemed to be dissolving, dissolving into component matter, dissolving.

Cassiopeia's voice returned in a sudden, piercing scream.

FROM THE ADAMA JOURNALS:

On the day when his petition to run for a minor political office on his home planet of Sagitara was granted, Adar came to visit us on Caprica. I was home on leave at the time, during one of those lulls that seemed to occur when the Cylons withdrew for a time from the fray. Ila was always happy to have Adar visit (at a much later time she asked me never to allow him into the house again) and the two of them had a great time chatting about the kind of literary and cultural matters that they enjoyed so much. I was content to listen to them and watch the antics of my two-year-old son, Apollo. (Athena and Zac were years in the future.) We had a tiny pet then, a rascally daggit whose main purpose in life was to trip up intruding human feet, and Apollo used to love to charge at the animal, hear it yip, run away, and then turn waiting for Apollo to charge it again. He loved that daggit and was terribly broken up three years later when it died from some mysterious daggit disease. Ila and I had a bad time convincing him that his pet's death was not in any way his fault.

Anyway, Adar could not hold in his good cheer during that visit. He bubbled over with happiness and optimistic hopes for the future. I don't remember much of what he said, but I suppose his main message was the one he used to much sinister purpose later—that he planned to push this business of the war to its finale. He felt the war was bogged down by the corruption of the politicians running it (I was glad, at least, that he didn't blame the military, as I'd just taken over the helm of the *Galactica* at the time and was quite sensitive about its record). The main goal had to be peace, he must have said. I don't actually remember what he did say. All I really recall was his joy and his enthusiasm. They rubbed off on both of us, Ila and me. Anyway, he was half in love with Ila and she was half in love with him.

On the day he left to go back and run his campaign, we joined hands, the three of us, and made a lot of foolish vows, none of which I wish to record here. All I care to remember is the touch of their hands, his and Ila's, and the smiles that we couldn't wipe off our faces. That we should hold hands and smile was, at the time, so normal, so steeped in the tradition of our friendships and loves, that we never suspected it was the last time the three of us would be together like that. Oh, we were together again a number of times, but Adar always brought a feeling of strategy to those visits, a sense that our times together in the past were part of a storybook whose tales were not particularly readable for him any more.

After Adar left, Ila hugged me for a long time. She seemed sad. I never did know why, though I asked the question often enough at the time. She said she just felt sad. Then the daggit, with Apollo after him, ran between my legs, and I fell to the ground. As Ila laughed and helped me up, she said she'd forgotten to ready anything for lunch and would I accept leftovers. I said what are you laughing at and yes I would. She said I looked absurd falling to the ground and would I fix us a couple of cocktails. I hugged her again. To this day I can feel vividly the way her body nestled against mine.

CHAPTER TEN

Adama kept a constant surveillance of the Carillon work activities. Shuttles from the agricultural project hastened toward the *Galactica* and other ships, with a harvest beyond original predictions of yield. The last request for a new Tylium load had been met with the usual Ovion polite phrasings that more would be sent soon, after they had corrected a malfunction in their processing machinery. Tigh, angry, complained that a number of tankers sat on the surface. Scanners showed them filled with Tylium in its volatile liquid form. Adama told his negotiators to keep trying. He was pleased to learn that one of the tankers had been dispatched, and he personally oversaw the meticulous landing of the battered-looking ship on one of the *Galactica*'s decks. An officer reported the successful boarding of the food stores, and Adama ordered all agricultural personnel to be shuttled off the planet. With the livery and agricultural workers returned, that left only the people collected in the casino for the awards ceremony still on the planet. His sense of timing suggested he wait a few moments before sending out a recall order. He would have liked to bring up Apollo immediately, but that was impossible. However, he put Tigh on alert, reacting to the Colonel's report that a group of Ovions in the casino were acting strangely.

Athena, who had been manning the scanners directed planetside, reported an unusual number of aircraft and a lot of ground movement on Carillon. The exceptional darkness of the planet made it difficult to specify, she said, exactly what was going on. At least one aircraft appeared to have emerged from the cloud cover now hanging over a large portion of the night hemisphere. The trajectory seemed to indicate the rather large aircraft had emerged from the dense center of the minefield.

"Is that possible?" she asked her father.

"Yes, if—"

"If what?"

"If they are in possession of information allowing them to pass through the minefield with safety."

"But such a large ship."

"Were you able to get a good outline of it for scanning?"

"Afraid not. The darkness and the cloud cover and the gathering precipitation—"

"Yes, I see. Very good, Athena."

"You have a suspicion about the ship, don't you, Father?"

Adama considered whether there was any danger in telling her. The time seemed to have arrived to employ Athena's strategic acumen.

"I think it just might be a troop carrier."

It took a moment for the information to sink in, then Athena said, "Cylons?"

"Possibly."

She returned to her duty. On the scanner screens, movements which had seemed strange to her previously now began to take on a military aspect.

A bridge officer turned away from a scanner console, and reported.

"Picking up a large body of objects closing toward us rapidly. They seem to have come out of nowhere."

"From behind an ambush screen, no doubt," Adama muttered.

"What was that, Sir?"

"Nothing. Scan the objects for life forms."

"Aye aye, Sir."

Adama glanced away from the console, into his daughter's concerned eyes. Obviously she had heard his muttering.

Before her father had alerted her to danger, Athena had been wallowing in self-pity about being left behind aboard the *Galactica*. Her mind had been filled with pictures of Starbuck chasing after that socialator. She wished she had not reacted so rashly, throwing the key down like that. If she had had any sense, she would have lured Starbuck to the guest quarters, used all her abilities to make him forget the Gemonese woman. It did not seem to her that men developed permanent relationships with socialators, and that comforted her for a while, until she recalled that Cassiopeia could not really be considered a socialator any more. She was an ex-socialator, able to use her considerable training within new social systems.

Now, however, there was no room for jealousy. If her growing suspicions were correct, and what was happening on the planet below and space above was another Cylon secret assault, then there was no time for petty emotions. Why didn't her father order up the troops, instead of leaving them in the casino? The odds were already against them, and the time wasted in lifting the warriors off Carillon might make all the difference between defeat and victory. She was not used to her father being hesitant in his command role. On the other hand, she had not been prepared for his resignation from the council, an act that seemed to indicate emotional disturbance. Was it possible that her father was cracking up, that under that tough surface pressure was building toward an explosion of madness? She shook her head, not wanting to even consider that.

Switching on the comline to Tigh, who had left his transponder open, she asked him for a report.

"The Ovions're collecting in droves," he said. "We might have to make a move very soon. If we can get this stupid crowd moving—"

"What do you mean?"

"They're buying every word Uri says. How can they? Listen, I'll turn up the transmitter, and you can hear...."

Uri was speaking.

"... to use this occasion to invoke in each of us a rebirth. A wiping the slate clean of animosities and prejudices against any living brother, whether a former friend or foe...."

The cheer that went up almost deafened Athena. The man's speech was effective, all right. How could their people be so gullible? She remembered her father saying once, panaceas were a cubit a dozen, but solutions cost much, much more.

"Athena?" Tigh came back on the line.

"Yes?"

"Tell your father I can't keep the lid on here much longer."

"Righto, whatever that means."

"You'll know soon enough."

Athena's fright seemed to have doubled as she turned away from the scanning console.

For the moment Starbuck and Apollo had outdistanced their Cylon pursuers. Cylons were not known for ground speed. Unfortunately their last turn had led them into a dead end.

"How do we get out of here?" Starbuck asked.

"I don't know."

"Am I correct in assuming that, in addition to finding ourselves in a cul-de-sac, we are also hopelessly lost?"

"That's correct, Lieutenant."

"Well, I always like to know the odds. Especially when they're a thousand to one against me."

"You can't always measure life in gambling odds, Starbuck."

"Is that right? Do you suggest an alternative measurement?"

"Starbuck, those Cylons'll locate us at any minute. This is no time to—"

"I agree. But what do we do? Go shoulder to shoulder, run out there blasting away like we did that minefield? And what about Boxey and that barking growling machine of his, what about—"

"Muffy's no machine!" Boxey protested.

Muffit perhaps felt the insult, too, for he started barking.

"Quiet, you daggit!" Boxey said.

The daggit started running away from them. He ran a few steps, then ran back.

"What's he doing?" Starbuck said.

"He wants us to follow him," Boxey said. "C'mon—"

"Boxey, I don't think now's the time to—" Apollo said, but before he could finish Boxey had leaped out of his arms and begun to follow the running daggit back up the corridor.

Apollo and Starbuck rushed after them. When they had almost caught up with the boy, the daggit turned into a dark area in the wall that looked like a shadow. Boxey followed him into it. Starbuck and Apollo exchanged glances. Closer examination showed the dark shadow to be a small tunnel that ran between the corridor and what proved to be, when the two men had crawled through the tunnel, a large cavern. At first Apollo thought it was just one of the mining areas until he looked closely at the ground.

"What're those?" he said to Starbuck.

"Looks like some sort of vegetable patch to me, but—"

"My God!"

They simultaneously perceived the humans inside the pods. Starbuck crouched down by a nearby pod and touched the plumpish young woman bound inside it.

"I think—I think I was playing hi-lo with this woman that first day I found the casino. Her name was—was—I forgot it already."

"Is she alive?" Apollo said.

"She's breathing. She's got a pulse. Let me see if I can—"

"What is it?"

"Her body. It's stuck here. Not only stuck. It's becoming part of the pod, blending with the leaves. Underneath, she's—Apollo, the back of her head and shoulders, they're breaking up into matter, into—"

"We can't stay here. C'mon."

"But this woman. The others. We can't just leave them, we—"

"And we can't sort out who's salvageable. We'll send a team back. Right now there's the Cylons. C'mon. Follow Muffit, he seems to know where he's going."

They crossed the chamber, carefully stepping over the pods, trying not to look at their contents.

Ahead of them, a group of Ovions entered the cavern, carrying four new pods. Apollo grabbed Muffy and crouched behind the nearest pod. Starbuck and Boxey fell to the ground beside Apollo.

"What's going on there?" Starbuck whispered.

"I think they've been siphoning off people from the casino, bringing them down here. That's the reason for the casino, the reason they keep everybody winning and happy and fat."

"But why? Why are they wrapping them in these pods and—"

"I'm not sure. Perhaps we're a source of food for the Ovions, maybe—"

"Food? Do you mean the casino is a foodlot? The Ovions are a race of cannibals?"

"No, Starbuck, that's not—"

"What do you mean, it's not—"

"Cannibals are species that eat of their own species. Ovions aren't eating Ovions here, they're—"

"You choose a fine time to nit-pick. You mean they're just fattening us up, like cattle, like—"

"That may be it. Those first pods they just brought in, the men in them look familiar."

Starbuck squinted at the pods, which were being delicately held up horizontally while Ovions attached tubing to them.

"They're the three men we were looking for!" Starbuck said.

"I thought so. Even from here the uniforms look like bad fits."

"And the other one—Oh no! It's Cassiopeia!"

Starbuck had stood up and begun to run before Apollo could stop him. He rushed toward the pod carriers like a competitive runner, leaping over the pods underfoot as if they were hurdles. With a last running jump Starbuck hurled himself on one of the Ovions who had just propped up the pod containing Cassiopeia for the attachment of its tubing.

Starbuck's move seemed to activate Muffit Two, who ran after him. Naturally, Boxey followed the daggit. Apollo, still crouching behind the pod, muttered, "Damn!" then started crawling toward Starbuck, around and over the pods.

Seetol, alerted to the disturbance by a messenger, rushed into the pod chamber. From another entranceway came Lotay, accompanied by the tall Cylon spy.

One of the humans, the brash young man Starbuck, was

struggling in the grip of two Ovion warriors. As Seetol approached, she heard him say:

"You can't turn her into—into *food*!"

"Not food precisely, Sir," Seetol said. "Although your nutrient substances are part of what is absorbed. They are diluted, in fact, into a liquid used to feed our babies at the time they hatch from the eggs."

Starbuck appeared to be sick.

"You're lower than—" he saw the Cylon approaching. "Lower than a Cylon!"

Seetol showed no reaction to his insult as she continued.

"Within these pods we are able to extract all that is best in your race. And other races, for that matter. Minerals, life-giving liquids, bones for building materials. We can even extract knowledge from your brains, information from your bodily cells. You might say, we use every bit of you usefully."

The Cylon centurion laughed harshly.

"Impossible to see a piece of human vermin as useful," he said.

Barking and yelling distracted Seetol's attention. The young human boy was pulling at the uniform on the leg of one of her warriors, while his detestable pet was biting at the Ovion's leg. The queen, clearly amused by the situation, walked to the scene, and with her long arms pulled the boy away from the soldier.

"I have special plans for this child," she said to the warrior, who had drawn a weapon. "He's mine. But, if you wish, you may dispose of the animal."

The Ovion coolly pointed the weapon at Muffitt Two, who was now leaping in anger. Squeezing one of its two triggers, she shot the daggit at the high point of a leap. Sparks flew from Muffit's hide as it fell to the ground in a crumpled, inert heap.

"Muffy! Muffy!" Boxey shouted.

"Why, you—" Starbuck shouted. Twisting his body violently, he pulled out of the eight-armed grasp of the two Ovion guards. Leaping up suddenly to Seetol's left, Apollo fired at the Ovion who had shot the daggit, sending a killing beam through her neck. Starbuck, in reaction, rolled to his left and came up shooting. His aim was true, as he sliced the Cylon's helmet in two. Suddenly the two men were blasting away, and an Ovion warrior seemed to fall with each shot.

Seetol ran recklessly through the fire toward Lotay, to protect her. Lotay held the child, who was now crying fiercely as he looked down at his fallen pet, tightly in her arms.

The firing behind her stopped. Looking back, she saw that all of her warriors had been killed by the two humans. Starbuck was now advancing toward her and Lotay.

"Stop right there, you ugly insect!" he cried.

Seetol moved sideways, placing herself deliberately between the two men's weapons and her queen. Whatever else happened, Lotay must be protected. It would be final proof of Seetol's love of her queen to die for her.

"Starbuck, stop!" Apollo shouted.

"I want to kill both of them. We haven't got time to—"

"You might kill Boxey, too."

Apollo's cautionary message seemed to make Lotay hold the boy all the more tightly.

"Disarm them, Seetol!" Lotay screamed, her voice shrill. Conditioned to respond automatically to an order from her queen, Seetol jumped at Starbuck. The man, surprised at the Ovion's lunge, nevertheless got off a shot at her which burned through one of her left arms. She finished her leap and knocked Starbuck off balance. Seetol grabbed at his arm to try to wrest the man's sidearm from his fingers. The move jostled his arm, made him accidentally fire the weapon. A high-pitched scream behind her ended in a gurgle. She turned to see Lotay falling, her head half-severed from her neck by the chance shot. Seetol's scream took up where Lotay's left off, and she ran to her fallen queen. Boxey, having been released from Lotay's arms as they went limp, ran to Muffit. Starbuck aimed his weapon toward Seetol's head.

"No, Starbuck," Apollo shouted. "We've done enough. Take care of Cassiopeia."

Starbuck ran to the pod containing Cassiopeia as Apollo rushed to the sobbing boy.

As soon as Cassiopeia had been released from the pod, she fell into Starbuck's arms, drugged, half-conscious, but alive. He hugged her to him briefly, then set her down while he released the three men in the Galactican uniforms. He was about to interrogate them, but he could tell from their glazed eyes they were in no state to produce any explanations at that moment.

At first Apollo did not know what to do about Boxey. He

figured that the crumpled daggit-droid's body must remind
Boxey of the death of the real daggit back on Caprica. Only
this time nobody had shielded the boy from his pet's fallen
form. Would the boy be able to get over such a loss again? Or
did it have to be a loss? Perhaps not.

"We've got to go, Boxey. We can't stay here."

"I won't leave Muffy."

"I know what you're thinking, but are you a Starfleet
trainee officer or not?"

"Yes, but—"

"Then get moving, young man. I'll bring Muffy, I promise
you that. Now let's go or I'll have you keelhauled."

Boxey, responding to the authority in Apollo's voice,
sprang to his feet. Gently Apollo picked up the daggit-droid.
A few wires inside it hung out, frayed and burned. Ordering
Boxey to start moving, they collected Starbuck, along with
Cassiopeia and the three uniformed men, all of whom could
respond to orders in a robot fashion. They made, Apollo
thought, an odd-looking platoon as they trudged toward the
entranceway of the chamber. Starbuck brought up the rear,
looking back with his weapon raised at the mourning Seetol.
He took aim at her, but Apollo said to leave her in her
sorrow. She was no threat now.

Seetol, aware of their departure, made no move to follow
them. There seemed no point. Lotay was dead. As in all
deaths of Ovion queens, the tiny sharp points on the skin of
her body had faded to a dull, nearly whitish, yellow. Soon
they would retract into the skin.

Without her queen, Seetol was without function. There
was nothing she could do to assuage her misery. Wounded by
Starbuck's shot, she could only sit and allow the life to drain
out of her body. For a long while she bent over the dead
queen and muttered prolonged, high-pitched sounds that
were the Ovion version of keening. Eventually, unconscious-
ness relieved her misery and she fell forward across Lotay's
body.

"I think I've got my bearings now," Starbuck announced,
after they had traveled some distance from the pod
chamber. "The elevator's that way."

"So's that bunch of centurions," Apollo shouted.

"Heck!"

Pushing the dazed men in uniform against a wall and forcing one of them to hold the inert form of Muffit Two, Apollo and Starbuck took cover behind a pair of jutting wall-rocks as the Cylons opened fire. Laser fire blasted chunks of rock from the wall. Starbuck and Apollo returned the fire, and two centurions fell.

"Do you have another weapon?" Cassiopeia, who had crawled up to Starbuck, said blearily. "I can handle a laser pistol. One of my many—"

Starbuck started to tell her to get back, she was still too drugged. Instead, he said, "See if one of those zombies has a pistol in his holster."

He pointed to the three uniformed men, then turned and shot at the centurions blocking the corridor that led to the elevator. His and Apollo's shots kept finding targets, and soon there was a pile of Cylons with nobody fighting back.

"Heck!" Cassiopeia said, unsteadily pointing the pistol she'd liberated down the corridor. "It's a fake. These guys are carrying fake pistols!"

"I'm not surprised. Let's get out of here. That shootout's got to draw some curious intruders."

Before he waved the group on, he touched the wall beside him. It was illuminated with a dim, but increasing, glow.

"Apollo!" Starbuck said. "You thinking what I'm thinking?"

"Yeah. With all this Tylium starting to burn, this could grow into a fire that could turn this whole bloody planet into a bomb."

"Um, let's tiptoe out of here, huh? This way, c'mon."

"Are you sure?"

"This is no time for a vote. Let's move."

A lone Cylon leaped out at them from behind the pile of corpses. He released one shot toward Starbuck which ignited more rock. Starbuck reacted quickly and killed the ambushing alien.

Maneuvering around the corpses, they traveled down another short corridor and into the lobby containing the elevator bank.

"What'd I tell ya, Captain. We're saved."

The door to the elevator that Apollo and Starbuck had tampered with opened suddenly, and a bemused-looking Boomer stepped out. He smiled broadly when he saw that

Starbuck and Apollo were standing across the lobby from him.

"Hey, guys," he said. "What's going on? You guys hot-wire this elevator? I looked all over—"

He was interrupted by laser fire emerging from the darkness of a corridor to his left. His weapon was immediately drawn and he went into a crouch as he fired at the source of the attack. Boomer's fire proved a cover by which Apollo and Starbuck could lead Cassiopeia, Boxey, and the three men across the open area. When they reached the elevator and herded his people in, Starbuck shouted, "We might get trapped in that thing!"

"Does it matter?" Apollo shouted back. "If those fires combine and spread and explode the Tylium, it doesn't matter where we are. Get in. C'mon, Boomer!"

Starbuck joined Boomer to allow him extra firepower in backing into the elevator. As Starbuck leaped into the elevator between the leading edges of the closing doors, a centurion appeared just in front of the car and took dead aim on the young lieutenant. The doors closed just in time but flamed briefly as the centurion's shot hit them dead center.

Serina had searched throughout the whole room for Boxey, and was rapidly becoming frantic. She tried to obtain Colonel Tigh's help but the commander's aide, intent on a small electronic device concealed in his hand, waved her away. She didn't know what to do. If Apollo would only return, she thought, he would know what to do.

On the podium Uri had brought the crowd to several cheers and a couple of ovations. He had reached the main point of his speech.

"And so I implore you all to join with me in the spirit of this great communion and put your faith in me and go to the Cylons. For I tell you that this night will be remembered as the foundation upon which the floor of peace was laid, to last for eternity. I give you the hope that—"

His speech was stopped abruptly by the charging of Apollo, Starbuck, and Boomer from the elevator. Apollo pointed his gun toward the ceiling and fired. Everyone in the room turned toward him.

"Everyone begin to move quickly and orderly towards the exits. That is an order."

"Stand where you are," Uri shouted from the podium. "I am in charge here."

Before Apollo could respond, a group of centurions had joined the Ovions at the entranceway and begun firing. Everyone began scrambling for cover.

"Listen to Apollo!" Uri hollered. "Do what he says. He's in charge here."

Boomer and Starbuck wiped out the entire contingent of guards at one doorway, and Uri was the first to hightail it through to the outside. The rest of Red squadron had produced weapons and laser fire crisscrossed in all directions. Voices screamed and lights, hit by random shots, began to sizzle and go out.

Serina dodged around tables and fallen chairs toward the elevator bank.

"Boxey! Boxey!" she hollered.

She discovered the boy cowering behind Apollo. She picked him up in her arms.

"Over that way!" Apollo cried. "That entrance is clear now!"

He led Serina and Boxey through the archway. Outside, rain stung their faces. Beams from Cylon helmets cut through the darkness. Apollo took Serina and Boxey to cover behind the grog fountain.

All around and inside the casino the battle raged.

"We haven't enough firepower," Apollo said to Serina. "There were too many fake guns among that fake Blue squadron."

"What fake Blue squadron?"

Apollo explained about the strange imposters in the squadron's uniforms.

"I don't know what was in my father's mind when—"

Over the hill near the fountain, a landram appeared, with Lieutenant Jolly mounted on a gun turret. The fat lieutenant started blasting away, and a group of centurions began to fall. Jolly had zeroed in on them by the light of their helmet beams.

Telling Serina to stay under cover, Apollo ran to the landram on which Jolly sat. Another two landrams had appeared, and their gunners were firing at centurions and Ovions.

"Assemble squadron!!" Apollo cried, as he reached the landram and scrambled aboard.

"Where in all that's holy did you come from, Jolly?"

"We're here courtesy of Commander Adama, Captain."

"But why—"

"He sent the landrams to cover for you guys in case any fighting broke out in the casino. Clairvoyant your father is, Captain. He also ordered us to collect Red squadron and shuttle them back to the *Galactica*. He's expecting a fight, he says."

"Red? Why just Red?"

Jolly smiled as he fired off another round, dropping several of the helmeted aliens.

"Blue squadron didn't get to go to the party, sir. Except for Boomer and Starbuck, who had to play hero with you down here at the councilor's little celebration. Guess all three of you had to go so Uri wouldn't get wise he didn't have all the military personnel at the party."

"Well, if the Blues didn't go to the party, who were those oddballs wearing their uniforms?"

"Anybody the commander could find up in the fleet to fill the uniforms. You shoulda seen the guy who got mine."

"I think I did, Jolly."

Shooting suddenly stopped. The Ovions were scattering, while the centurions were beating a retreat away from the casino.

"What are those damn Cylons up to now?" Apollo said.

"I'm not sure. Just before hell broke loose, I received a report that air activity had been tracked by scanner on the *Galactica*. They thought it might be Cylon fighters. Those guys might be returning to their ships."

"Then we better get to ours and damn fast!"

Apollo jumped off the landram. From the main entranceway, the rest of the guests—civilians, warriors, and civilians in warrior uniforms—scrambled out toward the landrams. The authentic warriors were being assembled by Starbuck and Boomer. Apollo joined them, explained as succinctly as he could what Jolly had told him.

"Red Squadron's got to go on ahead in the first landram. We may not have much time. Starbuck, you and Boomer take care of the civilians. Round them up and get them to the shuttles."

"But Captain," Starbuck complained, "I want to get to my ship, too."

"Do what you're ordered, bucko. Get up there fast enough

and I'll see if I can save you a couple of Cylon stragglers for target practice."

"Thanks a bunch, Captain."

Apollo gestured for the Red squadron to follow him to the first landram. Boomer and Starbuck began, with Cassiopeia's help, to calm the panicking civilians and get them organized. Tigh joined Red squadron. He was holding his left arm, which hung limp at his side.

"Are you all right?" Apollo asked. "A Cylon stray shot?"

"Yeah, but I got at least five of them first."

Serina, Boxey at her side, waited by the landram.

"They'll take you to the shuttles," Apollo said. "I'm sorry but—"

"We'll be fine," Serina said. "Get going."

Athena had noticed that the token force left on the bridge had grown to a full crew since the alert had gone out, but she had been too busy to wonder about it.

"Form scan positive," she announced as the information came up on her screen. "Multiple three-passenger vehicles."

"Centurion attack craft then," Adama said. Athena nodded.

"So they spring their trap. Recall all our personnel from Carillon."

"Evacuation activity has already begun," said a communications officer. "I just received a report. They had some kind of set-to down there, and Plan R is in effect." He listened for a moment longer. "Tigh reports that Red squadron has reached the shuttle and taken off."

"Good."

Athena, puzzled, looked toward her father.

"You knew the Cylon attack craft would be here?" she asked.

"Yes. Call General Quarters."

The claxon sounded immediately, as if an officer's finger had been placed on the alarm button awaiting the order. The screen showing the pilot's ready room switched on, showing countless warriors scrambling away from card games, reading, and sleeping.

"Father," Athena cried, amazed. "Where are all the warriors coming from? A full squadron is answering the call. There aren't that many pilots left on board."

"There are. I couldn't let you in on it, couldn't tell anyone who was not integral to the plan. Sorry, Athena."

On the launch board, squares of light flashed on, indicating each ship warming up in launch cribs. When all the lights had flashed on, Adama bellowed, "Launch when ready!"

"I see," Athena said. "You kept some pilots back. An entire squadron?"

"Yes."

"Exactly what I would have done!"

Adama smiled affectionately.

"I'm sure," he said.

They watched the launch through the starfield. The vipers, flying in pre-battle formation, were an awesome sight, and Adama felt confidence rise up in him. Each of the vipers peeled off and, as ordered, flew through the flight corridor the three heroes had formed with their exploit, and went out single file to confront the approaching enemy. A bridge officer reported that the Cylon task force was overwhelming, three entire flights.

"Our squadron won't stand a chance," Athena protested.

"They won't be alone for long," Adama said. "The others are on their way and, using the contingency battle plan, they'll be joining the first squadron."

"It may be too late. Where the hell are they?"

"Shuttle approaching landing deck," a bridge officer said.

"That soon enough for you, Athena?" Adama remarked.

But Athena was too busy staring at the screens showing the launching bay, and the pilots getting into battle gear on the run, to listen closely to what her father had said.

The rain was falling harder in the fields where the shuttles sat. Boomer and Starbuck hustled the panicky people off the landrams and up the gangways to each ready ship. A cold breeze drove the rain uncomfortably into their faces.

"I hate milk runs," Starbuck shouted.

"Look," Boomer cautioned, "each job's important, okay?"

"Ah, that sounds like one of the commander's lectures."

Cassiopeia, who had been helping people off the last landram, reported that everybody was off the vehicles. Her eyes showed she was alert now. Starbuck hollered at the last stragglers to get a move on.

"Boomer," he said, "soon as we dock these shuttles, we

head for the launch cribs. I want a piece of the action."

The rain lessened abruptly and Starbuck's attention was caught by a ship sitting on the slope of a nearby hill.

"What's that?" he said, pointing toward the ship.

Boomer looked.

"That's one of the Ovion Tylium freighters. It was supposed to be sent to—"

"Is it carrying a full load?"

"Well, yeah, must be. Why?"

"I'm taking it up."

"But that stuff's lethal. One attack and they could blow you out of the sky."

"Great. That's the way I always wanted to go. You take care of the shuttles, I'll—"

"I want to go with you."

"You've got your job, Boomer. Do it."

"But what do you know about flying an Ovion ship?"

"I can fly anything, Boom-Boom."

"You can fly your head into the clouds, that's what you can do."

"Goodbye, Boomer."

Starbuck started toward the tanker. Suddenly he was aware of Cassiopeia running beside him.

"What are you doing?" he roared.

"I'm going with you."

"But—"

"You can use me. I'll explain later."

Everybody on the bridge tensed as Athena announced, "First defense wing about to make contact with the attack force."

As the defense wing was revealed on the main console screen, Adama was struck by how pitifully small they looked against the wall of the Cylon armada.

"By all that's holy. . . ." one of the wing's pilots yelled over his com.

One of the lead Cylon ships went into a roll and fired as it flew by a viper. The viper took the hit full on, and exploded. Almost concurrently two more viper ships were wiped out by Cylons. Greenbean's voice resounded through the bridge.

"There're too many of them. Roll out, hit 'em from the sides!"

The Colonial vipers peeled off, but they looked too thinly spread to do much damage.

"Where's the Red squadron?" Greenbean hollered.

Turning back to the screen, he saw two more vipers exploding.

"So much for trying to hit 'em from the sides," he shouted angrily.

"Where are they?" Adama said.

Then his son's voice came through the comline.

"Revved and ready for takeoff."

The launch lights came on.

"Your wing ready, Jolly?" Apollo said.

"Ready, sir."

"Let's go."

Apollo's Red squadron streaked across the sky and into the minefield corridor.

"The shuttles are arriving, sir," a bridge officer said. "Reports show other ships rising up from the surface of Carillon."

"More Cylons?" Athena said.

"Running visual idents now."

On the comline Greenbean shouted, "Yaahoooo," as he observed the arrival of Apollo's squadron.

In the freighter's pilot compartment, Cassiopeia made Starbuck's jaw drop open. The tall young socialator obviously knew the ropes when it came to the bizarre technology of an Ovion tanker. Devices that seemed meaningless to Starbuck were duck soup for her. She started throwing levers and pressing buttons before she even settled herself in the copilot's seat.

"You been on one of these before, Cassie?" Starbuck asked.

"My dad, for the brief times I was allowed to see him, piloted a freighter. And you call me Cassie again and I'll see to it personally this ship blows up."

The ship began to rumble all around them.

"You want to take us up?" Starbuck said. "You seem to—"

"I'd do it, but I'm afraid I'll have to admit reluctantly that your instincts would serve us better just now."

Starbuck strapped himself into the pilot's seat and tried to get the feel of the strange ship from its rattling vibrations.

"Okay to lift off?" he asked Cassiopeia.

She smiled and raised an eyebrow. Studying the equipment, she replied.

"Okay. Lift off."

Cassiopeia had done her part of the job so well that they took flight just behind the shuttles. But the tanker was slower and too weighted down. It could not keep up. Starbuck watched the shuttles disappear through the clouds, leaving a brief red glow on their ominous black surfaces. It was a product of his imagination, he knew, but he thought he could sense the volatile liquid Tylium sloshing against the sides of its heavy containers. One good jarring shock and it was goodbye, bucko. Starbuck would be happy to deposit this payload upon the deck of the *Galactica* where experts could tenderly transport it to safe cargoholds.

"Scanner shows Cylon craft approaching us just below the level of the cloud cover," Starbuck said.

"Are the shuttles in trouble?" Cassiopeia asked.

"Nope. They seemed to have gotten off in time, or else the Cylons don't give a hoot about a pair of surface-to-air shuttlecrafts."

"They seem to give a hoot about us."

"I'll have to try evasion tactics. Hold on!"

Starbuck leveled off the tanker and headed it north, over the Ovion casino and Tylium mine and underneath the Cylon ships revealed by the scanner. The Cylons did not alter their direction, but instead started up through the clouds. Starbuck looked below. Some Ovions had emerged from the ground and were running around frantically. Starbuck wondered what their running amok was all about, when he heard a deep rumble from the ground area. It came through loud and clear over the rattle of the tanker.

"What's that?" Cassiopeia said.

"An explosion! In the mine. Something's setting Tylium off. We have to get the blazes out of here!"

Cassiopeia shrieked.

Starbuck knew exactly what was going through her mind. If the tremors from the underground explosion rocked the tanker, the Tylium in its holds would—he didn't want to think about it. The planet itself could go up. He headed the tanker toward the clouds again. If he got away from Carillon, if he got away from the perimeters of the mine explosions, if he successfully avoided pursuers, if he didn't encounter the attacking Cylon Star Force, if he could get through any fighters attacking *Galactica*, if he could execute the extremely difficult landing of a tanker full of volatile fuel upon the deck of a besieged battlestar—if he could do all that, everything else was easy. All he had to do then was climb in his viper and go off and join his buddies in the suicidal battle against the Cylons. Not to worry, he told himself, everything was just hunky-dory.

A second, more powerful explosion rocked the tanker.

"Oh, no!" Cassiopeia yelled, looking out the side window. Starbuck could see fire reflections on the glass and he knew immediately that something down on the Carillon surface, perhaps the mine itself, was on fire, and perhaps setting off chain reactions all along the surface of the planet. He aimed the tanker for a particularly dark cloud. As he went into it, he passed a Cylon warship coming out. He could sense it swinging around to follow, even though he now could see nothing but cloud outside any portal.

Apollo sliced a Cylon ship into ragged, burning fragments. Glancing to his left, he saw Jolly's plane in trouble.

"Look out on your wing, Jolly," he cried.

"Which one?" Jolly responded. "They're coming in from all over the place. They're—"

Jolly was interrupted by a hit on his tail. His fighter started rocking from side to side.

"There's too many of 'em, Skipper," Greenbean shouted.

"What do you mean, too many?" Jolly said. "I'm here, aren't I? Watch out at three o'clock, Skipper."

Apollo evaded the Cylon with a sweep left, a quarter turn and a spin to the right. Coming out of spin, he opened fire, cleaving his attacker across the middle. Both pieces started to go out of control and fall toward Carillon. Another Cylon fighter started tracking his wake and firing, and he put his viper into a reverse loop, coming down on the Cylon from above and running a line of fire along the top of the entire aircraft. A sudden explosion and the Cylon ship had been instantly transfigured to debris.

In the distance he could see one of the fighters of the Blue squadron shattering under the fire of eight Cylon attackers.

"Don't think we can hold out much longer, Captain," Jolly shouted. "Monk just bought it."

"Do your best."

"I'm doing miracles, sir, but it's not—"

Jolly's sentence got cut off by a trio of swooping Cylons. Apollo couldn't wait around to see the outcome of the attack, because he was abruptly faced by a dozen of the enemy trying to make him the spoke of their pinwheel attack.

A bridge officer reported to Adama that four of the Cylon ships that had sneaked onto the surface of Carillon were now emerging from the cloud cover, apparently to join the alien armada and attack the *Galactica*'s squadron from behind. However, they did not count on the artillery on the *Galactica* and the luxury liner *Rising Star*. Catching the Cylon craft as they attempted a flyby, both large ships opened fire with long-range beams. The four ships exploded almost simultaneously. The crew on the *Galactica* bridge cheered.

"Another unidentified vessel approaching," Tigh said. "Looks like, yes, it's one of those Ovion freighters. Could they be launching an attack? Might be trouble. Should I order it fired on?"

"NO!" screamed Athena from the communications console. "It's Starbuck. He just radioed. He's bringing a Tylium load."

"A Tylium load. Here? In the middle of combat?" Tigh said, incredulous.

Adama laughed, a bizarre sound to the crew around him, who had not heard him laugh so heartily for some time.

"That's Starbuck. Prepare the landing deck. Well, prepare it!"

The bridge crew sprang into action.

"Oh, no!" Athena screamed, as she stared at the scanner screen.

Just beyond the tanker a Cylon fighter had broken from the Carillon cloud cover, heading directly for Starbuck's ship.

"No, he can't be killed!" Athena yelled.

From another corner of the screen a viper, just launched from the *Galactica*, appeared.

"That's Boomer's ship," Tigh cried.

Boomer's viper raced on a course to intercept the Cylon

that was zeroing in on Starbuck. On the *Galactica*'s bridge, everybody held their breaths simultaneously. Just as it seemed the Cylon fighter would open fire on the tanker, Boomer guided his ship to a position in between the Cylon and the tanker, and opened fire. In a second the Cylon ship was a collection of specks that looked like momentary jamming interference on the viewing screen. Another cheer went up from the bridge crew.

"Look at that, will you, Tigh?" Adama said, pointing to the screen. Then he gestured toward other screens showing Cylon aircraft being hit by the smaller but more maneuverable Colonial Fleet vipers. "We're doing it. This ship, it's, I don't know, it's—"

"Coming back to life," Athena said, coming up beside her father.

"That's exactly it, it's as if the *Galactica*'s been sick, tainted by running away from the battle. Now we're proving ourselves again, we're—"

"Wait!" Tigh said. "Listen!"

He turned up a volume switch. Boomer's voice literally boomed throughout the bridge.

"Hey you guys, move over. Let me have some of this."

"Boomer!" Apollo said. "Where you been?"

"You know darn well where I've been. On *your* lousy milk run."

On the screen Boomer's viper started blasting at a trio of Cylon ships, all of which seemed to explode at the same time.

"Boom...boom...boom," Boomer said.

"Hey Boomer," Apollo said. "Welcome home."

Apollo's ship streaked into the picture. His and Boomer's craft seemed to touch wings as they headed toward a line of Cylon fighters.

"Hey guys," Jolly shouted, "we've got a fighting chance."

"You know it!" Boomer shouted. "In a minute we're gonna be filling this sky with fire!"

Adama turned toward Tigh.

"Jolly's right," he said. "We've got more than a chance. Are all our people back on board?"

"When Starbuck gets here with the fuel freighter, that oughta be everybody. Nobody else reporting in from Carillon. Things are bad down there anyway. Explosions." Tigh paused. "God, we lost a lot of people down there."

Adama nodded.

"Yep," he said, "and all that I can think of to say is, we've seen worse. Not very comforting. But we're turning it around now. I can feel it. We'll get those slimy—the *Galactica*'s alive again, do you understand, Tigh, do you?"

Tight looked at his commander as if he thought him on the verge of madness, but he nodded agreement anyway.

On the screens Cylon ships were blowing up all over the sky, as the human pests inside their vipers slipped in and out of the enemy's traps.

Concentrating their attention on a separate screen, Adama and Athena watched Starbuck's approach to the landing deck.

"Easy, boy," Adama muttered.

"Don't blow it now, bucko, please, *please* don't blow it now," Athena whispered.

The tanker seemed too large, too bulky for a smooth landing, especially under the present battle conditions.

"He's got to make it, Dad!" Athena cried.

"You're right there. If he doesn't, there'll be a hole in the side of this battlestar big enough to send it out of commission for a good long time, maybe forever. Watch it, Starbuck. That's right. Good. Easy, now."

One miscue, one bad bounce on the *Galactica*'s deck, and the tanker was sure to explode. And Starbuck was already notorious for flashy landings. Just before the ship made contact with the deck, both Adama and Athena inhaled sharply and audibly.

"C'mon, bucko," Tigh whispered.

Starbuck eased the tanker onto the deck so smoothly, so delicately, the fuel ship appeared weightless. When it gently glided to a stop, another unanimous cheer went up from the bridge crew. Adama could not help smiling.

"Precision flying?" Athena said to him.

"Exactly!" Adama shouted.

Starbuck ran down the gangway as the crew began unloading the tanker, rapidly but delicately. Athena's jubilant mood was momentarily diminished when she saw the tall socialator, looking quite self-satisfied, follow Starbuck down the gangway. But her anger was brief. At least Starbuck was alive. That was what counted.

• • •

Starbuck joined the battle by paying back Boomer his favor. One after the other he wiped out four Cylon ships that had Boomer caught in a pinwheel attack.

"Anybody want to fly over and touch me for luck?" Starbuck yelled.

"Starbuck...." Apollo said.

"Yo!"

"On your tail."

He looked over his shoulder. A Cylon fighter coming in from each side.

"Nothing to worry about," he said. But a Cylon laser torpedo came too close and the explosion sent Starbuck's ship rocking. He banked it over and away from the pair of Cylons, who continued pursuit.

"Boomer," Apollo said, "you give him a hand?"

"Again? Well, I'm trying."

Boomer swung over and began firing.

"Don't take too long, Boomer," Starbuck said.

Another explosion shook Starbuck's ship. Boomer got the attacker in his sights and pulled the trigger with a vengeance. The Cylon fighter made a thousand beautiful little pieces.

"C'mon, Starbuck, Boomer," Apollo yelled. "Let's triple-team 'em."

The three fighters quickly formed a triangular formation much like the one they'd used in blazing the path through the minefield, and they swept down together on the wall of Cylon ships, shooting left and right, up and down. Cracks seemed to form in the Cylon ranks. A series of explosions joined many of the close-flying craft. Apollo, Starbuck, and Boomer all together went into a tight turn and fled the counterattack.

"That's a few for the *Atlantia*," Starbuck said.

"And for Zac," Apollo said.

Other vipers from the Red and Blue squadrons came together and blasted away at the Cylon spacecraft. The wall of menace was quickly becoming a wall of fire and shattered fighters, Starbuck thought, as he swooped down on still another sitting duck target.

• • •

On the bridge the reports came in so fast that they were difficult to assimilate. Adama felt at the center of a vast network of communications.

"Commander! Scanner shows a series of mammoth explosions on the surface of Carillon. Half the planet is blowing up, looks like!"

A screen displayed the large fires on the planet's surface. Another one showed many explosions occurring in the sky above the mine.

"What're those?" Adama asked.

"Not sure, but we think it's the rest of the Cylon war party that sneak-attacked us down there. Appears they all didn't take off before the mine explosions started."

"Commander," Tigh reported, "the Cylon Supreme Star Force seems to be retreating, at least for the moment. Should we give pursuit? All our pilots are begging to pursue."

Adama wanted to give the order to pursue, but it was too dangerous to let the vipers get too far away from the main fleet.

"No," he said, "we must conserve our resources. There's too much to do yet."

"Should I order the vipers to return to base?"

"No, we better go out and meet them. Contact the *Rising Star* and the other ships. Tell them we're all heading through the minefield corridor. We've got to get out of this trap, then set all ships for the hyperspace jump back. I don't know for sure what's going on down on Carillon, but we can't afford to take chances—we've got to get moving in case the whole planet blows up. It gets any worse down there and, what with a working minefield on one side and an exploding planet on the other, we'd be between the devil and the deep blue."

"Yes, sir," Tigh said. "I'm on it."

Adama raced around the bridge as they set their course for the minefield corridor. He barked orders, directing the assembling of the fleet, the tricky flight through the minefield, and the subsequent landing of the flight squadrons.

The new crisis developed almost as soon as all the ships were outside the minefield. The Cylons had reassembled, rebuilt their attacking wall, and were heading back toward the fleet.

Adama turned to Apollo.

"All right, Captain," he said, "what's our potential? Can we give them a good fight, Apollo?"

Apollo punched out the information on the board below the main scanner, examined the data that came up on the screen.

"I'm afraid not, sir. There's still too many of them. In the long run, they'd wear us down. If we hadn't just been through a fight, we might be able to do something, but just now—"

"All right, all right. After the last time, I hate like hell to retreat from another battle. I don't want the military record of the *Galactica* to be tainted again."

"Sir, it's hardly taint when we're saving what's left of the human race."

"That's what I said the first time."

"You have the knack of always being right."

Apollo and Adama exchanged smiles. Adama saw, over his son's shoulders, that his daughter endorsed Apollo's words.

"And anyway," Starbuck interjected, "you know the old maxim: we're not retreating, we're just advancing in another direction."

"All right then, we'll make the hyperspace jump in—"

"Sir, there isn't time," Tigh said. "The Cylons'll close in on us before we can all make the jump. We have to set up a diversionary action."

"The Red squadron'll take care of that," Apollo said, then waited for Adama's response. After a brief moment, the commander nodded agreement.

"All right," he said, "but the *Galactica*'ll be the last ship to make the jump. Rest of the fleet'll go first. Apollo, you take your squadron out there and stall them, then get back here in time for the jump. Those are your orders."

"Aye, aye, sir!" Apollo began running to the elevators leading to the bridge, shouting back to Starbuck at the communications console, "Assemble Red!"

"Jolly and Greenbean're gonna love this," muttered Starbuck as he set the alert claxon ringing.

There was a moment of quiet on the bridge as everybody watched the pilots scrambling toward their launch cribs, and

.the fighters, now refueled and made ready by the *Galactica*'s
efficient flight crews, starting down the tubes.

Suddenly, as if to add insult to injury, Tigh shouted out,
"Oh, my God!"

"What is it, Tigh?"

"This is terrible. I just sent a message back through the
secret transmission channel to the rest of the fleet, the ships
we left behind. They sent back this." He waved the report
under Adama's nose. "An attack against them has just
commenced. A group of Cylon warships're surrounding
them and've begun firing."

"Have they any chance?"

"If they can hold off until we make the jump back there."

Adama turned toward Starbuck.

"Lieutenant?"

"Yes, sir?"

"Assemble the Blue squadron. I want it ready for a fight
as soon as we make the jump."

"Aye, aye, sir!"

Starbuck, waving back at Athena, made his run to the
elevators.

For the next few minutes, as the fleet made preparations
for the hyperspace jump, and Apollo's squadron blasted
away at the Cylon attackers, and the Blue squadron made
ready then settled themselves into gee-couches for the
hyperspace jump, the bridge of the *Galactica* was ablaze with
activity.

The timing had to be exact, and it was. As Apollo's
squadron returned to the *Galactica* after their hit-and-run
assault, the initial prejump mechanisms were set. After the
returning pilots were safely ensconced in gee-couches, the
jump was made.

A long moment passed, then suddenly the *Galactica*
found itself in the middle of the Cylon attack on the rest of
the fleet ships. Starbuck and his squadron raced to their
launch cribs, boarded their ships, and catapulted themselves
into the battle. The Cylons, so adept at ambush, seemed
surprised at finding themselves under sudden and unexpected fire.

If the Cylon's Imperious Leader could have viewed the
battle activity aboard the *Galactica*, he would have been

struck by the contrast on his own ship. Even the messages along his communication network had dwindled since the humans had begun fighting back, and winning. The losses on the Cylon side had no correspondence with any defeats in their previous history. Since his third-brain had more time than usual to contemplate the nature of his defeat, he could trace his mistakes quite far back. It occurred to him that his supreme mistake seemed to be dealing with humans in the first place. However he tried to interpret the meaning of the defeat, his mind returned to the havoc wrought by the human pest.

The universe had been in order until the humans had started asserting themselves. Even then, the Cylons had avoided actual encounters for some time. When they had tried to convince the humans to leave those areas in space they had usurped, the humans had not listened to reason. There had been no solution but war. Although the Cylons had made the first attack, it was in fact the humans who had precipitated the war by their stubborn interference in Cylon affairs and their refusal to give up their colonies and go back to whatever sector of the universe they came from.

The leader tapped the memories of previous leaders and examined every dealing the Cylons had had with the enemy. They were like a disease, these humans. Once they had infected an area with their presence, there was no cure; the disease spread until it touched all life forms. In that way they had infected the Cylons and brought them to this low point in their history.

The defeat of both Cylon task forces by the small contingent of human fighters had shocked the leader, especially the way his ships had fallen prey to the diversionary action of Captain Apollo and his crew. Embarrassing. The leader felt a pang of anger when he thought of Apollo—the man was, after all, the son of the hated Commander Adama, the prime source of all the human victories. Who would have expected, for example, that he would return to his near-derelict ships traveling slowly through space and ambush the Cylon attackers—the final horrendous defeat that Imperious Leader now had to consider. The whole campaign might have been salvaged if it had not been for those two men, Apollo and Adama. It was the leader's keenest desire now to rid space of these two reckless humans. He would experience great pleasure if he could personally torture the two men, father and son.

Well, he still had a chance at killing Apollo and Adama.

But, no, it was wrong to think such hateful, vengeful thoughts. It was unworthy of the possessor of a third-brain. He should not be brooding over the series of defeats, he should be planning the new strategies of attack.

Gradually, the truth of his position dawned on him. Any other Imperious Leader, realizing the import of the defeats he had suffered, would have resigned the position immediately and ordered his own death. It was the only logical thing to do. His death should be the price for allowing the humans to survive when their annihilation had been certain. But he could not do that. No, *he* must survive. It was essential. He must pursue the hateful Adama and Apollo, and the rest of their verminous race, to whatever part of the universe they would now travel to, with their renewed strength and their supplies of new fuel. All reports indicated that, after the defeat of the Cylons, they had taken their hyperspace and hyperspace-converted craft and vanished from their formerly camouflaged pocket of space. They had not been located since. Well, he would locate them. And he would go after them again. And he would slaughter them. He could not die until that final annihilation had taken place. He could not allow himself the questionable privilege of suicide as an historical failure.

It occurred to him that other leaders would not have had these qualms about giving up the position and dying. They would not have hated, they would not have desired revenge so obsessively. Why was he driven so, he wondered. And suddenly he knew why. He had been dealing with the humans so long, thinking like a human so long, that he had become like a human. His desire for revenge was quite humanlike. That was the final defeat, perhaps, that he had become like his enemy. Well, so be it. He would destroy what had become human within him by destroying the humans themselves. Adama, he would kill personally. For now he must wait.

Adama raised his silver goblet to signal a toast. All around the table that formed a circle in the middle of the bridge, the crew, civilians, and council became quiet. He took a moment to gaze at them, then past the gathering at the starfield portal beyond them. It seemed as if the stars in this part of space glittered more than any he had ever seen. He felt optimistic, hopeful.

"I toast our victories and the achievement of our goals," he began.

"Hear, hear," said Councilor Anton, who was sitting to Adama's right.

"And I ask you to remember for a moment the various men and women who died in the Cylon invasion of the twelve worlds and the subsequent events in which the members of the *Galactica* fleet acted so valiantly."

During the moment of silence many of the assemblage bowed their heads in prayer. Adama resumed his speech.

"I hope that out of this—all this tragedy—will come some good. I am sure we have not seen the end of treachery, either human like Count Baltar or alien like the Cylons."

He glanced toward Sire Uri, who slid down a bit in his seat, secretly glad not to be included on the commander's list of villains. Perhaps his resignation from the council had soothed Adama's anger toward him.

"I wish to take this occasion," Adama continued, "to officially announce my acceptance of the job as president of the council, and thank you for electing me."

"We didn't elect you," Councilor Anton interjected. "We merely took back and tore up your resignation."

"Be that as it may, I thank you. Now we go seeking a place for our race, a place to settle and people in peace. A place in the universe where we can test our potentials again. Perhaps we may find it on the planet our mythology calls Earth. I see no one scoffs when I mention Earth this time. Perhaps now you believe that our little ragtag fleet can do it, can perform this lonely quest as we flee from Cylon tyranny, discover anew the shining planet Earth. Ladies and gentlemen, as a toast I give you . . . hope."

They all drank and the meal, a simple feast prepared from food grown in their agricultural project during their brief stay on Carillon, commenced. Many in the company marveled at how much better this simpler fare was than the exotic delicacies fed them by the Ovions. The councillors, especially, agreed. Paye, through blood analysis, had established that Lotay had drugged the councilors' foods, making them susceptible to ideas they would not otherwise have entertained.

Serina, seated two places away from Adama, leaned his way and spoke.

"You really *do* believe we can find this place, this Earth, don't you, Commander?"

"Yes, I do. I realize what you're implying with your journalistic question, Serina—that we are chasing a dream. Sometimes dreams are worth the chasing. Along the way, who can say what we may find, what we may learn."

"Don't mistake me, Commander. I am on your side."

"I appreciate your saying that. There have been times recently when I was not entirely sure who was on my side, including some who were quite close to me."

Athena put a consoling hand on her father's arm, and Apollo nodded.

"But let's not, while everything is tranquil and our needs are being adequately supplied, dwell on such matters. It is a time for joy."

"I'm all for that," Starbuck said.

"Yes, aren't you?" Athena said, with a meaningful glance toward Cassiopeia, who was seated across from her.

"I am at peace with you," Cassiopeia said.

"See that you stay that way."

"No."

Athena glared at her, then broke out laughing.

"Okay," she said, "you're on."

"You sound like me," Starbuck said.

"Ten to one I don't," Athena said.

"Hey Starbuck," Boomer called from a seat farther down the table, "when you going to pay me off for saving your life out there?"

"But I saved your life right after that."

"And I saved your life again right after that, bucko."

"Swallow your fuel line, Boom-Boom."

Starbuck and Boomer's performance added to the party's festive air.

Apollo leaned toward Serina and whispered, "This is supposed to be a celebration. You look a bit down in the mouth."

"Does it show?"

"Yes, it does, and you're too pretty to look sad."

"Drop the military strategy, please. You know I'm receptive to you without it."

"Sorry. Can't easily get rid of my military instincts."

"Try."

Apollo smiled. Serina could barely resist that smile.

"Sure," he said. "But you haven't explained the sad look, Serina."

She looked down at her plate of food, swirled an asparagus stalk around with her fork.

"Well, it's—it's Boxey. You know how close I am to him, and, well, I just can't be happy with him so miserable."

"I noticed he didn't look so cheerful out in the hallway not long ago. What's wrong?"

"It's Muffit Two. Boxey's moping about losing him."

Apollo hit his forehead with the palm of his hand.

"I forgot! How could I? I promised him I would—"

Serina touched Apollo's arm.

"You couldn't be expected to do anything about it, not with battles going on and—"

"But I did do something. Where's Wilker? Wilker! Where are you?"

From far down the table the doctor yelled back, and stood up.

"Did you bring it?" Apollo asked.

"Of course," Wilker hollered back. "Just waiting for you to tell me what to do with it."

Wilker held up a large leather case.

"All right," Apollo said, and turned back to Serina. "Where's Boxey now?"

"I'll get him."

Serina was gone only a short time. She came back, dragging the obviously reluctant boy by the arm. Boxey appeared very downcast.

"Hey trainee," Apollo said, "what's got you down?"

As he addressed the boy, he signalled Wilker to come down the table.

"I'm okay. I wanta go back to my cubicle," Boxey said.

"But you're invited to our victory feast," Apollo said.

"Don't want anything to eat. I'm not hungry."

"Okay, we'll let Muffy take your place."

"Apollo!" Serina hollered.

"Doctor Wilker, you got the goods?"

"Right here."

"Open the case."

The doctor opened the case, and Muffit Two hopped out, right onto a plate of mashed potatoes. Extricating his paws from the food, he leaped into Boxey's waiting arms. The boy's face was completely transformed; his eyes glowed with happiness.

"You were saying?" Apollo asked Serina.

"What did you do?"

"Easy. Muffy's a droid, after all. All Doctor Wilker here had to do was straighten out a few wires, replace a few parts, patch on a new bit of fur here and there... right, doc?"

"It's a fairly easy repair job."

"Yes, and the doctor here has a Humpty-Dumpty complex. He makes sure everything gets put back together. The doctor's better than all the king's men and all the—"

"Oh shut up, Apollo, and let me hug you," Serina said.

Boxey, still holding Muffy, squeezed in at the table between Serina and Apollo. He managed to shovel quite a few spoonsful of food into his mouth. Serina raised a glass to Apollo and her mouth formed the words, thank you, my love.

Adama smiled at the happy Serina. She raised her glass again and addressed the commander.

"To Earth," she said.